SHE KNOWS TOO MUCH

SHE KNOWS TOO MUCH

IF ONLY SHE KNEW MYSTERY SERIES
BOOK 2

PAMELA CRANE

Tabella House
Raleigh, North Carolina

Tabella House
Raleigh, NC

www.pamelacrane.com

ISBN: 978-1-940662-329 (paperback)
ISBN: 978-1-940662-299 (eBook)

Thank you for supporting authors and literacy by purchasing this book. Want to add more gripping reads to your library? As the author of more than a dozen award-winning and bestselling books, you can find all of Pamela Crane's works on her website at www.pamelacrane.com.

To Jamie.

I'll always cherish our early days when you wouldn't give up on the slow learner in me. Even when it took handwritten notes back and forth until you had taught me enough sign language to get by. You gave me a most precious gift—sisterhood, connection, friendship—as you patiently revealed to me the beauty of American Sign Language. And I'm still learning!

Note to the Reader

This series features characters you may not be used to reading about, but who I chose for a specific reason:

Sloane: a Deaf woman who runs a popular event planning company that she built from the ground up. Inspired by my brother, sister-in-law, along with a Nigerian friend of mine, I sprinkled bits of Deaf and Nigerian culture and history into Sloane that will develop throughout the series.

Ginger: an older woman beleaguered by chronic pain due to poverty and a tough life that took a toll on her body. We often take for granted our ease of access to decent healthcare, mold-free homes, or fresh produce. But not everyone grows up with the same means, especially in rural areas. Those who are forced to battle daily illness or pain are some of the toughest people I know. Luckily Ginger's got a sense of humor and spunk that help her thrive.

And last but not least *Tara*: that co-dependent friend we all know and love who can drive us nuts but whose heart is made of gold. She's the kind of friend who makes you family—with all the good, the bad, and the crazy.

Why did I build a world around these characters? Representation matters. Growing up familiar with closed caption and TTYs (an early version of a phone for Deaf and hard-of-hearing people) and admiring Marlee Matlin, I always wanted to see more Deaf people in entertainment. So I decided to write what I wanted to read.

I also grew up on *Golden Girls,* but it showed a Glamour Shots version of what aging can be like. Not every hero can leap mountains. Not every heroine can scale tall buildings. Some have arthritis. Others are clumsy. And Ginger's here for those types of heroes.

I hope you enjoy my quirky cast as they draw you into a murder mystery that will fire up those brain cells! Their adventures—or should I say *misadventures*—are only just beginning…

Part 1
Tara Christie

Chapter 1

A breeze brushed over me, scattering dry dirt, revealing the pale gray of a recently buried hand. The waist-high dog fennel bent around my boots, and my hair whipped across my face, as if trying to cover my eyes from the grisly sight. But there it was, as undeniable as the dying April sun: a dead body hidden in my field.

Unfortunately, I knew who that hand belonged to. Let's just say we hadn't been on the best of terms. Some might even call us *archenemies* if we were characters in a Marvel movie. Which we weren't. So that, I guessed, made me a prime murder suspect.

After getting all the screams and gagging out of the way, I turned to my husband, wondering what we were supposed to do. Chris hadn't pulled his eyes away from the body since we found it. Only the hand was visible at first. Chris theorized an animal—a coyote, probably—had tried to dig up the body and gotten spooked.

"I'll call the police," he said, whipping his cell phone from his pocket. "Just…try not to say anything…incriminating when they get here, okay?"

Chris knew just as much as I did how bad this looked…for me in particular. As he wandered across the meadow, he held his phone out, trying to find a signal.

My sister-in-law's Great Pyrenees, Puffin, had been trying to dig up the rectangular patch of freshly turned soil ever since my scream summoned Chris and Peace to the scene. She was a beautiful animal, loyal and loving toward her human family, but the bane of foxes and coyotes stupid enough to menace the horses on Peace's property—the Christie family homestead that Peace had inherited after her parents' death. Although Peace's horse farm—the Rockin' C Ranch—was a solid five minutes away by car, Puffin preferred taking the scenic route through the fields where the edges of our properties met.

Puffin's usually immaculate white coat was stained sandy brown up to her chest. The harder Peace yanked on her leash, the harder the huge dog resisted.

"Peace, would you please take your wooly mammoth away from here? She is *really* determined to dig up that…whatever it is."

Puffin had managed to unearth another body part that looked to be an elbow in a torn chambray shirt, or was it a denim-clad knee, maybe? I wasn't sure which, and I didn't want to find out. My stomach was already in knots, on the verge of spewing lunch.

"I'm trying, I'm trying!" Peace finally managed to drag Puffin to where the edge of the hayfield met the wood line, then tied her up to a pine sapling along with the horses, cropping contentedly at the tall fescue.

The afternoon had begun innocuously enough.

It had been ages since I last walked the perimeter of the property line. The plan was to see where I could fence in more pasture, since our horse rescue was preparing to bring in a new herd of horses we saved from the kill pen. I figured I'd invite my best friend Ginger Mallowan and her widowed daughter-in-law Sloane Apara out for a leisurely trail ride. As it turned out, there was nothing leisurely about this.

Skipping like kids over ant hills and broken tree limbs, the mood light and breezy, I was pretty sure even Sloane, who was Deaf, heard my scream when I nearly tripped over the rotting hand, protruding from the shallow grave, like a cinematic jump scare. As the three of us stood shoulder to shoulder, I was the first to break the stunned silence.

"I…I know who it is."

"Get out of town," said Ginger. "How on earth could you know that?" She interpreted her question in American Sign Language for Sloane.

"You can recognize a man by his hand?" Sloane signed to me, though it took me a moment to catch the sign for *recognize.* "I look at hands all day and even I wouldn't be able to identify a person that way."

For several weeks, Sloane had been teaching me ASL in exchange for free horseback riding lessons. I wouldn't say I was fluent yet, but I could hold my own in a conversation.

It was a shock when Sloane mentioned wanting to ride, because somebody with her Instagram eye candy looks and a sumptuous treehouse-like pad worthy of a *House Beautiful* spread was definitely not the horse poop type, so I thought. The woman "gardened" in a white silk kaftan, for heaven's sake! So seeing this fashionista wearing Wrangler jeans and cowboy boots—and, naturally, looking drop-dead gorgeous in them—was almost as shocking as finding a corpse on the proverbial back forty. There was a reason her social media followers called her the "Lagos Deaf Duchess"—and it wasn't because she was actual Nigerian royalty. She just looked the part.

"Look at the ring." I signed the word for *ring*, then pointed at where a thick, putty-colored finger poked up from the ground.

I had instantly recognized the gold band with a ruby gem. It belonged to the one person who had the means to hurt me from beyond the grave. And his father just so happened to be the judge, whose money, power, and connections had enabled him to hold our little town of Bloodson Bay under his fat thumb for decades.

"That ring belongs to Victor Valance." The name slid off my tongue in a dreadful whisper.

"Judge Ewan Valance's son?" Sloane signed, eyes wide.

"The one and only."

"Oh, darlin', you're in deep do-do," Ginger said, patting me on the shoulder. She was old enough to claim her verbal filter was broken. "That's the one family you don't wanna mess with."

"Tell me something I don't know."

Chris approached the other side of the grave. "The police are on their way. As long as we stick to the facts, everything will be fine."

All three sets of eyes shifted to me—Ginger's full of terror, Sloane's full of confusion, and Chris's full of worry. I could already feel that rotting hand wrapping its ring-bejeweled fingers around my neck, choking the life out of me.

Chapter 2

The sky darkened. The stars flickered. And Victor Valance's broken face looked up at me. I had never seen a skull blown to bits before, but now I would never forget it.

"We really should stop meeting like this, Tara." Detective Martina Carillo-Hughes shook her head at me with a stern look, as if we had bumped into each other at Debbie's Diner, a popular local greasy spoon, instead of on my farm gazing down at a corpse.

"Do you think I like all this drama?" It was a rhetorical question, but Detective Hughes seemed to mull it over.

Drama was a bit of an understatement, but I didn't dare say the word *murder*. I didn't want to directly associate myself with that word in front of her.

"I'm starting to think you might. You seem to attract a lot of trouble, Tara. The deadly kind, if you catch my drift."

Detective Hughes, or Marti as I sometimes called her if I was feeling sassy, had a point. After Ginger's son Benson was stabbed to death last year, and my husband was arrested for it—and later released, mind you—trouble latched on to me like a foal to its mama. Last year my husband was the suspect, this year it was me. God forbid our daughter Nora should make the list next year.

"Officer Alonzo, make sure they bag him and tag him,"

Detective Hughes yelled over her shoulder to one of the policemen milling about.

"Yes, ma'am," the tallest and bulkiest one in uniform replied.

The forensics team had finished unearthing the entire body by now. The stench of decomposition was thick enough to cut with a knife. The macabre scene was lit by the headlights of the crime scene van, idling nearby. Two attendants manhandled the corpse by the shoulders from the grave, then rested a moment before finagling it, with some difficulty, into a body bag.

That was when I saw what I wish I hadn't.

The fragmented skull was a skull only in the academic sense, with chunks of brain tissue oozing out of the fissures. Where Victor's face should have been there was a red, pulpy mass, looking like a half-eaten wedge of watermelon with strands of flesh and hair clinging to it, and deep black craters in place of facial orifices. I thought I even saw seeds, but then the seeds *moved.* They were carrion beetles, flat and alien and creepy, burrowing through the layers of mutilated flesh. One of the men casually flicked the bugs off with his gloved hand, then zipped up the bag before he and his partner hoisted the body onto the gurney. As they wheeled it past me, I heard a singsong voice chanting beside me:

"The worms crawl in, the worms crawl out…"

Peace was grinning puckishly when I turned to look at her.

That's when I lost it.

Holding onto my churning gut, I ran into the brush and fell to my knees and barfed up my lunch. I sat back on my haunches, wiping the tears off my burning cheeks. I felt a hand on my back, rubbing small circles, and looked up.

"You okay there?" It was Ginger. And ironically I could go for a ginger ale right about now.

"The smell...the face...the bugs...it's...too much," I said as a drip of spittle fell to the grass. I rose unsteadily to my feet and watched them push the gurney across the pasture, barreling recklessly over fire ant mounds and chickweed patches in the advancing dark.

"Too much for your stomach to handle?" Marti said as she approached me. "I get it. It's not every day you see a man's head blown off. At least for most people."

"What's that supposed to mean?" I asked.

"You ever see something like this before?" Marti probed.

"Goodness no, Detective!" Ginger interjected for me. "Why would she have seen something like this before?"

"Oh, I dunno. If she's the one who did it."

"What?" My body stiffened. "Why would you think that I'm capable of killing a person?"

"Maybe if that person were someone you hated." Her long pause let it sink in. "I think you've got a good idea who this is."

I glanced sidelong at Ginger; her wide eyes said *don't say a word.* Then I remembered what Chris had said: *try not to say anything incriminating.*

"It could be any farmer from around here," I answered. "The boots, the snap-front work shirt, jeans. Your standard Tractor Supply wardrobe."

"An astute observation. But what about the ring, Tara? That didn't come from Tractor Supply, now did it?"

Marti was going to bulldog me until I cracked. Might as well get it over with. "I happen to know Victor Valance wore a ring like that. I'm not saying it's him, but it could be. I hope you appreciate my honesty, Detective."

"I do, Tara. Very much. But the fact of the matter is, the body's buried on your property. Everyone knows you and Victor had bad blood over the kill pen horses. I bet I don't need to dig deep to find motive. All we need now is the weapon, and I'm pretty sure you have a shotgun loaded with buckshot in your house somewhere."

"Around here, every farmer with livestock owns a shotgun loaded with buckshot," I pointed out. "Look, I know Vic and I weren't exactly on friendly terms, but I didn't kill him. And even if I did—*which I didn't*—what sense would it have made for me to call you and basically deliver the body to you?"

"To give the perception of innocence." Marti cocked her head as if she had just scored the winning point.

"That would have been pretty dumb of me," I retorted. "I wouldn't want to draw attention to a body when there's no way anyone would have found him way back here."

"Seems like you put an awful lot of thought into that logic."

I swore this woman was gunning for me and I still couldn't figure out why. My family was cleared of the murder charges when Ginger's son died. If Ginger could forgive me and move on, why couldn't Detective Hughes?

"You also wouldn't need to dig deep to find a whole lineup of people with motive to kill Victor Valance. We all know what kind of people he did business with."

The killing kind.

"We'll let the evidence speak for itself," Marti said. She started walking toward the forensics guys as they loaded the body, then turned to add: "In the meantime, don't go running off anywhere. I'll have my eye on you, Tara Christie. And I suggest you stay out of trouble going forward."

Easier said than done.

Chapter 3

"You'll never believe who got out on parole." Chris dropped the *Bloodson Bay Bulletin* he was reading on the coffee table.

I found it adorable that my husband still insisted on reading a crinkled and dew-dampened newspaper left in our driveway rather than follow the news online like every other millennial man in America. But my husband clung to the *good ol' days* as if he could stop them from slipping away.

"We know someone in jail? Who?"

I was only partly listening as I stood at the window, my reflection trapped in the glare of the glass. My gaze held fast to the field, bathed in twilight's golden haze, where we found Vic's body. I'd grabbed a jar of salsa out of the pantry for a late-night snack of loaded nachos and fiddled absently with the lid.

"Tara, you're supposed to guess." Chris leaned forward on the sofa cushion, waiting for a name I was supposed to pull out of my butt. "Not a single name comes to mind?" He looked at me expectantly, as if the answer was obvious. "Here's a hint: he's a ruthless murderer and traumatized us as kids."

Suddenly the name blinked into my brain. The only person I knew who was behind bars and deserved to rot there.

"Not Marvin Valance, I hope?" I ventured an educated guess.

"Yep. He was let out under the compassionate release

program because supposedly he has cancer."

I had heard about the law that allowed inmates, regardless of their crime, to petition for release if diagnosed by a physician as terminally ill, as long as they posed no risk to society. I never imagined that the man who in 1997 murdered a teenage girl I personally had known would ever see the light of day.

"I can't believe he's out," Chris grumbled.

Now that I gave it another thought, I actually could believe it. With Marvin's corrupt brother Ewan Valance as judge, our entire Bloodson Bay judicial system reeked of corruption. A little payoff between the judge and the prison doctor, and suddenly Marvin had terminal cancer.

"When was he released?" A chill prickled my spine just thinking about that killer running loose in our town. *My* town.

"A couple days ago." Chris stood up and joined me at the window. He wrapped his arms around me and rested his chin on top of my head.

"I hope the police are keeping tabs on him," I muttered, still working on twisting open the stuck salsa lid.

"What kind of judicial system releases a convicted child killer onto the streets? I'm just glad we don't have to raise any more kids in a world where murderers are allowed to run free. It's already bad enough knowing Nora's growing up in this."

Nora, my teenage daughter who had already seen the face of death way too young. She had been so traumatized by Ginger's son's death that nightmares of his ghost coming after her chased her out of her bedroom and into my bed for months afterward. Heck, even I hadn't gotten over seeing Ginger, covered in blood, sobbing over Benson's lifeless corpse, the knife sticking out of his chest…

I shuddered at the memory.

"Do you think Peace knows Marvin's free?" I wondered.

Peace had only been a teenager when she delivered the key witness testimony that put Marvin behind bars. After that, life grew quiet again until a publisher approached her about publicly sharing her side of the story. A budding, if unconfident, author since she was a kid, Peace jumped at the chance and received a nice advance that she blew on a car instead of college—along with earning an enemy hell-bent on revenge. And now that enemy was free and on the prowl. *If Only She Knew*, a true crime novel in the same vein as Truman Capote's *In Cold Blood*, became a short-lived bestseller before the fickle reading public moved on to the next sensationalized human trauma. If Peace had only known how that summer would change her life, she might never have written the book that forever put a bulls-eye on her back.

"I'll make sure my sister knows," Chris replied, "but we'll need to keep an eye out for her. I have no idea what Marvin will try to do to Peace."

The details of Marvin's court case clawed at my brain. Victor and his brother Leonard had testified against Marvin too. I reminded Chris of this fact.

"You know your family's rotten to the core when nephews testify against uncles," he laughed, breaking our embrace as he shifted to face me. "You think Marvin might have been the one to kill Victor?"

"It makes sense, doesn't it? Finally getting his revenge."

"On his own nephew?" Chris's eyebrow lifted with skepticism.

"The nephew who helped put him in jail for murder."

"Then why didn't he go after Leonard for testifying too? And Peace?"

"We don't know yet that he won't try. Maybe Vic's just the first."

A flash of movement at the front of my house yanked my attention away from the field. Where my driveway ran along a line of trees, I looked past my tired reflection and watched a pair of headlights swing across a break in the brush as a car parked in front of Ginger's yard next door.

A coat of pollen on the window—don't judge; I hadn't gotten around to spring cleaning yet—blurred my view, but it didn't look like her car. With Marvin on the loose, I didn't want to take any chances.

"Do you recognize that vehicle?" I asked Chris.

Propping his arm on the wall, he inclined toward the glass. His eyes narrowed into slivers as he scrutinized it. "It kind of looks like an unmarked cop car to me. Crown Vic. Blackwall tires. Ashtray hubcaps. Super-tinted windows. Dead giveaways."

"You watch *waaay* too many crime procedurals on TV. But why would they be parked there?"

"Surveillance, probably. A murder victim was buried in our backyard. I'm pretty sure they're going to be watching us for a while."

I backed away from the window, wondering if they could see us from there. "How long do you think they'll be watching us?"

Chris stepped back and shrugged. "Until they solve the case."

Another murder case with my family stuck in the middle…

I couldn't let Nora or my mother find out. The last thing I wanted was my daughter to have to deal with cops and interrogations and stress and fear all over again. After Ginger's son was killed and my family made headlines for it, I had decided to pull Nora out of school and homeschool her until things died down…no pun intended. But if you ever lived in a small town where nothing exciting happens, you'd understand that local yokels have long memories and short fuses. One misstep and your family slips from being part of the clique to clickbait.

While I hated asking Nora to give up wrestling and friends and everything she used to love about school, the Bloodson Bay High School gossip mill had churned out too many rumors about Nora's dad being a killer, even after his acquittal, that it was no longer safe for her there. My child became a pariah. At least Nora was in Myrtle Beach right now with my mom, hopefully steering clear of any Bloodson Bay news.

"After this murder case is all done," Chris said, breaking into my thoughts, "and we're cleared, I think it's time we move. Start over somewhere fresh."

The suggestion was so abrupt it nearly bowled me over. "Are you serious? But our lives are here in Bloodson Bay. And what about Nora? Her roots are here."

"Nora's not even going to her high school anymore, so we can finish her education wherever we go. And after that she'll be off at college. Even she couldn't stand being here…and we can't protect her from this town. You know how the people here are. They never forget. She'll never have a normal life here. And neither will we."

That part was true. Nora couldn't wait to get as far away as possible from the small minds of this small town. Her friends had abandoned her, and life had become so terrible that she opted to spend it away from us, in another town with her grandmother rather than endure another day here. Her only hope these days was studying hard enough to get into Duke University and leaving this cursed town behind.

"What about our work with the children's home? If we don't keep it running, who will? Those kids rely on us."

"Someone will step up in our place," Chris said.

It had been almost twenty years since Chris's parents, the founders of Loving Arms Children's Home, had died and passed the torch to Chris to carry on their mission. During that time no one had *stepped up* but us. What made Chris think that suddenly people too busy for two decades would lift a finger to help now?

"As a child who was adopted, Chris, I'd think you'd understand how important you are to those kids. You understand them. I just don't feel right abandoning them…"

Chris turned away from me, his head drooping. "Maybe I'm tired of giving and giving to everyone else and getting nothing but contempt in return. Maybe I want to do something for myself for a change."

"You don't mean that. You love those kids! And what about the horse rescue? Would Peace be okay running the Rockin' C Ranch by herself?"

For almost two decades Peace and I had been running her family's horse farm together, even after Chris decided to bow out in search of an office job where the cubicles didn't stink like manure and the work didn't give him callouses. I, personally, would take muck and blisters over cubicle confinement any day.

"I'm sure we could find a farmhand to help her. Or…" Chris

let the thought dangle.

"Or what?" There was no other *or* I could imagine him suggesting.

"Or maybe it's time to let the horse rescue go."

"Are you out of your friggin' mind! No, absolutely not. I've given everything to that farm. So has Peace. I'm not letting this stupid town chase us away from saving horses, Chris."

Chris threw his hands up. "It's been nothing but a burden lately with all the crap we've had with the Valances. You know we're on the verge of bankruptcy, don't you? Maybe Peace is just as eager to part ways with it as I am."

It felt like we were fighting now, but this was one fight I wasn't willing to concede.

"But with Vic gone, we could get back on our feet!"

Chris shuffled away from me, his gaze incredulous. "You sound like you're *glad* he's dead."

"Aren't you? Be honest. He was a thorn in our side."

"You want honesty? It almost sounds like you killed him." There was fear in his voice, and when I reached for him he stepped away.

"Honey, no…I'm not saying I'm *glad.* It's just that he was trying to ruin us…" Chris's expression betrayed revulsion now. I had to switch tactics. "What about our family and friends? And your job?"

"It's not like we're dropping off the face of the earth. And I don't know how stable my job will stay…"

I had been worrying about that very thing lately. Chris liked to provide, *needed* to feel relied on. I never tried to dissect why, but it was the reason I handed him the salsa jar, even though I had loosened the lid, and let him open it. Chris needed to be needed, so sometimes I played damsel in distress to reinforce my husband's purpose. Even if it was simply letting him open jars for me.

"If we leave, where will we go?"

This seemed to be the right question, because Chris's eyes instantly sparked back to life.

"We've always talked about traveling, so why wait? Let's do it!" Chris plastered on a smile, as if he could charm his way into winning this round.

It wasn't going to happen.

"No, Chris. This is way too big a decision, and it's coming out of nowhere. You're asking a lot of change for two people who still live in the small town they grew up in."

"That's exactly the point. We need a change. A good change—far away from here. Our *marriage* needs it, Tara."

I couldn't blame him. The moment Chris was arrested for Benson Mallowan's murder—and *acquitted* I had to keep reminding people—was the moment our lives irrevocably shifted. His co-workers still kept their distance, any chance for promotions disappeared, and he had been noticing fewer projects sent his way. Chris saw the writing on the wall, no matter how much I tried to pretend everything was fine.

Sometimes everything wasn't fine. Sometimes nothing was fine.

"Maybe you're right. A change of scene might be nice. We could finally go to Europe."

I imagined eating in a quaint Italian bistro, or sunbathing on a Grecian beach, or floating down the Seine on a flat-bottomed tour boat, hoisting my champagne glass at the peasants.

"Or we could tour the country in an RV," Chris added

excitedly. That had always been a family trip we'd talked about but never taken. "I'll start looking into it. Nora will be so excited to hear this!"

"Whoa, don't go saying anything to her yet," I warned. The Christie family had been a fixture in this town since the founding of Bloodson Bay. It wasn't something you just walked away from. "I'm not saying yes. I'm just saying I'll think about it."

The crooked lift of Chris's lips told me he probably wasn't listening to me and instead already planning our happily ever after far, far away. But as I glanced outside and saw the parked car beneath an upside-down ocean of starless black, I caught a glimpse of a face against a glowing cell phone. Eyes trained on me. Mouth a stern line. An ever-present threat.

I had a terrible feeling that there was no escaping this town, no happily ever after for the Christie family.

Chapter 4

A strange sensation prickled my skin. It felt like I had forgotten something. Or missed an important event.

I had just finished Facetiming with Nora. Only moments after hanging up I already missed my blonde baby girl who wasn't a baby anymore, or so she thought. She'd always be my baby girl to me.

"What's this I overheard about Nora's boyfriend breaking up with her?" Chris asked as I tidied up the living room on my way back and forth to the kitchen.

I detected slight relief in his question, the shield lowered from a father overprotective of his daughter against all manner of predatory boyfriends. At least that's how Chris saw them all, anyway. And Nora, a Daddy's Girl, lived to please him.

"Wow, don't sound so excited about it, Chris. You'll be happy to know Nora actually broke up with Keanu. I guess the long-distance thing isn't working and she wants to focus on school right now."

"Smart girl. I kept telling her she really should break up with that twerp. *Keanu.* Who names their kid Keanu? Gimme a break! Good riddance, I say. Teenage boys only want *one thing*. And I would know..."

"I couldn't agree more." I laughed, swiping my lips across his cheek as I bent down to pick up an empty plate and glass.

Already my teenage girl had experienced so many adult emotions. Fear. Loss. Heartbreak. Why did our kids ever have to grow up? Why did they have to suffer through this broken world we'd made for them? I wanted to wrap my arms around her lanky figure swallowed up in her Duke University sweatshirt, while she talked over every pro and con about enrolling in high school-approved community college courses. So driven, unlike me at that age. While I had cared more about filling my Caboodle with the latest wet n wild makeup, Nora was concerned with filling her college resume.

By the time I finished cleaning up for the night, Chris was sprawled out on the sofa, minutes away from falling asleep while watching *iRobot,* tuckering himself out on speculation over how close society was headed to AI world domination. Pretty sleepy myself, I picked up my phone from the arm of the chair and navigated to my calendar. No appointments for tomorrow. I swiped over to my email, skimming the junk mail as I cleaned out offers to enlarge the penis I didn't have or to claim a $2.1 million inheritance from a long-lost deceased aunt who lived in a country I'd never heard of.

Yawning, I had reached the end of my inbox when a name and subject halted my finger mid-delete. I sat forward, instantly wide awake. I checked, then double-checked, the date that the email had been sent, along with the sender.

"Crap on a stick," I whispered.

I sucked in my breath, clicked on the email, and read the message, the veins in my temple throbbing. The phone slipped from my hand, landing with a thud on the coffee table. This couldn't be right. And if it *was* right, I was in trouble. Big trouble.

"You alright?" Chris's groggy voice reached me through my swelling panic.

I looked over at him looking over at me, my mind firmly planted on the email. To be honest, nothing was alright. I was absolutely terrified.

"Honey, you're not looking so good." Chris swung his legs off the sofa and leaned toward me.

I reached for my phone and flipped it over, hiding the email.

"Oh, um, I'm fine," I sputtered rather unconvincingly.

I couldn't let Chris find out about this. Our marriage had barely survived the past year. My sanity was still hanging on by a thread. The glares at the grocery store forced me to shop right before closing time. The nasty, judgmental whispers around town had turned me into a veritable recluse. The situation had gotten so bad that even the kill pen had asked me to put a hold on bidding on horses, until they finally realized no one else was coming to rescue them and I was their last resort.

If I wanted to keep the peace, keep my marriage, keep my freedom, I couldn't tell Chris what I had done. Not unless I absolutely had to.

"Tara?" he asked again. "What's the matter?"

I had to think quick…which wasn't one of my better talents.

"I forgot to remind Ginger about our breakfast plans tomorrow, so I'm going to call her to make sure she doesn't forget."

See what I mean? Not the best excuse, but Chris bought it.

I paced into the kitchen, speed-dialing Ginger's number as I walked. As soon as I heard her chipper "Hi, Tara," I launched into a frenzied speech.

"You're the only person I can talk to, Ginger. Can we meet

up? It's urgent."

"What's got your panties in a wad?" Normal me would have teased her for the outdated phrase, but I wasn't normal me. I was distressed me.

"I can't talk about it on the phone. Are you free tomorrow morning?"

I had anticipated an instant yes, but I got radio silence.

"Weeeelllll..." She stretched out the word, making me think she was conjuring an excuse as she spoke. "I've got plans with Sloane."

Who stole my ever-available best friend and replaced her with a too-busy-for-me version?

"Like, all-day plans?" I pressed.

"No, just in the morning. How about we meet in the afternoon?"

I'd take whatever I could get, even if it was the scraps.

"Sure, that works. By the way, I think there's a cop sitting outside your house. Watching my house."

"What? That's creepy."

"Yeah," I agreed, "you'll see an unmarked car parked between our driveways. You can sneak up to his window and tell him I said hi if you get a chance."

Ginger sniggered. "Naw, he might drop his doughnut. Do the police think you had something to do with Victor's death?"

"I'm guessing so. But anyway, how about a late brunch at Debbie's Diner tomorrow? My treat."

"Cool beans." Ginger hesitated, then asked, "Hey, do you mind if I bring Sloane with me?"

I couldn't help but feel a little jealous at all the time Ginger was spending with her new bestie. And I absolutely did *not* want

Sloane there. I wasn't even telling my husband what I had done, let alone a woman I'd only known for a few months.

"I wouldn't normally ask," Ginger continued, "but Sloane has been feeling a little down after Bennie died..."

And there it was: the Ginger Guilt Trip. Ginger knew I still felt terrible about her son's death, and Sloane had been married to Benson, so of course I couldn't say no to a grieving ex-wife crashing my top-secret brunch with my best friend.

"Of course you can bring her. The more the merrier." I acquiesced to my people-pleasing nature. I really did want Sloane to like me. "What are your plans together tomorrow morning?"

Ginger suddenly got uncharacteristically secretive. "Oh, nothing much."

I was beginning to feel like Ginger's evasiveness was personal.

"Is everything okay between us, Ging? I hardly ever see you anymore and now you're always with Sloane. I thought we were best friends."

"We are, Tara," and then her defensive tone escalated, "but I don't have to tell you everything I do or spend every second with you. You don't have a monopoly on my friendship."

Wow, where did *that* come from?

"I'm sorry, you're right. I just worry that maybe you resent me because of what happened to Benson."

Ginger didn't respond for a long moment. So long that I thought the call disconnected.

And then her voice picked up a hint of annoyance as she went on. "I honestly don't know how I feel, Tara. His death wasn't your fault, and you know I love you. I just...I don't know what's going on with us, but we'll be fine. I just need a little…space. But I'll be there tomorrow for brunch, okay?"

"Okaaay." But it didn't feel okay.

It felt like my friendship was on the rocks, and I had no idea how to fix it. Or how to make my husband happy. Or bring my daughter home…if this was even still home for us. Maybe Chris was right. Maybe it was best if we just left and never looked back.

Ginger hung up, but I wasn't done yet. There was one other person I needed to speak to. Urgently.

I slipped outside on the back porch, scrolling through my contacts until I found the name I was looking for. The cold night air slapped my skin as a shiver ran over me. I wasn't sure if it was the spring chill or the creeping awareness of strange eyes spying on me.

When the call connected, I spoke barely above a whisper.

"You are literally the last person I would normally turn to, but I'm desperate. I need your help."

Chapter 5

The blushing sky turned my bedroom pink as an urgent pounding yanked me from a dull sleep. I woke up uncertain of the day or time, with Victor's pulpy face crawling with carrion beetles lingering in my brain.

Nightmares of his decaying fingers clenching my arms had plagued my sleep. I looked down at my hands. Red marks—like handprints—circled my wrists.

Had something happened last night? It was a ludicrous thought, but a nagging fear sat heavy in my stomach. I just needed more sleep, I decided, that's all.

I pulled the covers up over my head, drowning out the sun's glow. Another knock reached me through the downy blanket, and I realized that sound was what had woken me in the first place.

Now someone was leaning on the doorbell like it was a car horn. It was way too early for company, even by Ginger's "up with the chickens" standards. It had to be somebody else.

I rued the fact we didn't have a doorbell camera so I could see who it was on my phone, but money being tight, Chris had vetoed that idea.

"Chris!" I screamed at the bowels of the house.

Then I remembered he was probably at work. I threw off the covers and crept up to the window, peering down at the driveway. I didn't recognize the top of the car. The doorbell kept up its grating two-note song.

Whoever it is, I vowed, *I'll kill 'em.* Not the best choice of words, under the circumstances.

The scent of onion followed me to the bathroom. Lifting my arm, I sniffed the armpit of the shirt I had crashed in last night and winced. Yep, I was as ripe as our mini-pony Havoc's stall.

I had two options: hide out in my bedroom until whoever it was went away. Or answer the door looking like the Frankenstein Monster's bride. A joint chorus of knocking and ringing made the choice for me. Maybe my smell would scare them away.

"Coming!" I yelled as I descended the stairs, taming my bedhead as best I could.

I opened the door to find Detective Hughes standing there, one hand on her hip, the other mid-knock. Judging from her constipated scowl, she could use a heaping bowl of Colon Blow cereal—or maybe she was just still pissed at me. Behind her was Officer Joe Speers, the only cop who had reached out to apologize after Chris was released from jail.

"We need to talk, Tara," Detective Hughes demanded, brushing rudely around me into my living room. "Joe, go wait in the car while I talk to Mrs. Christie."

"But what about needing backup in case—"

"I thought I might need your help with the interview, but I just decided this should be a solo gig. I won't be long."

"Yes, ma'am," Officer Joe said, then offered me a quick, "Don't worry, Mrs. Christie. We'll sort this out. Have a nice day."

"It's good seeing you, Officer Speers," I said cheerily as he waved on his way back to the patrol car. To Detective Hughes I wasn't nearly as cordial. "Sure, make yourself comfortable," I grumbled, trailing behind her.

Marti didn't waste time unloading a file folder and notebook onto my coffee table.

"Want a coffee first?" I offered, mainly because I needed it before my brain could function.

"No, thanks. I've already had my quota for the day."

"Well, I won't make it through this conversation without one, so while I grab myself a cup, care to tell me what this visit is about?"

I should have felt awkward watching a detective barging into my home like she owned the place, but I was almost used to it by now. Marti sat down, and her unfairly cute-fitting slacks rode up slightly, showing off her typical sensible shoes. I wondered if her fit figure was from all the driveways she walked interrogating people like me, or if she belonged to a gym. It wasn't fair either way, when I spent countless hours doing farm chores and still managed to gain two sizes over the winter.

Marti flipped open a folder as I sat next to her on the sofa jolting myself awake with sips of caffeine.

"Take a look."

Pulling her spiral strands up into a short ponytail, a curly fringe of bangs framed her face. She looked like she was prepping to run a marathon, not go over paperwork. They almost felt like the same thing.

After pulling out several pictures, Marti scattered them in a half-circle around the table. It took a moment for me to make sense of what I was looking at. Then I realized it was Victor—faceless on a metal table. The same grotesque version of him I had seen when they unearthed him on my property.

Apparently these were the autopsy photos, and for some reason Marti wanted me to relive the terror that haunted my nightmares.

"Why are you showing me these?"

"You're the only one I know who had a lot of…dealings with Victor. And the only one who might be able to help me." Her tone softened from all business to warmth rounding out the edges of her words. "Tara, I was hoping you might be willing to tell me if you notice anything unusual about these photos."

"Other than his head being blown off by a shotgun?" My stomach was turning somersaults…which brought on the memory…and the smell… I closed my eyes and sipped my coffee, focusing on the caramel macchiato flavor.

"You identified the ring on the body as Victor's, but was there anything else that you recognized that made you certain it was Victor Valance? Any tattoos or physical markings?"

I hadn't taken the time to really give the body a once-over, considering Peace's dog was trying to chew his elbow off and I was trying to keep my lunch down.

"Wait, are you asking me to ID a man without a face?"

Marti sighed. "His mother refused to come down to the station to ID him. She's the only one I trust would know for sure it's him."

"I thought you could use fingerprints or teeth or something." At least that's what I learned from every crime show ever.

"If the prints are in the system, sure. But the body's fingerprints were burned off, and there are no teeth left to compare against dental records."

That was assuming Vic ever went to the dentist. I was shocked he even had real teeth, considering the brown color of them from all the tobacco he chewed.

"The medical examiner determined the victim had died approximately four days ago. We submitted DNA to the state crime lab for analysis," Marti continued, "but it'll be a few weeks until we get the report back. You know what it's like in a small town. No resources. In the meantime, anything you can tell me would be a great help."

"I still don't understand why you're asking me instead of his family. What about his father?"

Marti groaned and ran her hands down her face. Her fingernails were jagged and torn, like she had made a meal of them. As well put-together as she was, I realized what a stressful job Marti had. I didn't envy her.

"Judge Ewan Valance?" Marti huffed. "I don't trust him farther than I can throw him. I'm already getting pushback from him because he wants to oversee the autopsy."

"I'm sure his brother would know something."

"Leonard is hiding behind the protection of his father, so I can't get in touch with him. It's impossible to get anything done right when the judge is pulling every string he has to make my life difficult."

Welcome to the club, Detective.

"What do you mean?"

"He claims the body is Victor, but then throws a monkey wrench in the investigation and demands that the body be returned to him to have his own private autopsy done. It all seems so…suspicious. So we're currently fighting him on that, which is making all of this needlessly frustrating."

"A person can do that—withhold the body of a murder victim from the police?"

"Legally a family does have the right to demand their own autopsy, as long as it's after ours. So they gave our coroner one day to do his, then the judge had the body sent to his own pathologist. We had just enough time to get what we needed for a toxicology report, but like the DNA analysis, we're weeks from getting the results back from the Office of the Chief Medical Examiner. They always get involved in the case of suspicious deaths. And man, is this one ever suspicious."

"Why would Judge Valance do that?"

Marti shrugged. "He doesn't trust us. Just like I don't trust him."

At least the detective and I agreed on one thing.

"So you can't help me?" she confirmed.

I stared at the pictures, all various images of a naked man, from his cherry Jell-O head down to his gray toes. Sliding each one center, I examined the details carefully, moving them across the table until I'd looked at them all. Nothing immediately stood out to me at first. And then I saw it. *That hand...*

It was the one detail that was off. So off that it would blow everything about this investigation out of the water.

Chapter 6

The autopsy photo rocked me like a gut punch. That one detail stuck out like a painted whore on the front pew in church, to use one of Ginger's patented Southernisms. That one detail hung out there for me to pluck. Something far too strange to be coincidence. But I couldn't be certain it was worth mentioning yet. It would drag people into this that didn't deserve it. I had learned from dealing with the police before that worms didn't tend to slither back into opened cans so easily.

"No, I don't notice anything unusual," I lied. I'd figure this puzzle piece out later, away from Marti's scrutiny.

Marti stacked everything back into the folder, then turned to face me. I didn't like the intensity of her expression. As if she read my thoughts.

"Look, I believe the Valance family is hiding something. But I also think you're not being forthright either, Tara. If you know something, anything, you need to tell me. It's better if you tell me now than me figuring it out later. Especially considering the whole town knows you and Victor weren't on the best of terms."

"Whoa, I might have had a beef with Vic over the kill pen horses, but I'm not a killer. The guy was a known criminal. I'm sure there's a long line of people who wanted him dead."

Marti tucked the papers into her bag, all but one. I tried to lean in to read it, but she pulled it to her chest.

"But there is something unusual about his death, Tara. Something we've never seen before."

"You've seen a lot of murder victims with their heads blown to smithereens?"

"Well, you'd be surprised how many people are shot with a 12-gauge around here. But in the head point-blank from about five feet away? That's pretty personal, don't you think?"

"Then I imagine whoever did it probably has clothes covered in his blood. So feel free to search my wardrobe if you suspect me of something, because I have nothing to hide." Not everything I just said was totally true, but I wasn't hiding blood-stained clothes, at least. "I didn't know Vic very well, but it's no surprise that he died the way he lived—violently."

"That's actually the other reason I'm here," Marti added cryptically. "How he died."

"I thought—wasn't he shot?" I was afraid to ask, but I knew whatever she had to say was coming out whether I wanted to hear it or not.

"The cause of death wasn't from the gunshot wound. Based on the blood clotting, the ME determined he was killed prior to that. And while we're waiting to find out what the toxicology report shows, I found a Somulose kit with a missing syringe in Victor's Hummer...and your name was on the kit, Tara."

Just like that the air thickened. I gasped as Marti's dark eyes zeroed in on me, two black holes sucking my reaction in.

It was bad enough that I wasn't technically supposed to have possession of the prescription drug. It was worse that my name was on the kit used to kill a man.

"We both know you're pretty familiar with what Somulose

does and how to use it, which doesn't look too good for you, Tara. Care to explain how it got in his SUV?"

"I…I…" I reached for the slippery thread of an explanation, but it was too slick to grasp. "I don't know what to say. Maybe he stole it."

It was a lame suggestion, and I could tell Marti wasn't buying it.

Victor Valance's ghost had marked me for revenge, and no matter what I said or how far I ran, I was doomed to join him in hell.

Chapter 7

Since I was a kid, I'd been coming to Debbie's Diner for the loaded french fries. Debbie Dingle, the joint's rotund namesake, used to tease Peace and me about gobbling up the "heart attacks on a plate" she served, and never gaining an ounce. (She should see me now. I've "filled out," to use one of Chris's euphemisms for *damn, woman, you've sure gotten fat.*)

About ten years ago Debbie had the good sense to move away from Bloodson Bay when she married her fourth husband, the Snap-on Tools salesman who stopped in regularly to flirt with her over a cup of joe and a double slice of cherry pie. The rail-thin salesman professed a preference for "big-boned gals," and Debbie was his ideal. The last I heard they were living comfortably on Debbie's nest egg and the Snap-on man's pension in Pompano Beach, Florida.

Debbie handed over the keys to the diner to her daughter, who wisely didn't change a thing. Debbie's spirit lived on in the stick-to-your-ribs (and hips and everywhere else) comfort food, and in the melting pot atmosphere she'd cultivated. Everybody in Bloodson Bay—from the prim Seventh-day Adventist Church minister who secretly partook in midnight poker games at the firehouse, to the mellow neo-hippie girl who ran the drug store cash register by day and peddled home-grown weed behind the bait shack by night—came to Debbie's and were treated exactly the same. Even Judge Valance and his cronies were sometimes spotted, in the wee hours, occupying a favorite booth, plotting political strategies and smear campaigns. Debbie always said if you had a pulse and could pay the tab, you were welcome. Folks forgot their differences for a little while. They remembered to be friendly in a town where nursing a lifetime grudge was the favorite pastime and backstabbing was the main sport.

Within walking distance of the bay, the 1950s-style building didn't shine like it used to. The salty winds had gnawed mercilessly at the exterior, tarnishing the aluminum siding and chrome trim to a dull, flaky gray. The windows had a ghostly fog no amount of Windex or elbow grease could remove. Even the neon sign had grown weary of battling the elements; the "n" and "r" in *Diner* had burned out, leaving an ominous name in its place: *Debbie's Die.*

But the only *deadly* thing about Debbie's Diner was the banana cream pancakes and high cholesterol. It was always warm and cozy inside. Open 24/7, it was a haven for the sleepless and the restless, especially the local kids who had nowhere else to go in a town that rolled up the sidewalks at ten o'clock. The digitally-upgraded jukebox might crank out a tear-in-your-beer oldie from Patsy Cline one minute, a Keith Urban country-rocker the next, inspiring the bolder teens—and some boomer couples—to take a whirl on the checkerboard floor.

The little brass bell attached to the entrance door jingled as I entered, barely audible over the chatter of diners chowing down on Debbie's "world-famous"—or so the flyspecked sign in the window bragged—banana cream pancakes. (Debbie publicly claimed the pancake batter was a secret family recipe, but she once confided to Peace and me that she'd actually gotten it off the back of a Kiwanis Club calendar.) It was a town favorite, served one day a week, which happened to be today. The joint was packed—every stool at the L-shaped bar taken, every booth and table filled.

At Debbie's Diner, the gossip flowed as briskly as the sweet tea. Like Debbie used to say, if you were a quart low on gossip, you'd come to right place. "I should put gossip on the menu, right next to the gooseberry pie," she often joked. "If I charged for it, I'd be richer than John D. Rockefeller."

Today, I knew I was the favorite topic.

While Lisa Loeb's "Stay" played on the jukebox, a hush fell over the dining room as everyone's eyes followed me to the booth where Ginger and Sloane waited. Victor Valance's body—well, at this point everybody *assumed* it had to be him—being found on my property was the kind of ghastly but titillating story that twisted and turned until I became the killer and any number of rumors filled in the blanks.

I could feel the judgment in the collective stare as I ran the gauntlet of tables and booths, forcing a grin as I greeted people I knew—a cordial "*Enjoying the pancakes?*" to Mr. Soren Sosa, owner of the So-So Southern Motel, and a "*I know I'm overdue for a mani!*" to Miss Nellie, owner of Nails by Nellie. I eased into the red vinyl corner booth next to Ginger and across from Sloane.

"Is everyone still looking at me?" I asked, hiding my face with my hand.

Ginger interpreted in a couple quick hand gestures for Sloane, who turned in her seat and glanced around the room.

"I think the shock and awe have worn off," Ginger teased.

"Am I ever going to be able to walk into a room without people talking about me?" I groaned.

Ginger nudged me playfully in the side. "Stop attracting dead bodies and maybe they'll find something else to talk about."

"It's not like I seek out murder. It happens to gravitate to me like...stray animals and eccentric friends." I winked at Ginger, fetching a laugh. I hadn't realized how desperately I needed a distraction from everything.

"How's Nora handling the news about what's going on?" Ginger asked.

"I haven't told her. I just want her to focus on her schoolwork so she can get into Duke and get away from this place."

"She's going to Duke?" Ginger beamed, showing me a mouthful of chewed fries. "That's incredible!"

"Well, it's the plan, but we'll see what happens. So anyway, what were you ladies up to today?" I signed the words I knew for Sloane and hoped she could piece together the rest from lip-reading.

Sloane glanced at Ginger with a question on her face, as if seeking permission to tell me about some classified mission they were on. I now fully understood the Fear Of Missing Out kids referred to these days. #FOMO

Sloane signed several words I didn't recognize—ending with a G cascading down her hair.

"What's that mean?" I asked, turning to Ginger.

"Oh, that's my sign name," Ginger explained.

"Sign name?"

"A sign name is a sign that represents your name, and only

a Deaf or hard-of-hearing person can give it to you. For me, she's using a G for Ginger, and it's cascading down my hair because of my red hair."

"Oh, that's neat! What's my sign name?"

Sloane looked uncertain as she signed her reply. "I don't really know you well enough to give you a sign name yet. Sorry."

"Oh, no worries," I answered, feeling supremely dumb. "You never said what you were up to this morning. Anything fun?"

Sloane shrugged off the question. Ginger glanced away, saying, "No, not *fun* exactly."

"Is there a reason you're being tightlipped about whatever you did?"

"No, it's nothing. We're just spending time together."

Their secrecy was planting all kinds of paranoia in my mind. Why wouldn't they tell me? What were they hiding?

"I can't help but feel like you're angry with me about something."

"Tara, honey, you know I love you like family. Stop overthinking it," Ginger said.

She was asking the impossible, because I overthought everything. "Okay, if you say everything's fine, I'm trusting you'll tell me if it's not."

"I didn't want to tell you because I didn't want to make you feel bad," Ginger added tentatively, "but we went to visit Bennie's gravesite together. I only wanted it to be me and Sloane because, well…"

Ginger didn't need to finish the explanation. I got it. It was because I had always disliked Benson and trusted him about as far as I could shove my foot up his butt…which I had wanted to do on many occasions when he treated his own mother like garbage. Plus, my family was partly responsible for his death. Clearly she wouldn't want me there, and yet…I still wanted to be there for my best friend.

"You could have told me that. I would have understood," I replied.

"I just…I didn't want to make you feel left out, but I'm still processing my feelings. To be honest, Tara, I kind of resent you for what happened, even though I know it's no one's fault but his own."

An awkward silence descended on our booth. I rested my arms on the table, the sleeve of my shirt clinging to a blob of maple syrup. I didn't know what Ginger wanted from me. An apology? A time machine? A miracle to bring Benson back from the dead? Luckily Ginger broke through the tension with, "What are you getting to eat?"

I stared at Ginger's pancakes and my stomach did a flip. As little as I had eaten since finding Vic's dead body on my property, I had no appetite. I guess being a murder suspect was an effective way to diet.

"Since it's past breakfast but not quite lunch I couldn't decide between loaded fries or pancakes, so I ended up getting both. And I highly recommend both." Ginger grinned, this time a mouthful of pancakes peeking out between her teeth.

"I think I'm just going to get an iced tea," I said.

Ginger shoved her half-empty plate of fries toward me. "Help yourself. You've always been my favorite mooch."

"That's because I'm your only mooch."

"So what did you want to talk to us about?" Ginger asked.

While I hadn't intended the *us* to include Sloane, at least I knew she could keep a secret, since she'd already done it for Ginger.

"Detective Hughes stopped by this morning," I launched into it. "She said the medical examiner thinks Victor was killed by Somulose, though she won't know until the toxicology report comes back in a few weeks."

"S-O-M-U-L-O-S-E?" Ginger asked, finger spelling the word out for Sloane.

"It's a drug used for the humane euthanasia of horses," I explained.

Ginger snorted. "So somebody put Victor Valance to sleep, huh? A fate much too kind for the dirty skunk, if you ask me."

"That's not all. The kit had my name on it. It was the spare one we kept in the barn in case of emergency, like if a horse broke its leg or something."

"Or if a power-hungry psychopath threatened you," Ginger mumbled. "You didn't do it, did you? I wouldn't blame you if you did."

"Of course not! Why would you ask that?"

"The thought has probably crossed the mind of most of the people in this room."

"Well, I didn't kill him. But I went to check the barn and sure enough, our Somulose kit was gone. I told Detective Hughes that Vic must have stolen it, but I don't think she believes me."

"I'm more confused than a termite in a wooden yo-yo. So the police think you're a suspect?"

"I guess so. But that's not what I was calling you about last night. It gets worse."

Ginger's jaw dropped. "How can it possibly get worse than that?"

I couldn't tell anyone exactly what I had done that could put me behind bars for Vic's murder. Not Chris. Not even Ginger. There was no way any of them would understand why I did it. But there was something I needed her help with. I handed her my phone, hoping she'd reserve judgement until after I explained.

"What is this?" she asked, looking from me to the phone screen in her hand.

"Read the message."

Ginger placed the phone in the middle of the syrup-sticky table, reading the message with Sloane leaning toward her. As their gazes locked in on the words, I watched them, waiting and praying for some kind of affirmation that it wasn't as bad as I thought it was. When Ginger hugged me, I knew right then it was even worse.

I was afraid to meet Ginger's washed-out olive eyes that held more wisdom than her tongue.

"You are as screwed as a dog in heat, honey."

The phone buzzed, vibrating a couple inches across the Formica. A green text bubble popped up on the screen:

This isn't over.

Another bubble pulsed to life and I snatched up the phone:

Your family is next.

Chapter 8

Staring out the window, I focused on a breath, willing my heart to slow down. Through a smudged handprint I could make out a trawler pulling into the bay with the catch of the day. Two pre-school kids were running along the beach trying in vain to launch a mile-long dragon kite on a windless day. I knew just how they felt.

Ginger read aloud the email I'd received from Vic, dated the day before we found his body. This put a big question mark behind his time of death, because Detective Hughes said he had died four days ago. This email was sent two days ago. Either Victor Valance wasn't dead, or it wasn't Vic who emailed me. Neither scenario was good, because that meant someone else knew too much. They knew my secrets. And they planned to reveal them:

You think I've forgotten you, but you're wrong. You and me have a special kind of history. I know you see me as the villain and you as the hero. Your self-righteousness wouldn't let you see us any other way. Somebody's going to knock you off your high horse someday. It might very well be me.

Despite what you want to believe, it's not over between us, and if our history proves anything, we will never be over.

A long time ago I gave you a chance to pick me instead of Chris. "Why do you waste your time with losers?" I had asked you. It turns out I was right. Chris is the worst kind of loser, the kind that can't even keep a job and take care of his family. You had your chance with me, Tara, and you blew it. Now you're going to pay the price.

Consider this email my final warning.

I have something very interesting that I bet the police would love to hear. I recorded our parting words. Pretty smart of me, right? But before you get any crazy ideas, if anything happens to me, Tara, they'll receive a copy of the tape. Unless you're willing to do something for me. Perhaps we can work together after all. This time on my terms.

Don't want to sell your soul to the devil? Tough. There's no hiding what you did. And soon everyone will know who you really are—a murderer.

Ginger stared at me, her expression a mask of confusion, waiting for an explanation I didn't want to give.

"What…what is he talking about?" she asked. "I don't even know where to begin with the questions. First of all, why did he call you a murderer?"

I didn't know where to begin either, just as I didn't know

where this would end. I hoped not with me behind bars.

"It's not what you think. This email is misrepresenting what happened."

"Then tell me what really happened."

"About a week ago Vic and I had a huge fight at the horse kill pen because he kept outbidding me on every horse, when he knows my farm is struggling to stay afloat."

"Your horse rescue is struggling?" Sloane interjected.

I nodded sadly. "It's been a long time coming. Chris, Peace, and I are pouring everything into it, but it's not enough. We're spending endless dollars keeping horses off the chopping block without any return."

"Then why are you giving me free riding lessons if the ranch is struggling? You know I'd be happy to pay!" Sloane signed, her gestures vigorous and her facial expression sympathetic.

"You're teaching me sign language," I reminded her. "We had a deal and I don't want to accept payment from a friend."

"I have plenty of money!" Sloane insisted. "How much do you need? I can help. And if you won't take it, then I'll make Peace take it. You're both doing this work to save horses—it's a tax deduction anyway."

Sloane picked up her camel Hermes Birkin bag—I had no idea she had *that* kind of money—off the seat and rested it on the table. Who brought a $20,000 purse to a dive like Debbie's Diner? And set it on a syrupy tabletop to boot? Someone who had a money tree, that's who.

She pulled her phone from the overpriced purse, pecked it with her acrylic nails, then showed me the screen. A money transfer app was open, with the amount left blank.

"Type in what you need," she signed, pushing the phone

toward my hand.

I waved her offer away. Principle held me back. "I appreciate it, but the day-to-day costs are only getting worse. Hay prices have gone up. Grain is three times more expensive than it's ever been. And to top it off, the whole town of Bloodson Bay aligns my family name with murder, even after Chris was acquitted. No one wants to do business with us. We're not able to resell any of the young trained horses, and our sole survival is based on Chris's job…which lately has been looking tenuous at best."

The farm problems continued full circle until they became a noose around my neck.

"Back to this email," Ginger persisted. "What happened between you and Victor?"

"After he kept outbidding me on horses at the kill pen, I suggested we make an arrangement that we both could benefit from. I'd let him bid low on the horses without any competition from me, and I'd buy the horses off of him at a profit to him. It was a win-win deal."

"What did he say?" Sloane asked.

"He agreed. Or so I thought. I ended up letting him bid low on a dozen horses, then when it came time for me to buy them off of him, he reneged on the deal. Then he laughed in my face—I swear, an actual evil villain laugh, just like Dr. Evil—and told me he'd been waiting a long time to watch our family crash and burn. But that's basically all that happened."

Sorta.

The conversation didn't quite go that smoothly. I may have said a thing or two I regretted. Deeply. In the moment they seemed harmless. But now that Vic was dead, they were incriminating.

"But that doesn't explain whatever you *did* to him."

"I don't know what he's referring to." I hated omitting details, but Peace and I had made a pact. No one could find out what had happened—not even Chris. I hated lying to my husband almost as much as I hated keeping Peace's secret. But the less I said, the better for everyone.

"I may have *mildly* threatened him while he was recording our conversation, which I didn't know he was doing, by the way. But I never acted on it, of course. I was pissed and lashed out. If someone has that recording, I'm worried it might make the cops think I killed him."

"Any ideas on who that someone might be?"

"No clue. But I don't know how Vic could have sent this. Or maybe he told someone about our conversation, knowing he had a target on his back. Read this—doesn't it sound like he was using this to blackmail me into protecting him?"

But before you get any crazy ideas, if anything happens to me, Tara, they'll receive a copy of the tape.

Sloane's eyes flashed angrily. "But how could *you* protect him? And why the heck would you protect him after everything he's done to you?"

"Back in the day," Ginger began, offering Sloane a CliffsNotes version of the Christie family's history, "Chris's father had been the mayor with a lot of connections. In fact, his family was the founding family of Bloodson Bay. I'm guessing Chris still has some of those connections…and I think Vic was banking on Tara using them to protect him from whatever bad situation he had gotten himself into…again."

"I know I'm late to the party here," Sloane cut in, "and I don't know much about this Victor guy, but were you two lovers or something?"

"Ew, no!" I physically gagged, spitting a spray of sweet tea. "What makes you think that?"

"He said he had given you a chance to be with him. I just figured…"

"No, he's referring to when we were teenagers, back when I had first started dating Chris. Vic hit on me, I rejected him, but it was nothing more than that."

Sloane's expression fell, as if she was disappointed there wasn't a juicier story there.

"Then who hates him enough to kill him? And hates you enough to bury him on your land in order to frame you?" Sloane probed.

I made a sweeping gesture signifying the entire dining room.

"Ever since my family made headlines for murder, it's pretty much everyone in town."

"So what are you going to do?"

Run? Hide? Bury my head in the sand? But those weren't realistic options. I had a daughter to protect, a horse farm to save, and a town to prove my innocence to.

"Wait…I think I might have an idea…" I started. To which Ginger shook her head vehemently.

"No, no, no. Anytime you have an"—Ginger crooked her fingers into air quotes—"*idea,* it always makes things worse."

"How much worse can it get? My hometown hates me. My daughter practically has PTSD. And now Detective Hughes thinks I killed Vic. What choice do I have? I have nothing left to lose."

As it turns out, I still had plenty to lose.

Chapter 9

I could hear Vic's specter mocking me, his threat growing more corporeal every waking minute. There was only one way to fix it, and Ginger had been 100 percent against my *"very stupid, very reckless, very dumb plan."* Her words, not mine.

"Don't forget about tonight!" Chris called out to me from the kitchen with a mouthful of sandwich.

I envied my hubby's always ravenous appetite. I had shed a few pounds on my stress diet and imagined I was starting to look like one of the walking dead. One of these days I hoped to get my appetite back. I wondered if they carried human brains in Kroger's deli?

"They opened up that new drive-in in town," Chris added. "We can relive our teenage glory days."

"I'll be home in time for our date," I promised him, kissing his chipmunk cheek as I grabbed my purse from the counter.

We both knew me better than that, though. The last time I had been on time for anything was when I was in labor with Nora and made it to the hospital before popping her out. I'd been late to everything else ever since.

"Oh, and I have some news to tell you tonight," Chris added.

"What kind of news?" I didn't want to wait until tonight. Along with being perpetually late, I was equally impatient.

"I don't want to get into it now. We'll discuss it later, okay?"

That made it sound bad.

"Is it bad?"

"I never said that," he replied.

"Then it's good? Did you get that promotion you applied for?"

I was reaching for any hint I could get.

"One of these days you need to learn patience is a virtue, Tara."

"So is chastity," I reminded him with a wry grin. "You wouldn't want me to learn *that* too, wouldja?"

"Uh…"

"I didn't think so."

I mentally planned out what time I'd need to be home in order to fit in a quick leg shave—or up to my knees, at least—in case Chris was serious about reliving our teenage years, and what outfit would be most weather-appropriate for an April evening at the drive-in. Weather in North Carolina was as capricious as a woman on her period. Tank tops and shorts by day, sweaters and sweatpants by night. It made my laundry room a war zone.

I opened the front door, calling out, "I'll be back in—*holy crap*!" I stumbled against the foyer wall, clutching my chest. "Ginger, you scared the life out of me!"

Ginger sported a solid black outfit consisting of skinny jeans, turtleneck sweater, and heavily studded motorcycle jacket—a hodge-podge of thrift store finds, apparently, and way too snug on her frame. She looked like a bargain-basement Michelle Pfeiffer as Catwoman. I couldn't help but giggle.

"You know it's not Halloween, right?"

Ginger took mock umbrage. "Well, excuuuuse me! If I would have known I was that hideous, I would have put on more makeup."

As if her slathered-on-with-a-trowel red lipstick and blue eyeshadow wasn't enough.

Sloane, posing with supermodel poise beside Ginger, was a vision in black. She wore skintight leather pants, thigh-high Stella McCartney boots, and a zip-up Rick Owens leather jacket that hugged her svelte figure. Her makeup was impeccable, of course; her dark hair was gathered up into a fetching chignon. She looked like a Bond girl who had come to steal my plans for world domination—or to kill me.

"You gonna invite us in, or what?" Ginger said.

"Yeah, sure." I stepped aside, and we went into the living room. "I was just going out myself, but—why are you here, anyway?"

I was pretty sure Ginger was here to stop me after she had told me what a terrible idea it was to break into Vic's house to look around. I just needed to make sure nothing else connected me to his death. Because while *I* knew I was innocent, I had no idea what Detective Hughes knew. Or what she would find when she searched his house…if it wasn't too late.

Ginger stood with hands on hips, five feet and change of pure attitude. "You didn't think I would actually let you go—"

"Don't! Just don't. You know I have to. Nora can't go through another parent being accused of murder. She's been through enough, and this is the only way I can find and get rid of that recording."

"If you'd let me finish," Ginger sternly cut in, "I was going to say you didn't think I would actually let you go without me..."

"You're both here...to help me?"

"Does a cat have climbing gear? We'll call ourselves Tara's Angels! Pretty nifty, huh?"

"Terrific," I muttered.

"So what's the plan, Stan?" Ginger smiled big, globs of her signature red lipstick flecking her teeth.

"It's pretty simple, really. I'm just going over there to snoop around. See if I can find the recording before the police do."

"How do you know they haven't already?" Sloane asked.

"I don't, but I'd assume Detective Hughes would have shown up on my doorstep already if they had."

"I brought something to help." Ginger hefted onto the couch a hideous supersized carpet bag—literally made out of carpet—decorated with pictures of pro golfers wearing outfits they'd apparently stolen from circus clowns. I imagined it was one of Ginger's 1980s fashion statements that should have stayed buried deep in her closet. "Say hello to my little friend," she added with a terrible *Scarface* impersonation. Then she pulled out three ski masks. "I brought these just in case."

"We're not robbing a bank, Ginger."

"You have no idea who might be watching his place. I wouldn't be surprised if he had criminal ties to Jimmy Hoffa."

Sloane looked me up and down, eyeing me with disapproval. I almost thought it was judgement for what I was about to do until she grabbed my hand and dragged me upstairs to my bedroom.

"You can't wear that," she signed.

"What's wrong with it?" I asked, looking down at my

striped sweatshirt that matched my green moto leggings perfectly. I thought I looked pretty darn cute.

"Where are your shirts?" she asked.

I pointed to my dresser drawer, which she promptly rummaged through until she whipped out a plain black top.

"Here," she said, thrusting it at me. "Black. When you break into someone's house, you wear black. Not bright stripes that will draw everyone's attention. And put on black leggings and meet us downstairs."

While I felt like all three of us dressing like cat burglars appeared more suspicious than dressing like normal women, I was outnumbered. I quickly changed, feeling a fine dew of sweat breaking out on my forehead at the ridiculousness of what we were about to do.

Chris was in the foyer wearing a *what now?* look when I bounded down the steps to meet the girls at the front door.

"Don't ask!" I said, sailing past him.

Chapter 10

At three stories tall, Victor Valance's home had stirred up a hornet's nest of controversy during its construction. The massive ten-bedroom dwelling completely obstructed the ocean vista his hopping mad neighbors had paid a premium for. Of course Vic and his daddy's army of lawyers skirted around all the zoning ordinances, and he built it even bigger and gaudier than originally planned. It was no wonder the douchebag had so many enemies. He went out of his way to create them.

Tatters of clouds drifted across the early evening moon, huge in the burnt umber sky. A cool briny breeze sighed. The house was dark and empty when Tara's Angels—as Ginger had dubbed our intrepid little trio—arrived. I'd parked my car a block down the street and we'd walked the rest of the way. You'd think three women clad all in black would attract more attention, but only a cocker spaniel glanced disinterestedly as she did her business on a manicured lawn.

The ground floor appeared to be a multiple-car garage, where a staircase split around both sides of the garage doors, meeting at a landing a few steps below the front porch of the main house. Luckily it looked obscured by enough palm trees and crape myrtles to hide us from view. Hopefully.

We climbed the stairs up to the landing, peering in through the glass wall. I was tempted to smear dirty handprints all across his pristine windows…but I behaved. Only because it would have been stupid to drop fingerprint evidence right in Detective Hughes' lap.

There didn't appear to be any cop cars parked on the street, which I suppose made sense since the only person who lived here was now dead. But I couldn't shake the feeling that I was being watched.

I tilted a potted clematis up, searching for the housekey. There should have been one there.

"How are we getting—?" Sloane signed. I was having trouble seeing each word as dusk settled in around us.

I turned to Ginger for clarity.

"I missed part of what Sloane said."

"She wants to know how we're getting inside," Ginger explained. "Does anyone know how to pick a lock?"

Sloane and I both shook our heads.

"What exactly *was* your plan?" Ginger asked me.

"There was supposed to be a key out here somewhere." Nothing under the doormat, the bench cushion, or even above the door frame. I couldn't find it.

A car turned up the driveway, its headlights swiveling toward us. The beam of light swooshed right over my head just as we all ducked.

"Someone's here!" Ginger whispered; she and Sloane hugged up against the wall.

A car door slammed shut as I frantically looked around for an escape, but the railing held us captive on the porch that dropped two stories down.

The vague shadow of a person passed across the floor under the glow of a streetlight, then paused at the first step. There was no hiding now.

“Tara?” a voice called out.

I stood up tentatively. “Leo?” I verified.

“Why is Victor’s brother here?” Ginger demanded.

“I called him when I saw the email from Vic and asked for his help getting inside.”

Ginger came out of hiding; Sloane followed her, a little more cautiously. “What the hell, Tara?” Ginger fumed. “Why didn’t you just *tell* us there was a key?”

I couldn’t tell her I’d just donned my black duds just to humor her. “And miss out on all this intrigue?” I said. “What kind of boring caper would that have been for Tara’s Angels?”

Ginger mulled this over. “I guess you’re right!” she said with a grin.

By now Leo had reached the top landing. “Ah, the things one would do to destroy incriminating evidence,” he chided. “You know I went out on a limb for you. If the cops or my father knew I was letting you inside…”

“I know, I know. I owe you big-time, Leo. Please tell me you got Vic’s phone…” I searched his face for affirmation.

“About that…” he began, then skimmed the front yard with his gaze. “I’ll tell you inside.”

“Where’s the key you said you’d leave out here?” I asked as he headed to the front door.

“You don’t need a key. I left the door unlocked. Did you even try the handle?”

Ginger and I exchanged a guilty look, wondering how it had never occurred to any of us to check.

Leo let us inside, leaving the light off as we wandered around the glass-encased living room checking out the place. I felt exposed to the world, unable to fathom how anyone would *choose* to live in a see-through house.

Clearly the police had already been here as drawers were open, couch cushions out of place, and overall the place looked clean but disheveled. Definitely not the mess of a slob, but an organized mess, if that made any sense. I made my way to the dining room—more windows, no surprise there—and watched the darkness saturate the lingering orange hues, turning the sky the color of black coffee.

"Break the news to me, Leo. Were you able to get his phone or laptop?" I asked.

Leo nodded, and the crushing weight instantly lifted.

"Yeah, I got his phone and laptop before the cops arrived. I cleaned out his emails and destroyed both. They're long gone in the bay."

"Bless your heart, we've got a knight in shining cowboy boots here!" Ginger exclaimed.

"Were you able to find the recording he threatened to use against me?"

This time Leo didn't look so promising. "There were no audio files or anything like that on either device, so I don't think so. He must have saved it somewhere else."

How the heck were we going to find it in this monstrosity? That is, if it was even still here. It had to be. If Detective Hughes had found it, I'd be arrested by now…or at least sitting in that 1970s throwback interrogation room sipping stale coffee while they drilled holes in my defense.

So if the cops didn't have the recording, and it wasn't on Vic's phone or laptop, where could it be? I felt like this was one of those moments where I was supposed to think like Vic in order to figure out his hiding place…but God help anyone who was forced to burrow inside a mind that evil.

Chapter 11

"It's not here," Ginger groaned after we had searched the entire first and second floor of unnecessary bedrooms for some kind of thumb drive that Vic would have saved the recording on.

"If it's not here, then either the cops have it or he was bluffing," I concluded.

I was too weary to keep searching, and Chris would kill me—with kindness, that is, because as I had told the police countless times last year, there wasn't a murderous bone in his body—if I didn't make our date night tonight. I couldn't waste a good leg shave, could I now?

"Is it absolutely necessary we find it?" Ginger pressed. "I mean, I don't know what exactly you could have said that would incriminate you. Even if you did threaten him. People make threats all the time and don't get pinned for murder because of them."

"How many people do you know who threaten someone, then find their body buried in their yard, and *not* get convicted?" I threw back at her. It wasn't *her* head on the chopping block. It was *mine*.

Ginger shrugged. "At this point, what else can we do? We've searched every square inch of this house."

"Wait," Leo interjected. "Except for the man cave."

"Did you say Batcave?" Ginger and I echoed

simultaneously.

"No, *man* cave. It's…something else. Follow me."

Leo led us to Vic's office, where a large bookshelf stood against one wall. With the toe of his boot he stepped on a mechanism along the baseboard and pushed the bookshelf to one side, opening up a hole in the wall that led down a set of carpeted steps.

"No. Friggin'. Way!" Sloane exclaimed, this time using her voice.

"Jeez," Ginger said, "who would have thought a peckerwood like Victor Valance would have a secret man cave? No offense, Leo."

"None taken. Actually, peckerwood is a compliment for somebody like Vic." Leo switched on a light, illuminating the stairs. "Be careful walking down."

Ginger frowned. "Darn, I was kinda hoping we could slide down the Batpoles."

"You know, Ging," I said, "the way you said that, it sounded kinda dirty."

She snickered. "That's exactly how I meant it. Lead the way, Alfred," she said, and gave Leo a hard shove that almost sent him sprawling.

At the bottom of the steps Leo flicked another switch. Track lighting blazed to life, illuminating a sprawling, knotty pine-paneled room that was every adolescent's fantasy come true. Victor's man cave had everything: a billiard table with a tacky poker-playing-dogs light overhead; three ginormous wall-mounted flat-screen TVs; a mechanical bull like the one in *Urban Cowboy*; foosball coffee table, walk-in beer cooler, and full-service wet bar; a stone fireplace surmounted by a giant moose head—and even more toys, toys, toys. My mind reeled, trying to take it all in.

"Impressive, Leo," I said, "but I don't understand why your dear departed brother's man cave had to be kept secret."

"Actually, it's not unusual for guys to have secret entrances to their man caves. It's all part of the fantasy. But you haven't seen the big secret yet. Come with me."

He led us through the maze of manly-man leather furniture, past the walls plastered with neon beer signs and posters of busty bikini-clad babes hoisting assault rifles and straddling Harleys, toward the back of the room. Curiously, the crown of a straw cowboy hat was sticking up over the back of one of the chairs. As we passed it I turned to look.

"Aaaah! There's somebody here!"

A stunning young woman with silky shoulder-length blonde hair propped her tanned arms on the armrests, one manicured hand clutching a Budweiser can. A pink crop top revealed her enviably flat stomach and belly button ring. The cowgirl sat cross-legged in her Daisy Dukes, smiling vacantly. Her cherry lips never twitched. Her big green eyes never blinked. Sloane and Ginger joined me in gawking at her flawless gams like three jealous stepsisters.

"Wait just a minute," I said, giving the blonde goddess an experimental poke on the arm. The silicone dummy didn't flinch, just kept smiling that mindless Barbie doll smile.

Leo chuckled. "That's Laura. Vic's...companion doll." He stroked her cheek affectionately with the back of his index finger. "Incredibly lifelike, huh? I forget what he paid for her, but he said she was worth every penny. Totally poseable. And anatomically correct down to the, uh, last detail."

I felt my flesh crawl. "Gross! Leo, your brother was one sick puppy."

"Tell me something I don't know."

"Companion doll, my ass!" Ginger snorted. "Just goes to show that money can't buy class."

I turned to Leo. "Let's get on with it. This place gives me the creeps."

Leo reached under a corner of the wet bar and pushed a hidden button, activating another sliding panel, and flicked on the fluorescent lights. We stepped into a plain, medium-sized, unventilated room with cinderblock walls and a cement floor—quite the contrast to the palatial man cave. There were numerous shelving units and stacks of boxes against the walls.

"This is where he kept his, uh, *private* business stuff."

"So that doll wasn't kept private?" Ginger mumbled under her breath.

"Dad insisted on Vic adding this room off of the man cave to keep him from getting caught in his…more nefarious dealings," Leo continued. "Anything important—and potentially incriminating—he kept down here. I'm guessing that recording would qualify."

All four of us meandered around the room, searching boxes and shelves and every other nook and cranny. As I finished rooting through yet another dead-end container, my phone pinged. This was now eight reminder texts from Chris pelting me through my pocket about our date night, and I was almost ready to give up on this quest. There was no way to know what exactly we were looking for or where Vic would have hidden it.

"Check this out," Ginger commented, setting her carpet bag down on a shelf where several old electronics sat. "He's got a

VHS player here."

Ginger blew away a layer of dust, then sneezed. She blew her nose on a tissue she whisked from her sleeve like a magician and scrunched it up.

"You're not going to put that back up your sleeve, are you?"

Although I teased Ginger about her hoarding tendencies, it wasn't her fault. Ginger grew up so poor that her family repurposed everything. And I mean *everything.* A paper towel might be used to wipe a face, then the counter, then the floor until it disintegrated. The same with tissues. Ginger stored tissues up her sleeves and reused them until they turned to dust. It was why she couldn't get rid of her entire wardrobe from 1985. If it still fit or could be used for something, Ginger refused to let it go.

I sidled up to her, checking out the stack of VHS movies, most of which appeared to be from the 1990s. "Someone was a Schwarzenegger fan. *Terminator. Twins.* He even has *Kindergarten Cop* here!"

The movies revived a nostalgia for those Friday nights when a teenaged Peace, Chris, Jonah, and I would head to Blockbuster to pick out a flick. I remembered one night in particular when my brother Jonah and Vic got into a fistfight in the parking lot over the last copy of *Men in Black.* I don't know what they were trying to prove, besides being testosterone-driven idiots. Even back then trouble plagued our two families, and the passage of time had done nothing to forge a truce.

Next to the VHS player was a tape deck, almost identical to the one I played countless mix tapes on as a teenager. I'd lay on my bed for hours listening to random music collections…along with a few *for-your-ears-only* romantic collections Chris had made me. Ah, the good old days of recording your favorite songs from the radio, trying to time it just right so that you didn't get the DJ talking over your music.

Along with the cassette player was a box of Memorex cassettes with a pink and yellow stripe across the bottom. I remembered using the same exact ones to record the Spice Girls album from Peace, who was cool enough to have the technologically advanced Sony dual cassette player-recorder that I had begged my parents to buy me three birthdays in a row. I eventually ended up with a Walkman, which defeated the purpose of illegally recording music.

My daughter had no idea how easy kids had it these days.

I picked up a cassette with *Alice in Chains* written across the edge of the case. At least Vic had decent taste in music.

"Man, I haven't heard this group in forever."

"Who is that?" Ginger asked, peering over my shoulder.

I grinned. "I guess you never listened to alternative rock?"

"Is this the same as Alice Cooper? I used to really dig him. What a cool stage show he put on! Snakes, guillotines, dancing skeletons. Saw him in concert once in Raleigh at the—"

"Different Alice, different era." I picked up the tape deck, testing to see if the batteries had corroded; they were good. "Here, I'll see if I can play it for you." I popped open the cassette player and slid the tape inside. "Welcome to the wonderful world of grunge. You'll probably hate it."

I pressed the *play* button, expecting the slow buildup of electric guitar and the opening "oooh" of "Rooster" to ooze from the tiny speaker. Instead it was just a boy talking.

"Pfft! I'd say Alice Cooper has got Alice in Chains beat all to hell," Ginger declared superiorly.

Sloane, noticing my perplexity, waved my attention to her from across the room. "What is it?"

"It's not music. It's just a kid talking," I signed back.

"Didn't that email you got mention a *tape*?" Then she pointed to the cassette player.

I pulled out my cell phone, opened up the email. No friggin' way. Sloane was right. No one used the word *tape* unless they actually meant a tape.

"Do you think Victor recorded your fight on one of these tapes? There's almost a dozen of them," Ginger speculated, rifling through the plastic cartridges.

"Maybe. Though I didn't think anyone still used tape recorders. Where would somebody even find tapes?" I wondered.

"Are there still Kmarts? I used to buy tapes there when vinyl records went out of style," Ginger said.

"Jeez, you are a dinosaur, aren't you? But I love ya anyway. No, I'm afraid Kmart's a relic of the past, Ging. I just don't understand why he'd put a blackmail recording on a tape."

"Because no one would suspect it," Sloane suggested.

Considering the box full of them, how many people was Vic blackmailing? And if these were as old as they looked, how long had he been doing it?

"Something was important enough for Victor to hold on to these for so long," Ginger observed, echoing what I was thinking.

"Well, there's only one way to find out."

Ginger punched the play button, and the tape began with the most chilling words in the most ominous tone I'd ever heard: *"I've done something terrible, and this is my dark confession."*

Tape 1
Alice in Chains

1995

[Cassette tape clicks on, muffled sound in background]

[Young male, whispering] I've done something terrible, and this is my dark confession. I decided to record this in case anything goes south, someone would know the truth.

If anyone finds this tape, or finds her body, I didn't do it. I didn't kill her.

[Rustling of paper in background]

[Young male] Oh, dude, I probably should give some context. So there's this secret I've been keeping. Only since yesterday, but it's heavy. It's so bad I haven't even told my bro. The worst part is I don't know how to feel about it. Proud? Ashamed? A little of both?

At first I was pissed that Dad picked me to do this. It's bogus to put your own kid in this position. But whatever. I'm starting to see why he chose me. 'Cause he didn't trust anyone else.

See, I've been staying in a bunker. Yeah, totally the gun room in *Tremors* kind of stuff, as in an underground, damp, cinderblock room with fluorescent lights, one outlet, and a toilet room. It's boring as hell in here, but at least there's a generator. My job is to make sure it's got enough gas to run, and to keep the supplies stocked.

You might be wondering why I'm even here. This is where it gets dark. Like Buffalo Bill kind of dark.

[Woman distantly pleading] Please let me go!

[Young male] *Her.* My most important job is to keep an eye on *her.* Dad didn't tell me why she's here, but it's for something heinous, I'm sure. *Don't ask, don't tell* is our family motto.

[Woman] Did you hear me? Please, I am begging you to let me go home!

[Chink of metal in background]

[Young male] Stop spazzing out, lady! I can't free you. I don't have the key to your shackle thing. Besides, it's only been a day. I'm sure you'll be out of here soon.

[Crinkle of a plastic bag]

[Young male] But just in case, I brought you some clean clothes. From The Gap. These looked to be about your size. I grabbed them from my mom's closet, so hopefully she won't notice they're missing.

[Furby chatters in the background]

[Young male] Oh yeah, I forgot—I brought this thing too. It's like a little annoying toy pet that talks. I figured if we ain't got cable, at least this will entertain us. Here, take it.

[Woman speaks weakly] Thank you, but I do not even know why I am here. Please...you can let me go. I will not tell anyone if you let me go.

[Young male] No comprende English, lady? I already told you I don't have a key to unshackle you! Plus, if I break orders I'm dead meat. And you'll be fine as long as you don't do anything stupid. Just take a chill pill. Jeez!

[Woman] So we are both just...stuck here? For how long?

[Young male] Your guess is as good as mine. Until my dad gets what he wants, I guess.

[Woman] If someone would just tell me what he wants, I swear I will do it. I just want out of here...

[Young male] Well, he ain't here to ask, so we just have to wait.

[Young male chomps, then spits]

[Woman, growing hysterical] Why are you spitting your food out? Is there poison in the food you've been giving me?

[Young male] Oh my God, will you stop wiggin' out? You're not poisoned. You never see chewing tobacco before?

[Woman] You *did* chain me to a wall, so it is not crazy to think you might poison me too.

[Young male] Hey, I'm not the one who put you here. You got a bone to pick, take it up with my dad.

[Woman] Who is your father? I do not even know who brought me, or how I got here.

[Young male] You seriously don't remember anything?

[Woman, growing frantic] No, the last thing I remember was being in my own bed in my own home. The next thing I know I am waking up chained to this wall!

[Chain rattles in background as woman strains at her bonds]

[Woman, calmer now] Look, I am trying to help you. Whatever the reason your family has for locking me in here, they have the wrong person. And it is illegal. If someone found out, which is going to happen because I have friends and family who will start looking for me, you will go to jail. You are a young man—do you want to destroy your future, all because your father told you to hold a woman prisoner?

[Young male scoffs] You think you can trick me into releasing you? I'm not lying when I told you I can't free you.

[Woman] But you can go straight to the police and have them rescue me. I will make sure they know you saved me! I promise to protect you. You will not get in trouble.

[Young male] So you want me to turn my own dad in to save a stranger? First of all, I have no idea what you did, but he never gets the *wrong person.* You're here for a reason. And second of all, I'm no narc.

[Woman breaks down into sobs]

[Young male's voice loud in the recorder] I swear, I don't know what my dad has planned, but if this lady dies, I didn't kill her.

[Tape clicks off]

Chapter 12

"Search every square inch of this house if you have to!"

The tape had just clicked off when we heard the booming voice in Vic's man cave.

I *knew* that voice.

"Leo," I whispered, "is that your—"

"Dad! Crap! What's he doing here? Y'all better hide."

Ginger pulled her carpet bag off the shelf and dropped down to hide behind a cardboard box curiously marked *Sugar*—I suspected it contained something much more potent—while simultaneously pulling her ski mask over her head. She signed to Sloane to do the same.

Sloane cocked her head. "Seriously? You think a ski mask will stop him from shooting you dead?"

Ginger shrugged and replied in sign, "I thought at least if he misses and we escape he won't know who he needs to come after."

Ginger had a point, so I grabbed my own mask and took cover behind another stack of boxes.

"No one leaves until it's found!" Judge Valance's voice was louder now as his footsteps clicked along the man cave's hardwood floor.

"Alonzo," the judge barked, "get in touch with Corbin Roth. He'll know a buyer for the drugs."

Corbin Roth. The sleezy real-estate mogul who dipped his hands in investments scams and apparently drugs too.

"Yes, sir," the man replied.

I peered around the boxes, recognizing the tall, bulky Alonzo as one of the officers at Vic's crime scene. Now that a corrupt cop was added to the mix, my chances of getting out of this whole murder mess were growing slimmer by the second.

"Metal shelf!" Leo mouthed as he scooted past me.

Metal shelf? What about a metal shelf?

While we scrambled to hide deeper in the room, I overheard Leo talking to his father in the man cave. I couldn't make out their whole hushed conversation, only bits and pieces of Leo's explanation for being there. Something about him making sure the cops hadn't discovered the secret storage room during their search, which bought us enough time to slip into a dark corner before the judge headed in our direction.

"There's something down here I need to check on," the judge said, closing in on our hiding place.

Sloane must have read Leo's lips, because she was already standing beside a large metal shelf in the corner, mostly empty except for a few tools. Fluttering her fingers over her head, she drew our attention to where she dropped and crawled along the floor, pushing at the shelf and feeling around the base of it.

A mental lightbulb flickered on.

Of course! The *shelf*!

I dashed over to her just as she found the same type of floor mechanism that had activated the other sliding panels. She signed to Ginger the word *exit*, jabbing her finger at the sliding shelf door. Weaving around stacks of boxes full of who knows what illegal substances—my guess was cocaine, I mean *sugar*—

Ginger finally joined us just as the judge strode purposefully toward the middle of the room. Leo was walking ahead of him, clearly trying to block his view.

"We could totally take him! He's ancient!" Sloane signed, ending with a good old-fashioned flick-off.

"Not if you don't want to go to jail for life—he's the most powerful man in Bloodson Bay," Ginger signed. "The evilest too. I'm pretty sure he drinks the blood of virgins."

"Good luck finding one around here," Sloane signed back. They both snickered.

Watching Ginger and Sloane converse so companionably, I felt a sharp pang of envy. Still, I made a mental note: keep learning and practicing sign language, because it came in handy when you needed to communicate silently!

"Stop yakking," I whispered, "and start pushing!"

The shelf, heavier than it looked, gave way with a shrill squeal. We abruptly stopped pushing, waiting for the judge, who had migrated to just outside the storage room near Vic's "companion doll," to notice the sound. I was too terrified to breathe. When nothing happened, we hefted one last push and it groaned open, letting in a fresh waft of ocean air.

"Did you hear that?"

Judge Valance must have heard us, because he shoved past Leo, heading back inside the storage room now. The judge's gaze roved over the shelves and boxes as Ginger, Sloane, and I huddled beside the door in the shadows out of sight. At least I hoped we were out of sight.

"That was me," Leo said. "There's so much crap in here it's impossible to move around."

That seemed to satisfy Judge Valance enough for him to

lose interest in investigating further. Leo, ambling casually around the room, glanced in our direction and gave us a surreptitious jerk of the head while mouthing the word *go*.

By now the secret door was open just enough for us to slip through. Impressively, it matched the exterior siding perfectly, blending into the wall as if they were one.

We were standing outside, my shoes filling with sand while nudging the door slowly closed, when Ginger shot me a hangdog look I knew all too well.

"Well, what have you done now?"

"I, uh…"

"Just tell me!" I whispered when I wanted to yell.

"My tissue—I left it on the counter," Ginger squeaked. "With my snotty DNA inside!"

I had to laugh. "What are the chances he'll touch your used tissue? Don't worry about it. We gotta go!"

As I was closing the secret door the last sliver, I watched Judge Valance approach the spot where we had found the tapes…and where Ginger's nasty tissue sat front and center.

"Leo, was anyone else down here?" he bellowed, picking up what looked like a tape, flipping it over.

"Uh, Tara?" Ginger whispered. "I think I left one of the tapes behind."

"Well, it's too late to do anything about it now." I sighed, catching a glimpse of the word written across the tape: *Exposé*

The judge was staring at it curiously. "And Alonzo, in case your pals at the precinct come back, get rid of anything incriminating that could lead back to me. We need to clear out this room tonight. It's only a matter of time before Detective Hughes discovers it."

Judge Valance turned around, only a pivot away from seeing me through the gap, when Officer Alonzo jogged into the room. I couldn't hear what he said, but it clearly made Judge Valance angry.

"Someone was here, and I'm going to find out who!" the judge boomed as the door sank silently back into the wall.

Chapter 13

Tara's Angels took off like a trio of scalded dogs, to borrow Ginger's expression, back to our waiting getaway car.

I was a couple miles down the road when my nerves stopped spazzing. I was pulling up my driveway when my brain stopped buzzing. And I was putting the car in park when I realized what I had left back at Vic's house.

"Shoot! I forgot to grab the tapes."

Even if Vic's decades-old *dark confession* didn't directly prove my innocence in his murder, it was at least enough to show someone else had motive to kill him—the mysterious woman on the tape. I wasn't the only one in Bloodson Bay who hated him. The enemies he'd made along the way were as countless as his sins.

Ginger laughed for a long moment, signing something to Sloane behind my back as I wondered what was so hilarious.

"It's not funny, Ginger. That tape was the only proof we had that could have saved me. And it could even help take down his whole criminal family."

"You mean *these* tapes?"

Ginger pulled the cassette player, along with a stack of tapes, from that gaudy supersized carpet bag I would never make fun of again.

"Oh my goodness, I love you so much! You're brilliant!"

"And I will never get tired of hearing you say that," Ginger said, hugging me from the side.

"We need to turn the tapes in to the cops," I said. "Once they hear this evidence, there's no way Judge Valance will stay in power. We'll finally show the town the monster behind the mask."

"Whoa, hold your horses." Ginger stepped out of the car, lugging her carpet bag with her. "I'm all for turning them over to the fuzz, but not until we listen to all of them. I want to know exactly what kind of person we're dealing with, and I have a feeling these tapes will tell us a lot." Ginger lifted the bag, the plastic cassettes clattering inside. "Because if it gets out that we're the ones who turned these in…will the cops even be able to protect us once Judge Valance finds out? Because you know he'll find out who turned them in, and God knows what he'll do…"

God probably had a pretty good idea what the judge would do—and Vic's wouldn't be the only body buried. I had long speculated that the judge had some of the cops on his payroll; Officer Alonzo showing up at Vic's house with the judge was proof of that. Which meant I couldn't trust anyone. Not anyone at the Bloodson Bay Police Department. Not even Detective Hughes.

If the tapes did manage to fall into the hands of an honest cop, Judge Valance would stop at nothing to discredit or destroy them. Along with the unlucky fools who had stolen them. Which was us.

"What should we do then?" I asked.

"We need to find a cop we can trust and turn them in anonymously…after we make duplicates," Ginger said. "Do you know any trustworthy cops at BBPD?"

"I think so." There was one cop on the force that I had a feeling wanted to take down the Valance family almost as much as I did. I just needed to figure out a way to test this cop's loyalty.

We got out of the car and headed up the walkway to the house. I hadn't even reached the bottom porch step when the door swung open. Chris stood in the doorway holding a sweatshirt.

Nora's royal blue Duke University sweatshirt. The one we bought last year after touring the campus of her dream college where she planned to study political science, and hoped to use her knowledge to help restore some semblance of ethical principle to her venal hometown government. A noble aspiration, even if it did sound wildly idealistic. I vividly remembered Nora taking that shirt with her when she left.

Which could only mean…

"Great, Nora's home!" Grinning with joy, I brushed past Chris. His hand on my shoulder gently but firmly spun me around.

Only now did I notice there was no *our-baby's-home* smile, nor was he dressed up for our date. And instead of his usual pre-date *I'm-having-sex-tonight* smirk, a look of dread creased his brow.

"Nora's not here, Tara. I found this on the porch, and when I called her, she told me she had her sweatshirt with her. So…I was hoping maybe it was yours."

I shook my head. "It's not mine, Chris."

He opened his mouth to speak, then thought better of it.

"What it is?" I demanded.

"Don't freak out, but there's something else..." Chris opened up the sweatshirt, and dotting the blue devil mascot were red flecks.

"Snap my garter!" Ginger blurted out. I had forgotten she and Sloane were still standing behind me. "Is that blood?"

"I need to call Nora. Right now!" I was already picking up my phone, scrolling to the call screen, when Chris yanked the phone from my hand.

"I said not to freak out! Will you just wait a minute before you needlessly scare the crap out of her? She's been through enough, Tara. If she finds out about everything going on...she won't sleep, won't eat...you know how fragile she is."

He was right, but how could I *not* freak out? If this wasn't Nora's...then someone had specifically bought the same shirt and planted it here. No one, not even the friends she lost over the past year, knew she wanted to go to Duke, so this person had done some deep digging into my family to come up with this sick calling card. Was it a warning? A threat? Every terrible scenario flooded my imagination.

"And no, it's not blood. Probably ketchup stains or something." Chris aimed his words at Ginger, who didn't like being singled out.

"How do you know, Mr. Smarty-pants?" she fired back.

"Hydrogen peroxide bubbles up if it's blood. I already tested it. So please, everybody...just take a breath and calm down. Especially you, Ginger."

Ginger had given Chris up for adoption when he was a newborn. Ever since he'd learned she was his birth mother, Chris seemed to single her out for abuse. I understood his ambivalence, but it was hard on poor Ginger.

"Any idea who left it?" I wondered aloud while Ginger pouted.

"Maybe it's just one of the children's home kids playing a prank," Chris speculated. "Or maybe one of her old high school friends trying to punk her."

"Maybe..." I mumbled, though it seemed unlikely. Especially after having just uncovered a corpse in the backyard. "Oh my gosh, Chris, do you think someone would hurt Nora?"

"No, because I won't let them."

How was Chris going to protect our child from hundreds of miles away? A fierce mama bear instinct pulsed through me. I had to figure out who was behind this, if it was the last thing I did. Without telling Nora or my mother, who had a habit of making things worse. While Eloise's heart was in the right place, her meddling tended to backfire. At least I knew where I got my own savior complex from. Thanks for that, Mom.

I searched the empty street, wondering if the Peeping Cop was still there and had maybe seen something. Under the distant glow of a streetlight I could tell that the unmarked car was gone, but I'd be sure to stop and talk to Detective Hughes to find out who was posted in front of our house, and what they witnessed.

"Just come inside," Chris urged. "I'll make a pot of tea, and we'll think this through."

Chris led everyone into the kitchen. Ginger, unprompted, filled my long-suffering husband in on the exploits of Tara's Angels, embroidering the details a mite for dramatic effect, but mainly sticking to the facts, which were bizarre enough. Chris made occasional groans of disbelief as he made and poured the tea. I'm here to tell you, I have a helluva understanding and indulgent hubby...most of the time.

"Okay," said Chris, sitting, "so you broke into Victor Valance's house, and you claim you've got proof his clan is Bloodson Bay's answer to the Corleone family. Let's see it."

"O ye of little faith!" Ginger produced the tape deck from her cavernous carpet bag and placed it ceremoniously on the table. "On the tape we listened to Victor confess to holding a woman hostage in a bunker," she began, before I cut her off.

"I'm wondering if whoever killed Victor is the woman in these tapes. If you were held captive against your will in a bunker, wouldn't you want to kill the person who abducted you?"

"You're assuming she's still alive…" Sloane added somberly.

"There's only one way to find out," I said, pressing the button that took us back in time to the circumstances that set the mystery in motion.

Tape 2
Little Red Corvette

1995

[Tape clicks on]

[Young male] I'm bored out of my freakin' skull. Keeping an eye on this chick has gotten old fast. If she dies, I'll be an accessory to murder. Yeah, I looked up the charges on one of my runs to town. Hell, I might get murder one, even though I'm underage.

[Woman, teasing] You know that talking to yourself is the first sign one is going crazy, do you not?

[Young male] Shut up!

[Woman] I will not shut up until you release me.

[Young male] I said shut up, or—

[Woman] Or what? *Daddy* is counting on you to keep me alive. You do not have the backbone to shut me up!

[Sound of hand slapping skin]

[Woman gasps] You hit me! Is that how you were raised—to beat on women? You deserve to burn in hell. You and your entire family of degenerates!

[Young male, after a pause] I'm already in hell, lady! Just be quiet. Please. I've gotta sort this out in my brain.

I'm starting to worry that Dad isn't planning on letting this lady go. It's been two days, and while I'm supposed to keep her fed and watered like a horse or something, Dad hasn't given me any idea what's going to happen. I'm starting to think maybe I should turn myself in.

[Woman, pleading] Of course you should go to the police! I do not even know why I am here! But you can make it right if you let me go. The police will not charge you if you step forward.

[Young male sighs heavily] Yeah, so my dad can kill me instead, and then still kill you. Do you know what he'd do to me if I don't obey his orders?

[Woman] Let me guess. Your father will take away your brand-new cherry red Corvette. I know your type. Spoiled rich brat who would rather let an innocent woman die than lose his toys or sully his family's reputation.

[Young male scoffs] Actually, it's a Nissan Skyline R33 GT-R, not that a chick would know anything about sports cars. But I'm not doing this over a car. I'm doing it for survival, lady. Just like you need to do whatever he asks to survive too. It'll be over soon.

[Woman] So you can guarantee he will not kill me?

[Long silence as a bag rustles]

[Young male] You know I can't guarantee anything. But hey, I brought a variety of tapes and plenty of D batteries so we can listen to music. I know there's some Smashing Pumpkins in here, or are you more of an Alanis Morrisette kind of gal? And I'll bring a TV and VHS player tomorrow to help us pass the time.

[Woman] Exactly how long will I be here that I need music and movies? You know my family and friends will be looking for me, do you not? It is only a matter of time until they go to the police.

[Young male] Ha! My dad has half the BBPD in his back pocket. You might as well get comfortable.

[Woman] How can I get comfortable with shackles on my wrists?

[Clink of chains rattling]

[Young male] I meant get used to being here for the long haul. Oh, I almost forgot. I brought you

Jurassic Park since it was the only book I had, though I personally would skip the book and watch the movie.

[Woman begins weeping]

[Young male] Hey, if you like a different genre I'll head into town tomorrow and pick up something else. Oh, and I got us Twinkies and Doritos.

[Woman] You can shove them up your ass!

[Young male] Whoa, language, lady. Listen, if you tell me a fast-food place you like, I'll pick you up a decent meal tomorrow. What about Wendy's?

[Woman] Wendy's is a decent meal to you? I want out of here! Please, I have a family. A child. How would you feel if someone did this to your mother?

[Young male] My mother wouldn't have done whatever you did to get yourself in this mess. You must have done something to piss my dad off. What did you do, anyway?

[Long silence]

[Young male] If you're not going to tell me, then I'm not going to help you. And if you ever want out of here, you better stop complaining and just do what I say. Got it?

[Woman] I do not know what I did, I swear! Where exactly is *here,* anyway? I have no idea where I am.

[Young male] You're in a bunker near—oh, nice try, lady! I'm not as dumb as I look.

[Woman] I find that hard to believe.

[Tape clicks off]

Part 2

Ginger Mallowan

Chapter 14

When you've been around as long as I have, you've seen it all. Good things, like the civil rights movement. Couples of all types being able to marry—why should they be any less miserable than the rest of us? Bad stuff too. The breakdown of the family. Red states and blue states practically going to war over petty politics. Back in the sixties, the catchphrase was *don't trust anyone over thirty*. Now it seems like no one trusts anyone. Whatever happened to the peace and love generation?

And don't get me started on technology! I guess I've got a love/hate relationship with it. When I was girl in the fifties, television was a miracle. Then came the end-all be-all transistor radios of the sixties. Now the sum of all human knowledge—for what it's worth—is on a little rectangular device you carry around in your pocket. One of these days I swear I'm going to master my smartphone...maybe even before artificial intelligence makes mindless slaves of us all. It was the one thing Chris and I could agree on—our shared fear of self-evolving technology.

"I almost slipped and told Tara our secret after breakfast yesterday..." I had just signed to Sloane through the video screen.

I used to think texting was complicated until Sloane introduced me to video calls. Half the time I accidentally hung up on her while trying to connect, and the other half I held the phone too close for her to see me sign, instead giving her a closeup of my nostrils. Finally I was getting the hang of it. This particular evening, I propped the phone up against my sexy leg lamp, an exact replica of the one in *A Christmas Story.* Tara said it was hideous, but then Tara has a stick up her butt half the time anyway. (Don't tell her I said so!)

This time there was no awkward tour of my nostrils as I signed back and forth with Sloane.

"I won't be mad if Tara finds out. Why not just tell her?" Sloane suggested. "What's the worst that can happen?"

Ha! It was obvious Sloane didn't know Tara at all.

"She would take it personally that I didn't involve her. Then get jealous. Stop being my friend. Hate me forever. The options are endless…"

"Oh stop! She can handle it. She's not as dependent on you as you think."

Sloane was a godsend after Bennie died. We hadn't kept in touch as much as I had wished after she and Bennie separated. In a way, I kind of blamed her for not hanging in there with him. She was the only good thing in his life, the only person who kept him grounded. So when she ended things with him, I ended things with her.

Our reconnection was bittersweet as our long conversations brought back a rush of good and bad memories. A mixed bag. That's what relationships were, weren't they? A heap of love, and a heap of pain. Because those closest to us knew how to hurt us the most.

"Do you ever miss Bennie?" I asked her, feeling the heat of my face flushing, tears rising.

"Of course. We were married, and I loved him deeply." Sloane appeared so stoic as she said this that I wondered if it was true. "But then he changed. You know that about him. I don't miss that version of him."

"I can't seem to move on." I was pleading for that same stoicism. I was tired of grief and wanted to feel nothing for once. "I don't know how."

"I wish I could help you. I guess I learned young how to harden my heart against emotions. Probably because I knew death before I knew life."

I vaguely remembered something about her mother being a widow, though I never knew the details of what happened to her dad. She had always been closed off about her family.

"I never told you this," Sloane continued, "but my dad died before I was born, so I never had to go through loving and losing him. He has always been a ghost to me."

"What about the rest of your extended family?"

"They're all in Nigeria, and I haven't seen them since I was a teenager." Sloane glanced off-screen, counting on her fingers. "Wow, how has it been over twenty years?"

"Aw, darlin', I'm sorry to hear that. You know I'll always be your family, don't you?"

"I appreciate it. And my mom appreciates how good you've been to me also. It's lonely in a hearing world where no one signs...thank you for caring enough to learn, G."

I adored her sign name for me—that cascading curling G. I felt so hip. And to me it meant she saw me as a true friend, not some old battle-ax of a mother-in-law.

"Well, it's not totally selfless. I remembered a little ASL from when I was younger and took classes thinking I might want to be a speech therapist someday. While that never panned out, I'm glad it came in handy. Besides, my hearing ain't so good these days, and I'm already using closed captions. If I turn my television volume up any louder, my neighbor will complain!"

"Isn't your neighbor Tara?"

"Exactly! Nobody messes with that woman's quiet time."

It was well after my bedtime, so we finalized tomorrow's plans and hung up.

I'd been in the middle of painting my fingernails lime green when Sloane had called, so I finished the task, then added tiny yellow stripes on top. As I was sealing the bottles, I noticed I'd gotten a couple of blobs of polish on my shirt. Not that it mattered on this old rag. A vintage Cyndi Lauper concert tee that Rick had bought me back in 1984, when Cyndi was at the height of her popularity. I adored her—her songs, her witty personality, her wild wardrobe, the whole schtick—and Rick knew it. He surprised me with tickets that he'd worked overtime at his weekend job at the auto repair shop to afford. It was a long haul to Winston-Salem, and we barely made it in time, but the concert at the Veterans Memorial Coliseum was fantastic. After the show, over my rather meek protests, Rick had insisted on buying me the ridiculously overpriced T-shirt. It showed Cyndi in her outrageous get-up from the "Girls Just Want to Have Fun" video, and sported the legend She's So Unusual. She sure was, and so was I; we were kindred spirits.

Anyway, I wore that shirt with pride for years, then put it away when it began to fade and stretch out of shape. The sentimental value had long since worn off. Nowadays it was my go-to top for slopping around the house, since now *I* was kinda faded and stretched out myself. I guess I've shrunk a little in my advancing age too; the shirt fits me like a short dress these days. Usually, like tonight, I wore it with nothing else but my panties. Hey, a girl has a right to be comfortable.

Rose and Dorothy from *The Golden Girls* were getting into some kind of mischief in a rerun I had probably seen a dozen times. Careful not to ruin my nails, I clicked off the television and headed into the kitchen to make my nightly bedtime tea. While waiting for the kettle to boil, I turned on the radio to a station that claimed to play the *oldies*, though everything on it was from the 1980s. They had no idea what true oldies music was.

"Haven't you ever heard of Elvis Presley or The Supremes?" I yelled to no one in particular. One of the advantages of living alone is you can say whatever you want, anytime you feel like it. But there were times when I got so lonely I wished there was someone around just to tell me to shut up.

"Do You Really Want to Hurt Me?" was playing. That was a good tune, so I really couldn't complain. Good video too. I was busting some Boy George dance moves around the kitchen, and singing along, as I finished loading the dishwasher with the pathetic single plate and cup I had used for dinner, when the doorbell rang.

"It's unlocked, Tara!" I called out. At this late hour it could only be Tara.

But the doorbell rang again. Maybe she hadn't heard me.

"Come in!"

A dull thump—not a knock, more like something big slumping *against* the door—reached me all the way in the kitchen.

Maybe it wasn't Tara. Maybe it was that undercover cop. Maybe he had a problem.

"Alright, alright, keep your shirt on!" I hollered, scampering to the foyer. "Unless you're Brad Pitt," I added to myself.

I peered out through the peephole. Blackness. Another thump.

Against my better judgement, I unhooked the chain lock and flung the door open. The specter that tumbled against me muffled my scream as I collapsed to the floor.

Chapter 15

"Rick?" I awoke to the ghost of my estranged husband hovering over me, so vivid he looked real. I was surprised to feel warm skin and prickly stubble when I reached up to touch his face. "Is it really you?"

I hadn't seen Rick Mallowan in almost forty years, and yet here he was. In the flesh.

In blood-soaked flesh.

I scrambled to sit up, crab-walking backward, away from his dripping torso. I didn't know what to think, what to do. My mind grew oddly quiet.

Then it was suddenly loud with questions.

"What in the Sam Hill happened to you?"

"Oh good, you're awake." Rick glanced back at the darkened street, then stumbled past me through the doorway into the house. "Sorry I knocked you down. It was all I could do to prop myself up against your door. I need your help, Gingersnap."

There was a special level of fury reserved for those you love who betray you. It was a red and blinding anger that lurked in memories and revealed itself when *your song* played, or the scent of his cologne wafted over you, or your child asked where his daddy was. And right now it flooded me as he spoke his nickname for me—*Gingersnap*—like we were lovers.

"You want *me* to help *you*? Where was *my* help when I needed *you*?" I screamed at him.

My brain was running a mile a minute. Noticing the blood seeping from what appeared to be everywhere. Wondering how he even found out where I lived. Hoping that this was a hallucination from the mushrooms I ate on my pizza and not real life. For a long minute I sat on the floor, frozen, lost in a fog of shock.

"I'm sorry! But I really need your help before I bleed to death."

"Maybe you should. It'd be justice for what you did to me."

"Are you actually going to watch me die here in your foyer?"

"I should. But I won't. Even if you are as worthless as gum on a boot heel."

I stood up and guided Rick into the kitchen where I sat him on a stool, calmly grabbing a hand towel to give him to stop the bleeding. It was odd how calm and collected I was when I couldn't care less if he died.

Rick lifted his shirt up, probing his abdomen with his fingers and yelping when he found the wound.

"Lord have mercy!" I felt a little woozy when I saw the muscle tissue peeking through. "That's a stab wound, and it's deep. You're gonna need stitches, Rick. Let's get you to a hospital."

"No!" I stepped back from him, startled. "No hospital," he insisted.

I had a bad feeling I knew why. Stabbings drew questions, and questions drew the police. What had Rick gotten himself into this time?

Kneeling down, I took a closer look to see what exactly I was dealing with. Something inside his flesh glimmered. Was that…

"It looks like a piece of glass is wedged in here. What happened, Rick?"

"Bar fight," he groaned.

It was believable, but it wasn't true. I always could sniff out his lies. Slipping my fingers into the open seam of skin, I clamped onto the shard and pulled it toward me while Rick bit down on the towel to muffle his scream. Warm blood coated my hands while I swapped out the glass for the towel, pressing the fabric hard against his body.

"Let me get something bigger to make a torniquet out of. It's bleeding too much."

I walked—not ran, because Rick wasn't worth exerting the energy for—to the linen closet and grabbed a sheet, the only thing long enough that could tightly wrap around his entire chest.

"This will hopefully stop the bleeding until I can find some bandages. Just sit tight."

"You can still sew, can't you?" Rick asked weakly. He was turning paler by the moment as blood literally drained from his face.

"You don't expect me to sew up your…skin, do you?" The toughest fabric I had sewn was microfiber, and that was no picnic. There was no way I could sew up human flesh…without passing out. I shook off an image of Leatherface's homemade skin mask in *Texas Chain Saw Massacre.* "Nope. No can do, Rick."

"C'mon, Gingersnap. I'm practically a goner."

"Don't *Gingersnap* me," I grumbled. "And if you tell me your life is flashing before your eyes, so help me I'll shove that piece of glass back inside you and finish the job!"

"Same old Gingersnap. Regular Irish spitfire."

He tried to laugh, and an awful rattling sound bubbled up in his throat. He looked so pitiful and helpless; in spite of myself, my heart ached. No matter how much I hated the man, I still loved him and couldn't let him die.

"Shake a leg, Ginger!" Rick urged.

I refused to hurry. Grabbing my sewing kit, I took my sweet time going back to the kitchen. I cut the end of the thread, pinched it between my fingertips, and sucked it for a second to moisten it—just like Mama had taught me. I made threading the needle look harder than it was while Rick sweated bullets in front of me.

"You know the old saying, 'This is going to hurt me more than it hurts you'?" I said.

Rick, brightening, managed a half-smile. "Yeah."

"Well, not this time. Hold on to your butt."

I positioned the needle next to his skin, popping the thimble on my finger because my hands were way too shaky to risk stabbing myself.

"Oh, I forgot!" I jumped up and headed to the liquor cabinet, returning with the bottle of rum I soaked the traditional Claxton Fruit Cake—it's a Southern thang—with every Christmas. In my opinion, that's the only way to make the hard-as-granite dessert with the weird candied fruit edible.

"You don't have any rubbing alcohol or peroxide?" Rick asked.

"It's not for you. It's for me." I guzzled a mouthful to calm my nerves as I sewed a line of hot pink across his abdomen while Rick cussed a blue streak between savage bites on the hand towel.

I couldn't help but grin sadistically as I shoved the needle in and out, again and again, watching him suffer a fraction of the way he had made me suffer.

Chapter 16

Thirty minutes and four arthritic knuckles later, I was done. Rick ran his fingertips over the sealed wound experimentally. "Pretty neat job, Ginger. But hot pink? You didn't have a more neutral color thread?"

"Yep, I got plenty of those. But I thought this would look better. You're welcome." I stood up, pointing him to the bathroom. I could have really gone for a couple Tylenol right about then, but I remained planted in place. My swollen hands throbbed from the sewing strain, but I wasn't about to let Rick see my weakness. "You'll probably want to clean it with rubbing alcohol and there's some antibiotic ointment in there too."

I couldn't spend another moment in his presence right now. I was tuckered out and needed some space.

"I came here for a reason."

I watched Rick disinfect the wound in the reflection of the bathroom mirror. It was strange how much I missed his face in my mirror when we used to brush our teeth together every night. For a long time I hated that empty space beside me, until I simply gave up hope.

"And what reason is that? To draw me back into your world so you can hurt me again?"

"No, of course not." Rick appeared in the hallway outside

the bathroom door, his shirt off, the bygone years showing. I had learned to embrace that about aging—youth was fleeting, a mirage. Embracing the way time imprinted itself on us was the *real* virtue.

My gaze traveled over the man I had spent countless nights naked under the covers with back when we were together making babies. He hadn't changed much—a new pooch on his stomach, more curly gray hairs on his chest—but the main contours of his body felt familiar. Like his arms that used to pull me into him, picking me up and—

"Are you listening to me?" Rick stood in front of me now, head cocked challengingly. "I said you should warn your friend Tara Christie to be careful...and you need stay away from her."

The unwanted flush of heat Rick's arms had inspired chilled instantly. "Tara's my best friend. I'm not *staying away* from her."

"You don't understand. Someone is after her and I don't want you getting caught in the crosshairs."

"Then tell me who is after her. Whoever it is, I'll cream his corn!" I was baiting Rick and he knew it.

"I...can't tell you." Rick shook his head, refusing to give me a name. "Tara's dangerous to be around. Promise me, Ginger!"

"And I can't do *that*." I turned away from him, putting distance between us. I couldn't trust anything he said. "She's not dangerous. I've known Tara forever, and I trust her far more than I trust you."

The rum was working its way through my system, and I appreciated the numbness enough to grab the bottle and gulp down another swallow. Then I flopped onto the sofa to rest.

Rick joined me, glancing at the rum bottle longingly, which I held out of reach.

"Oh no you don't. This stuff is partly to blame for ruining our marriage, so you're stuck with pain pills and water. Other than showing up for a quick stitch and trying to turn me against Tara, what brings you here?"

I wasn't sure I wanted to know the truth. Because I already knew it wasn't because he missed me. It didn't take a man forty years to realize he missed a woman and suddenly act on it.

"Okay, you got me." Rick lifted his hands in surrender. "I do have an ulterior motive."

"Which is?" I chuckled because I *knew* it. The second I saw him I knew he either wanted money, a place to hide out, or an alibi. I couldn't wait to find out which one it was.

"I want to start over."

My chuckle erupted into a laugh. It was the most ludicrous thing I'd ever heard.

"Get real, Rick. Start over with what exactly?"

"With you, Gingersnap. Isn't it obvious?"

I stiffened, then lowered my gaze to my knees. "Wow, that's pretty insulting of you to assume I'd still be single all these years later."

"I looked you up. I saw you hadn't changed your name, so I assumed as much. Whattya say? Give a guy another chance?"

"Uh, considering I haven't seen hide nor hair of you in decades, and you missed our boys growing up, and basically left me to do everything on my own without a dime of support, I'd tell you to go screw yourself, but I'm too much of a lady to do that." Tiny pause. "On second thought: go screw yourself!"

With a pained groan Rick leaned toward me. Cupped my

chin with one hand, and held my hand with the other.

"I realized something that took a lifetime for me to figure out, and I'm sorry it took so long. But I need you. I can't live without you." His eyes watered. My eyes were as dry as the Sahara. "I've quit my old life and just want another chance to prove to you that I can make you happy."

I twisted my face from his grip, ripped my hand out of his. "You're fresh out of chances, Rick. And judging by the wound I just sewed up, it doesn't look to me like you've quit your old life."

"That's okay. I didn't expect you to take me back right away, but I'll wear you down eventually. You know I'm persistent, Gingersnap, and I plan to woo you till you crumble."

"Well, you better bring your A game, because I stopped missing you long ago." That was a bald-faced lie, but I folded my arms across my chest defiantly.

"Speaking of missing, what have I missed out on?" He looked so genuinely curious I couldn't help but scoff.

"What did you miss out on? You mean your family's entire lives? How do I catch you up on a lifetime of being a single mom, juggling working two jobs with helping with homework and toting them back and forth to soccer practice? You missed it all, Rick. Every last moment and every precious memory!"

"I'm sorry I wasn't there for you and the boys, but I want to make up for lost time now, if I can."

"It's too late, Rick."

"Why? Do you think they'll speak to me?"

"Darlin', it's a lot more complicated than that."

"What do you mean? Did I screw them up?"

I couldn't endure feeling his body heat another moment. I

stood and walked to the window, needing room to breathe.

"You tell me if you screwed them up. Because your one son is dead, your other son just got out of jail, and the third one lives next door and never knew we were his parents."

Chapter 17

The cool night air emptied me of all the emotions boiling inside. Nursing a full glass of rum, I sat in the corner of the back patio, listening to the metallic chorus of katydids and crickets. The sweet scent of honeysuckle perfumed the light breeze.

"Hi." Rick appeared at the back door, waiting. Waiting for what? An invitation? Forgiveness? He'd be waiting until hell froze over.

"Hi," I replied, my gaze focused on the lightning bugs flickering yellow sparks in the black-dark firmament of the piney woods. I couldn't look at him.

"I didn't know you went through all of that with the boys…"

"How could you know? You weren't around. And I don't blame you for what happened to them. Lots of single moms have kids and don't mess them up like I did. So it's all on me. As you can see, I did a bang-up job of raising them."

It hurt to speak the truth, but what else could I say?

The screen door shrieked as Rick pushed it open, slipped out into the darkness with me. He still knew me well enough to stand on the other side, far away from where I hid my tears from him.

"Gingersnap…" His voice was soft, soothing, the way I remembered it from our early days together when we didn't have a pot to piss in and were actually naïve enough to believe love would keep us together. "I'm the one to blame for everything, not you. I chose the bottle over you, and my freedom over family. I set you up for failure. And I don't care what you say, you were an incredible mom. I always knew you were way too good for me and better off without me."

"Is that what you tell yourself to help you sleep at night?" I turned to face him. I wanted to know the truth, and his eyes always told the truth.

"Nothing helps me sleep at night."

"Well, I can't say I'm sorry to hear that. You don't deserve anything better after what you did to us."

"You're right. Y'know, you haven't aged a day since I last saw you in 1986. You're just as beautiful as ever. Same flame-red hair. Same dancing green eyes."

I absently fluffed my hair. Couldn't let his BS get to me. "You're laying it on with a trowel, don't you think?"

"I'm not laying anything on. I remember everything about you back then."

"Everything, huh?"

"Yep." He took a tentative step toward me. I caught him admiring my bare thighs—if I do say so they ain't bad for a "mature" lady—which was a pretty big turn-on. "I remember that shirt you're wearing, for one thing. Cost me a damn fortune, but it was worth it to see your face light up. That was some concert, wasn't it?"

I chuckled. "Sure was. Best I've ever been to. And remember that crappy motel we stayed in after the show? I woke up to find a cockroach on the bed and screamed, and you thought someone had broken in and was trying to kill me."

He took another step, eyes locked on mine.

"I always respected that about you, Gingersnap. There wasn't a man tough enough to scare you off, but a harmless little bug sent you runnin'."

And another step. I could almost feel his body heat. "I can easily kick a man where it hurts. But bugs…they're all creepy crawly coated in body armor."

One more pace as he whispered, "I can't believe you still have that shirt."

"I can't believe I still fit into it."

This last step brought him directly in front of me before he dropped to his knees.

"I know you're hurting. But you can't deny that the past was pretty good, wasn't it, Ginger? Remember our passion? I still got my Mick Jagger moves." He chuckled and shimmied his hips.

I remembered those moves well—on the dance floor and in the bedroom. "You always did like it when I called you Mick."

"You know that nickname stuck with me for years?"

"Because you're *nothing* alike?" I snorted a laugh. "I remember teasing you that you'd leave me for Mick one day. Was I right? Was that who you were running around with all these years?"

My joke didn't land as Rick turned solemn. "I'm sorry. I really am. But us—the good part—it could be that way again…"

We lingered there in a painfully nostalgic silence, his eyes searching mine, until finally he pressed his cheek to my lap. I rested my hand on his head, running my fingers through his hair like we used to do in bed while talking the night away.

"Which son…passed?"

The question jolted me, and I felt myself clenching his hair until the feeling slipped away.

"It wasn't as calm as passing. Bennie was stabbed to death. Just this past year, actually."

"That's horrible." Rick wrapped his arms around my waist. "And who was in jail?"

"Jonah—well, you knew him as Cole, but his other mother renamed him Jonah."

"Other mother?" Rick lifted his head to look at me. I could see he wanted to know the full story of how Jonah ended up being raised by another woman—Tara's mother, in fact—but it was too long and complicated to get into now. Not like this. I shook my head.

"And I'm guessing Chris is the one who lives next door?"

"Yes, but I gave him up for adoption, so we're still working through building a relationship now after all these years." I sighed. "It hasn't exactly been smooth sailing. Sometimes he gets on my last nerve. And he thinks *I've* turned funny."

Rick's lip curled up at my Southern-speak for being off one's nut. My mother had used the expression all the time, and now here I was like mother, like daughter, despite my teenage self vowing never to turn into her.

"Wow, Ginger, I had no idea…"

"I know." I inhaled a strained breath. "I often wondered if you were around, would all three of my boys still be alive and well? Would I have a passel of cute grandkids, and big Irish family dinners?"

Rick couldn't answer that and I couldn't expect him to. The tension grew long and awkward, but I wasn't going to make it easy for Rick to just waltz back into my life and turn my heart upside down after all the damage he had done. He dared to show up at my doorstep begging for me to save him, but I was tired of doing the saving. Sometimes a girl just wanted to be rescued.

"I'm sorry for everything, Ginger. I truly am."

"You know, I almost wanted to let you bleed out and die right there in my kitchen while I watched, but somewhere deep in my empty heart I still love you, Rick Mallowan. Flaws and all."

He released me and stood up. Rising from the patio chair, I found myself drawing closer to him. Rick's charisma had pulled me into his orbit since the moment we met. And damn it, it still had a hold on me. I didn't want him to leave, but I didn't want him to stay, either.

"You'll see. I'm going to prove to you I've changed and I'll do whatever it takes to be worthy of that big empty heart again."

"Why now? It is because your employer is dead?"

"My employer?"

"Yeah, Victor Valance. I know his family are the ones who convinced you to leave me way back when, dragging you into working for them doing whatever crooked things they needed done."

Rick shuffled back, shaking his head. "I don't know what you heard—"

"I heard enough to know better than to let you dump all that backwoods *Godfather* crap on my doorstep."

"It's over, I promise. I cut ties with the whole family."

That's when it dawned on me. The gaping hole in his stomach. The too-convenient timing of his return. The sudden desire to get back together. Was he hoping I'd protect him? Was I his last-minute alibi?

"Rick, I want the truth. Did you kill Victor Valance?"

Chapter 18

"Did you kill Victor Valance?" My question hung in the sliver of space between us, while Rick's silence was the only answer I needed.

I should have kicked Rick out right then and there. I knew he had been doing some shady stuff all these years, but murder? That crossed a big, fat, bold line.

"You think I'm capable of murder, Ginger?"

"I think you're capable of anything, darlin'. You proved that when you left me for a life of crime."

I had never quite pieced together what crime exactly the Valance family and their cronies had been dabbling in. All these years I had assumed it was drug dealing. A little marijuana here, a little cocaine there. But ever since hearing that woman's voice on tape, now my mind wandered to more sinister places. Like human trafficking. What other purpose would someone have for holding a woman captive in a bunker?

I couldn't fathom the love of my life, the father of my children, agreeing to do something so horrifying as selling people. But I didn't really know Rick anymore, did I? Had I ever?

The memory still felt as fresh and bitter as the night he had left me for the last time. I had two boys at the time—Benson and Cole—and was pregnant with our third, Chris. Rick and I had fought terribly earlier that evening, something about our finances. It was always about money. Him blowing it at the bar. Me blowing it out of proportion. We blew up a lot in those last days.

When Rick had stormed out after an expletive-ridden tirade, I couldn't help myself. I needed to know what exactly lured him away from us. What was worth giving up his *children*, losing *me*? Booze? Another woman?

The neighbor had agreed to watch the boys while I followed Rick to the bar where he spent most of his evenings…and most of our income. While I nursed a soda at a table in a dark corner, I watched Rick approach one of Ewan Valance's goons at the end of the bar. I later found out from the bartender that all it took was $1,000—which was two months' pay back in the early 1980s—to draw Rick in on a random job transporting the unknown contents of a van from point A to point B.

"It's easy money, and there's no risk," Rick had told me when I confronted him after he got home that night. But I knew the truth. Nothing about working with the Valance family was risk free. That night he packed a bag, telling me he'd be home in a couple days after he'd made the drop-off. He never unpacked that bag or returned home, and it turned out I was right. Rick risked his family, his future, and lost it all when he discovered breaking bad suited him, then realized too late he couldn't walk away from it.

"All I can say is, you're not denying killing Victor. As far as I'm concerned, you're guilty as sin." I nudged past him to head inside, weakening at the feeling of his breath on my cheek. His hands on my hips stopped me.

"You want me to say it out loud? I didn't kill Victor

Valance!"

I chose my reply carefully, because Rick knew how to play politician with his words. Winding them together just so, in order to avoid lying, but also to avoid telling the truth.

"Did you have *anything* to do with Victor's death? This stab wound wasn't some kind of retaliation?"

Rick groaned. "No. And I don't want to talk about Victor. I want to talk about us, Gingersnap."

I hated how much I loved hearing my nickname on his tongue. My mind slipped back to the first time he called me Gingersnap. I was seventeen, and we were sitting in his fix-'er-up hotrod when he leaned over and kissed me. *"You taste sweet and spicey, like a gingersnap cookie."* A compliment like that would make any girl a little weak in the knees.

"There's nothing to talk about. You made your choice back then, and it wasn't me. It wasn't our family. I've moved on, Rick. I'm done."

It was all a lie, because I had never gotten over Rick. He was the only man I ever truly loved. And while it sounded completely unbelievable to love a good-for-nothing SOB, Rick wasn't always *this* Rick. Before the Valances lured him in, he had been romantic and thoughtful, the kind of boy who danced barefoot with me on the beach. The man who sat across from me in a peeling red vinyl booth at Debbie's Diner until the sun came up, listening to my life stories like they were gold pouring from my lips. A husband who spoiled me with flowers just because—even if they were stolen from our neighbor's garden. He cooked, he cleaned, he brought me breakfast in bed. He loved me, and I loved him, and we were perfect together.

Until.

Until he chose the Valances over me.

That's when we broke, a fissure so deep it cracked through time and space.

Through the window screen in the kitchen "The Lady in Red" played from the radio, and it brought a tear along with a memory. Rick always thought I looked good in red, no matter how many times I told him that as a redhead, red was my least flattering color.

Pulling my hips towards his, Rick scooped my palm in his and pressed his other hand against the small of my back. Under starlight we swayed. Beneath moonlight we moved. It was just like old times, with my cheek to his chest as his heart thrummed in my ear while I held on to his neck twirling strands of his hair around my fingertips. Rick sang to me a familiar song on his familiar lips in a familiar dance.

When "The Lady in Red" segued into "Brick House" by The Commodores, he looked at me and I looked at him. I couldn't look away, no matter how strong my sense of self-preservation was.

Leaning in, he kissed me and it felt like a lifetime of kisses all wrapped into one delicious moment. When he pulled away, all I could think about was how painful this pleasure was.

"You killed me when you left me, Rick. I became dead inside because of you."

"Then let me revive you."

I giggled at his cheesy line, but it worked.

"You'll always be the only woman I love."

They just so happened to be the only words in the universe that could reach inside me and rekindle life. Love pulled me toward him while fear pushed me away, until I found myself stuck in the middle with a dangerous desire.

My reply slipped off the tip of my tongue: "One."

He looked at my quizzically.

"One?"

"Yes, one. One more chance, Rick. But if I fall for you again and you hurt me...*again*..."

"I will never put you through that again, Gingersnap."

It was a promise he had made once before, and I briefly wondered how much damage he would do to me this time. My silence was weighted with everything I didn't dare say, for fear Rick would fly away again.

Rick assured me with another kiss. Before I knew what was happening, he had scooped me up in his arms and was carrying me through the house toward the bedroom like he had on our wedding night. I was a lot younger then, and a lot slimmer, but Rick betrayed no strain. I realized I wanted this more than I dared admit. I wanted him back. I wanted *us.* Sometimes you love someone so much that you can't bear a taste of his lips, or breathe the same air because you risk wanting it all.

He held me in his arms, bedside, tracing my face with his eyes.

"We're not in our twenties anymore," I murmured. "You can't make the past go away with one night of..." My voice trailed off hopelessly.

I thought he might toss me on the bed playfully as he used to do, but he placed me on the bed almost reverently. He was gentle and sweet and romantic and passionate. In the lovely, caressing night, the future cracked wide open with expectation.

Chapter 19

The sun slipping through the blinds was cheerful. The covers draped over my body were warm. Bliss poured over me at the thought of last night with Rick. I felt young again, so alive. Today felt like the best morning of my life.

Sex was a lot more complicated than I remembered. Mama never told me that when you get older, it takes a great deal more patience and ingenuity to get the pistons firing, so to speak. Rick and I approached the challenge with good humor. All I can say is, the Lord bless whoever invented K-Y Jelly.

"You definitely had moves like Mick Jagger last night," I murmured.

When Mick—I mean *Rick*—didn't reply, I raised up, stretched, and yawned languorously. The candle I'd lit sometime during our lovemaking had burned down almost to the nub. I blew out the dying flame, then flipped over to where Rick had been sleeping, holding me in his arms as night turned to day and I finally fell asleep.

Now his side of the bed was empty. His covers cool. And apprehension filled me.

I listened for the sound of cupboard doors opening and closing in the kitchen, the scent of breakfast being cooked, like he used to do every Saturday morning when we lived together. Silence. No aroma of fresh-brewed coffee or bacon frying. All

I could think was, *it smells like sex in here*. My nostrils crinkled with disgust and shame. Suddenly I felt cheap. And stupid. And used. By my own damn husband.

Rick was gone.

I should have known.

And the best morning of my life instantly turned into the worst.

I grabbed Rick's pillow—no, not Rick's pillow, *my* pillow, because he didn't live here and he was gone now and I was here alone—and I tossed it at the closet door. How could I have fallen for his trite old line? And what was the purpose of it all? Just to torture me, like I hadn't had enough when he left the last time?

And the worst indignity of all: there was my Cyndi Lauper tee, wadded up on the floor where I'd flung it in the heat of passion.

I jumped out of bed, threw on a nightie and a robe, and stormed into the living room. I desperately needed to vent. I grabbed my cell phone and pulled up video chat. Sloane answered brusquely.

"Hey, I can't chat right now. I'm in a meeting with a client. I'll call you after I'm done." She looked at me in the screen, then added, "Are you okay?"

Not wanting to let on that something was wrong, I offered a weak smile. "Which Hollywood celebrity is throwing a party this time?"

Sloane's party planning business, Feel the Noize Party Planning, was inspired by her teenage introduction to Quiet Riot, the hair band infamous for the head-banging song "Cum On Feel the Noize." Being Deaf, Sloane couldn't hear music in the conventional sense, until one day her high school friend,

Peace, decided it was time Sloane discover it for herself. After ordering Sloane to lay down on a huge speaker, Peace cranked up the sound and blasted the song as Sloane felt it pulse through her. That's when her love of music was born. And the parties she planned were just as adventurous as Quiet Riot's wardrobe choices.

Her business had taken off after she got "Instagram famous," whatever that meant. I had barely gotten used to Facebook when this other social media platform became all the rage among young people with apparently nothing better to do than look at photos and videos all the livelong day, and blindly take life directions from strangers pompously called "influencers." It sounded to me like a colossal waste of time. Another sign the world was going to hell in a handbasket!

I didn't try to understand it all, and I didn't begrudge Sloane her success. In fact, I admired her tremendously. She had worked her butt off attracting legions of "followers"—a creepy term, if you ask me—with her clever posts, which showcased her dusky beauty and flair for haute couture to irresistible effect.

So, it was no wonder Sloane's business was booming. Now everyone up and down the East Coast wanted her services, and a few West Coast celebrities too.

"It's the actor Zach Galifianakis," Sloane told me. "He's a North Carolina native, but I'm sure you never heard of him." She started to fingerspell the long, unusual name for my benefit when I interrupted.

"Child, you cut me to the quick! I've seen *The Hangover* twice. Laughed my butt off."

"You mean you *like* raunchy comedies?"

"Why not? Just because I'm old doesn't mean I'm a prude.

Good luck. And tell Zach I said hi."

We hung up.

My fingertip hovered over the phone screen to call Tara, but she was already going through so much with the whole body-buried-in-her-backyard situation. Then again, maybe my drama would be a nice distraction from her own.

Tara picked up on the first ring, sounding eager to hear from me. "You're up early."

"If I tell you something, do you promise not to yell at me?" I began cryptically.

"Can you give me a hint?" she asked.

"It's about Rick," I answered simply.

Nothing further needed to be said between us. Tara could read me like a psychic read tarot cards. "I'm on my way over."

I barely had time to change out of my nightie into a sweater and skirt before Tara showed up, calling to me from the entryway.

"I'm here and I brought coffee and chocolate!"

Tara was always good at enabling my chocolate addiction. I rounded the corner and found her holding out a huge chocolatey muffin and head-sized mug of coffee.

"Any chance that's a mocha coffee?" For double the drama I preferred double the chocolate.

"Carmel macchiato." Tara pretended to take the mug back.

"I can deal with it." I greedily reached for the sweet offerings, eager to get the taste of Rick's kisses out of mouth. "Homemade?" I asked with a mouthful of muffin.

"Nothing but the best for you." Tara winked.

"So Chris baked them?" I teased.

"Of course." Tara laughed, then headed to the kitchen table.

She looked awkward as she sat down with her mug, gaze elusive, like she was hiding something. I could always tell when she wasn't quite herself.

"You're not telling me something," I blurted out, sitting across from her. "What's going on?"

"I'm not here to talk about me. I want to talk about you," she insisted.

"No, you first. How was your date with Chris?"

She shrugged. "We didn't end up going out."

"Because of the sweatshirt he found? I'm sure it's nothing—"

Tara's cheerful expression wilted. "It's not just that. He wants to put the house on the market and use whatever we make from selling it to buy an RV."

This sounded like a huge life change, and Tara didn't handle change very well. Maybe with the right positive spin it wouldn't sound so bad.

"A lot of people downsize once their kids move out. You ever watch those tiny house shows? That sounds nice and cozy."

"It gets worse. He wants to sell the ranch and leave Bloodson Bay. For good."

I couldn't believe my ears. "No! You're my best friend! I need you here."

"I don't want to leave, but I also don't know if I can stay. The looks I get, the whispers, Chris's job being uncertain…and not having my own daughter here with me…and now whatever this threat is against Nora. What's the point in staying where we're clearly not wanted?"

"Because you *are* wanted. By me and your family. I don't think leaving is necessarily the answer. There's loads of remote jobs now. Chris could find another job…"

"That's not what he wants, though. He wants out of here." She covered her face with her hands, wiping away the sniffles and sadness. When she looked at me again, she wore a happy face that I wasn't buying. "Enough about me and my miserable life. You mentioned something about Rick."

I didn't want to bring Rick up after hearing about Tara's life-changing problems, but I couldn't hide it. Not from her.

"Rick appeared out of nowhere last night and needed my help."

This perked her up. "Help with what? Relocating him to the other side of the continent, I hope?"

Oh boy. Here we go…

"He had gotten stabbed or something, and he wanted me to sew him up."

Tara's jaw dropped to her knees. "He got stabbed? And you helped him?"

"Of course I helped him! I wasn't going to let the father of my children bleed to death. It wasn't as bad as I thought sewing up human flesh. A little slippery, but not terrible."

Tara gagged.

"Anyway, I'm hoping you jabbed him extra hard with that needle and sent him on his way, right?"

"Um, not exactly. But there was definitely some…jabbing going on."

I grinned while Tara grimaced.

"Oh no you didn't!"

"Oh yes we did…twice! He…sweet-talked me into taking him back."

She gasped. "Man, that must have been some sweet talk!"

"Oh crap, who am I kidding, Tara? He fed me a line of BS, that's all there is to it, and I fell for it." Long pause. "I *hate* that I love love. D'ya know what I mean?" She grabbed my hand, squeezed it; she knew *exactly* what I meant. "And now he's gone again."

Tara eyed me with pity. "I'm so sorry, Ginger. You know it's not you, right? He's broken, and he lives to break other people."

"I know. I just don't understand how I could be so dumb to fall for him…again. Everything felt so real last night. I had forgotten how amazing love was. The butterflies in your stomach, your heart thumping out of your chest…" This conversation felt far too heavy to handle right now. "Now I realize it was probably just indigestion. '*So you see, my son, there is a very fine line between love and nausea.*'"

Tara did a movie-worthy spit take of coffee across the table.

"Did you just quote James Earl Jones in *Coming to America*? You're unbelievable."

"I always loved his voice. So deep and sexy. I wonder what pillow talk with him would be like?"

"Ew, I do *not* want to imagine that!" Tara crumbled into a full-body laugh now, and I was relieved to join her.

"Hey, I've got an idea." Tara squeezed my hand, then looked down at my fingers. "How about we spend some girl time together? Go get a mani-pedi? My treat."

I examined my nails, realizing last night's paint job must not have had time to dry before Rick showed up. My cute little neon stripes were smushed and smudged.

"I'm not sure you've left anything for them to paint." I pointed to her chewed-off nails.

Then my gaze trailed to her wrists. A random web of fresh red scratches and gouges stood out on her pale skin. There were long, pinkish scars visible too. I noticed the wounds continued up her forearms.

"What happened there?" I touched one scar. Tara flinched and pulled her arm back.

"It's nothing. I work on a horse farm. Lots of barbed wire." Tara grinned, but she hadn't sold her story well. I knew she would never use barbed wire. "C'mon, Nails by Nellie takes walk-ins. We both could use a little pampering after everything that's been going on."

"As long as I get to drive," I insisted. "You drive slower than my dead grandmother."

We left my house, leaving all thoughts of Rick and Victor and threats and moving behind.

Chapter 20

Nothing hit me quite like the scent of acrylic and nail polish. As Tara and I walked into the glass storefront at the end of a mostly empty strip mall, Nails by Nellie smelled to me like youth and beauty. Tara didn't seem to agree as she coughed the moment the door jangled closed behind us.

"Mornin', girls. Don't let the air conditioning out." Nellie, whose Russian last name somehow went unknown by the whole town, treated Tara like she was the same careless teenager from the 1990s.

"Good morning, Miss Nellie." And Tara still addressed Nellie like the perpetually old lady who had intimidated her since the 1990s.

"*I love the smell of napalm in the morning*," I said as I picked my seat and fiddled with the massage settings on the pedicure chair.

Tara smiled thinly at my *Apocalypse Now* joke. "Yeah, those chemicals are pretty strong today." Tara held her sleeve over her nose while Nellie, the only nail technician here today, prepped the pedicure tubs.

"No stronger than any other day." Nellie busily filled the soaking tubs with warm water and teal beads that burst into foamy foot goodness.

"You at least should be wearing a charcoal mask," Tara

continued educating Nellie about a subject the woman seemed to care absolutely nothing about. "That's formaldehyde, and it's not healthy for you to be smelling all day."

Nellie glanced up wearily at Tara from her stool at the base of my foot tub. "Honey, the sooner somethin' kills me, the better off I'll be." Then she picked up a nail file, ready to tackle my toenails.

"You might need a chainsaw for those," I joked, handing her a coral nail polish I spent a good ten minutes going back and forth deciding on.

The massage chair kneaded the knots that had been forming in my shoulders since this morning. Already Rick was undoing me and he had only been back—and gone—within twenty-four hours. I was doomed.

Nellie hunched with a grunt over my feet, and I watched the sinewy muscles of her arms and hands flex beneath sun-spotted, wrinkled skin not much younger than my own. I saw more scalp than hair on top of her gray head. She was probably close to my age. Well past time to give up this backbreaking work, if she wanted a chance to enjoy her golden years before they tarnished.

"I thought you were planning to retire soon, Nellie," I said.

"Me too." Nellie kept sawing away at my nails while she talked. "But things don't always work out the way we expect."

"Why don't you hire someone else to take over? Or sell the business?"

Nellie let loose a mirthless cackle. "This place ain't worth nothing. No one wants a dying nail salon in Bloodson Bay. I only got one other nail tech, so I gotta do everything else myself. Which means we can't take on as many clients, and that means less money. And when your grocery bill is almost as high as your rent, well, retirement becomes a fantasy. I'll probably still be working two jobs after I'm buried six feet under just to afford my tombstone. I'm sure my мать would be so glad she immigrated from Russia just to give me this wonderful American dream."

"I'm sorry to hear that."

And I truly was. Bennie had left me with a nice chunk of savings to live off of when he passed, but without it, who knows how I'd be surviving. My Social Security checks sure weren't cutting it.

"I meet myself comin' and goin' every day at this dump. Eh, but who needs sleep anyway? It is what it is," Nellie concluded without a trace of emotion.

While Nellie filed away chunks of skin and turned my toes from a troll's back to a human's, Tara turned to me.

"You never told me why you think Rick came running back after all this time."

"I think it's more like he's running away from something," I clarified. "I think he might be in trouble with the law."

"What kind of trouble?"

I had never told her much about Rick, because there wasn't much to tell. I didn't know where he had gone to, or what he was up to. But now I was starting to piece a lot more together about who he was and what he might have done.

"All I know is he used to work with Victor, and suddenly he's dead and Rick shows up with a huge gash in his side. The kind of injury that might happen from a retaliation. That can't be coincidence…can it?"

"You think he *killed* Vic?" Tara gawked. "That seems like a stretch."

"Victor Valance had a lot of targets on his back." And that's why everyone called the nosy nail technician *Nebby Nellie.* I had almost forgotten she was there, scrubbing and soaking and swiping color across our toes, until she stuck her big fat nose into our conversation. "It was only a matter of time before someone pulled the trigger...figuratively speakin'," she added with a chuckle.

A crack of thunder rattled the large windows, and I turned my attention to the storm brewing outside. Across the empty parking lot a flotilla of ashen clouds billowed across the darkening ocean vista. Fat drops of rain splattered on the concrete, a foretaste of the frog-strangler I knew was coming.

"Anyone in particular who wanted him dead?" Tara fished.

"Oh, more than one person. I know a lot about the Valance family sins." Nellie rose to her feet and stretched her arms until the joints popped. Shadows clung to the angles of her face, and her acid-washed blue eyes dimmed to an unnerving shade of gray.

"How do you know so much about them?"

"I used to be Miss V's housekeeper. But I did a lot more *cleaning up of their messes* than cleaning up their messes, if you catch my drift."

The rain was pouring down in buckets now. Tara leaned forward, drawn in by Nellie's admission. "Are you saying you witnessed their criminal activities?"

"I did more than witnessed. I also overheard Mr. V bragging to his friends about his *conquests*...all the mistresses he bedded. That man had no shame."

The mistresses—one of them *had* to be the woman from the tape! "Did you happen to overhear any names for those mistresses?"

"No, he never used names, only descriptions. Busty Bombshell. Black Beauty. Skinny Skank. As you can see, he was real classy about it."

Shoot! We were back to square one.

"I shouldn't be saying this." Nellie's voice dropped to a conspiratorial whisper. She glanced around at the empty salon, as if someone could have snuck through the jingling door without detection. "But I got them out of a bind or two. Things I never told anyone, mind you. You could say the Valances owe me for my silence."

Tara turned to me, and I could read her thoughts before she spoke them. "Did you ever overhear anything about a…bunker?"

Nellie perked up, as if Tara had just handed her a twenty-dollar tip. "You know about the bunker? I didn't know they still used that old place up in the mountains. Ugh, what a snake pit! Straight out of a horror movie. I would have thought nature had taken it back by now."

"I'm not sure if it's still in use or anything. But yeah, we heard about it. What exactly were *you* doing there?"

The fine hairs on my arms stood at attention. Had Nellie been the woman in the tape?

"Doing what I always do. Cleaning up their messes."

Chapter 21

I nearly bolted up out of my massage chair as Nebby Nellie dangled the key that could put Judge Ewan Valance and his whole corrupt brood behind bars. Tara had a much cooler reaction as she grabbed my arm and shook her head at me, forcing me to stay grounded.

Act cool, Ginger. Don't scare her silent.

"So, um, what kind of messes did you clean up in the bunker?" Tara asked, trying to sound only casually interested.

"Oh, honey, you have no idea." Nellie sucked in a breath, fixing to launch into a juicy story, when the door jingled.

We all turned our heads toward the front of the salon. A bedraggled figure stood there, hair sopping wet, clothes dripping on the tile floor. In his hands he held a soggy bouquet of flowers and a paper to-go bag from Debbie's Diner.

I couldn't believe my eyes. "Rick? What are you doing here?"

Tara stood up, jaw clenched, nearly tripping as she stepped out of the pedicure tub.

"You stay away from her!" she yelled, advancing on him with balled fists. "Haven't you done enough damage yet?"

I grabbed her wrist. I wanted to hear his explanation, regardless of whether it was the truth or not.

"Wait, just let me explain," Rick pleaded.

"No one here wants your explanation, Rick!" Tara spat before I could squeeze a word in.

"I do. Tara, let him speak." Slipping on a pair of foam flipflops, I shuffled over to him, careful not to mess up my nails a second time.

Rick glanced at Tara as if asking for permission. "I went out to pick up breakfast while you were sleeping, but when I got back you were gone. I didn't know what the heck you thought happened to me, so I've spent the last hour running all over town searching for your car."

"You expect her to believe that?" Tara cut in.

I knew Tara was only trying to protect me, but this was between me and Rick. I seized his hand and led him outside under the cover of the awning while the rain pelted the cracked concrete slab around us.

"Are you telling me the truth?" I desperately hoped it was. Although my hand released his, my heart refused to let go.

Rick held out the paper bag. "This cold, wet egg and sausage biscuit is proof."

"Okay, then show me the receipt."

"Don't you believe I got it from Debbie's? Because the bag says so right here." He pointed to the logo—two intertwined Ds rising from a steaming mug.

"No, I want to see what time you bought it, which should be on the receipt."

"Okay, I guess I can't blame you for doubting me." He dug around in his pocket until he retrieved a crumpled paper with a faint timestamp on it.

Sure enough, he had bought it over an hour ago.

"Why didn't you leave a note?" It seemed like a logical

thing to do, but then again, Rick had always lacked good old-fashioned horse sense.

"I wanted to surprise you. I didn't think you'd wake up and assume I ditched you."

I didn't want to say the nasty reply I was thinking, so instead I said nothing. I chuckled, feeling giddy despite the downpour and silly that I had overreacted. But then again, history had taught me that Rick was prone to walking out and never coming back. I stood on my tiptoes, wrapped my arms around his neck, and gave him a big, wet smack. When I stepped back, my body felt hot despite the rain's chill.

"I guess you forgive me?" Rick knew the answer before he asked. "Since breakfast was a bust, how about I make you a fancy dinner tonight."

"Sounds perfect," I agreed.

"I'll put your flowers—well, what's left of them—in water at home." He paused. "Is it okay that I call it home?"

"That depends on if you live there or not."

"I'd like to. With you. Eventually, if you'd have me."

"We'll see."

I winked at him. He kissed my hand.

As he ran to his car, he tossed one last look at me, signing the universal gesture for *I love you.* I couldn't believe he still remembered it from back when I had been studying to be a speech therapist a lifetime ago, showing him the signs I was learning in my class.

I returned to my pedicure chair floating on cloud nine. I caught up with Tara and Nellie in the middle of a conversation about the bunker, how Ewan Valance built it in the 1980s during the Cold War for fear there'd be a nuclear war between the

United States and the Soviet Union.

"Can you believe he thought my family were Soviet spies? I had to prove that my parents were deported under Stalin before he would hire me. But eventually I earned his trust, and that's when he showed me just how terrifying he could be."

As far Nellie she knew, the bunker sat vacant for over a decade before one day—it was the 1990s, but the exact year was a blur—she was in the middle of cleaning out Judge Valance's office when he asked her to do the strangest thing.

"It was almost quitting time when I had finished up with Mr. V's office desk—and don't get me started on the papers I came across in there! It was enough to put the good ol' judge behind bars for life, but I knew better than to tell anyone. Anyway, he comes into the office and shuts the door, acting real hush-hush. Then he makes the oddest request."

She paused, knowing Tara and I were hanging on her every word, and she was enjoying every excruciating minute of it.

"Mr. V asked me to do a special off-site cleaning, and in exchange for my trouble he'd give me ten grand."

"Ten grand? I'm guessing you said yes?" Tara said without missing a beat.

"Of course. I needed the money, he needed my services. No way was I passing that up. So Victor—he was just a teen back then—drives us all day up to some random spot in the woods in the mountains near Six Devils where there's a metal door in the ground. An actual door in the ground, I kid you not!"

Tara grabs my hand, never taking her eyes off Nellie.

"The bunker," Tara whispers, as if that much wasn't already abundantly clear.

"So in we go, and it's an absolute mess with piss and dried

crap and blood and half-eaten food and God knows what else. Victor asks me to clean it thoroughly, so I do, no questions asked. And they reiterated at least a dozen times that I must never tell anyone about it."

Nellie paused. I wondered if she was having second thoughts about spilling the beans on the Valances. But then a huge *what have I got to lose?* grin spread across her face.

"I kept that promise for an awfully long time, but I ain't always been the most loyal employee. Come on, girls, follow me."

Nellie led us into a storage room in the back of the salon. Along the walls were metal shelves stacked with chemicals, endless rows of nail color, and a few boxes along a bottom shelf. She pulled one cardboard box out, rooting through it for a few minutes until she yanked out a large yellow envelope and handed it to me.

"It's time I do the right thing," Nellie said. "We've had a kangaroo court in this town for far too long. Somebody needs to serve up the *real* justice the Valances have comin' to 'em."

"What is it?" I asked, feeling the object through the envelope and already opening it before Nellie had a chance to tell me.

"I took this tape from the bunker while I was cleaning. Play this and you'll have all the answers you need to help clear your name, Tara Christie."

Tape 3
Mad About You

1995

[Tape clicks on. Television blares in background as intro song to *MADtv* starts]

[Young male] It's been three days and I still don't know what Dad's plans are. I'm starting to wonder what the whole point of this is...and I'm worried that Dad might tell me to do something I don't think I can do.

[Woman] Hey! Can you stop talking to your recorder and listen to me? I have asked several times to use the bathroom!

[Young male] And I didn't realize how nasty it would get down here. It smells all the time.

[Woman yells over him] It smells because you force me to use a children's potty instead of a proper bathroom!

[Young male] Stop complainin', lady. You're alive, aren't you? And fed. It could be worse.

[Woman] Please, I am begging you. I need to use the bathroom!

[Young male] You know where your toilet is.

[Woman scoffs] A children's potty is *not* a toilet. It is humiliating and degrading to make a grown woman use that when right across the room there is a proper adult toilet with a wall for privacy.

[Young male] You think it's any better for me having to clean that nasty kid's potty?

[Woman] The simple solution would be to unshackle me so I can use the other toilet.

[Young male laughs] So that you can escape and make things worse for us both? I don't think so! Suck it up and use the damn kid's potty.

[Woman] Could I at least have some privacy?

[Young male] Fine. I'll leave you to do your business. I need to run into town for a bit to get supplies. I'm hoping this is over soon.

[Woman] It is over when you say it is over! You could go to the police now and free me. I will not tell anyone you were involved. I do not even know your name or who your father is. So I can disappear without a word. Please!

[*MADtv* skit plays on television in background]

[Young male] You know I can't do that. But I'll try to make you as comfortable as possible. Do you like *MADtv*? I recorded these first few episodes on VHS. They're pretty funny. I figured it'd be a good distraction while we're here. Though you're probably not the show's target demographic.

[Woman] Can you at least tell me where we are?

[Young male] Why? So in case you escape you'll know if you can make it on foot to the nearest town?

[Woman] How about just a hint? Like a game. See if I can figure it out.

[Young male] Okay, I like games. I'll give you one hint: even the devil wouldn't come here.

[Woman] Let me think. I am assuming the closest town cannot be too far because the fast food is still warm when you arrive here. And I am guessing it is a couple hours from Bloodson Bay. And the devil would not come here? Hmm. Are we near Six Devils?

[Young male] Righteous! You're legit good at this game. I didn't think you'd ever figure that out.

[Woman] This is not a game. It is my life...and that of my daughter. Will you at least tell me why your father kidnapped me and is holding me hostage?

[Young male] All I know is he told me this is supposed to send you a message and make sure your secret stays hidden.

[Woman] What secret? I do not understand. And who is your father? If I knew who he was, I would give him whatever it is he wanted.

[Young male] I don't know what he wants. Look, you seem like a nice lady. And honestly, I couldn't care less if my dad went to jail for this. He deserves much worse, and I'd love to see him rot in prison. But it's my mom I've got to protect. If she found out about what he's doing to you, it'd...push her over the edge.

[Woman pleading, near tears] As a mother I appreciate that you try to protect her, but I am also a mother. If anything, she deserves to know her husband is a monster! The best way you can protect her is to make sure she gets away from him!

[Young male] She'll never be able to escape him. He'll never let her. He owns my mother just like he owns Bloodson Bay.

[Woman gasps] Wait...you said he had the police in his pocket too. Is your father...Judge Ewan Valance?

[Young male] Um...no.

[Woman] Oh my goodness, it is Ewan doing this, is it not? Is it because of his daughter?

[Young male] He doesn't have a daughter.

[Woman] So you do not know...

[Young male] Are you...are you my dad's mistress? I can't believe this! He knocked you up and now he locked you up? This is hella heavy!

[Woman] No one knows but him...and now you. And I will make sure it stays that way. But to let him kill me simply because I asked for some money to help my daughter have a better life than I had...I do not need his money. I do not even want it anymore!

[Young male] Let me get this straight: you and my dad had a kid, and now you want child support money? I hate to tell you, lady, but I know my dad, and you're not getting a penny from him. Worse than that, there's no way he's letting you leave here alive.

[Tape clicks off]

Chapter 22

The long drive up to Six Devils dragged along with each dreary mile. The gale raged. Rain pummeled the windshield. Wind rocked the car. Puddles sent our tires skidding. Thunder reverberated through my bones.

The storm felt personal, as if it carried a warning on its gray, heady shoulders. And it didn't isolate itself to the sky. It had crept into the car, where Peace, Tara, and I got stuck in a fight no one wanted to concede.

"Okay, I've had enough, I want you to take me home," I informed Tara when we were an hour outside of Bloodson Bay. I was as nervous as a cat in a room full of rockers. "There's practically zero visibility. And the car keeps hydroplaning. It's only a matter of time before we skid off the road into a tree."

"Look, I'm driving as safely as I can," Tara said. "Got my emergency blinkers on. We've come this far and there's no way I'm turning around now."

I looked over my shoulder at Peace in the back seat. She had insisted on coming when Tara called to tell her we were going to see about a bunker. "Can you believe her?" I said.

"Absolutely. She's a control freak." She didn't glance up from the game she was playing on her iPhone—Bejeweled Blitz, I think, or some other equally mindless time-waster. "Always has been, always will be."

"Thank you," said Tara. "I'll take that as a compliment."

"Wasn't meant as one."

Tara was like a dog with bone, determined to uncover what clues the bunker held. I didn't know how Peace and I let her talk us into coming on this mission, as she insisted on calling it. Breaking into Victor Valance's pad was one thing, but this was just plain foolish. I guess insanity loves company, right?

"Okay," I sighed, "since you're determined to kill us one way or another, would you mind putting some *good* music on the radio?"

Tara frowned over at me. "What's wrong with Billie Eilish?"

I was well aware that Tara did her best to appear "hip" at any cost—even if it meant listening to contemporary music she really didn't care for.

"Nothing," I said, "if you like some wacky pop tart whispering nonsense lyrics instead of belting out *real* lyrics. Let's have some Motown, for pity's sake. Let's listen to some Aretha Franklin!"

Tara stared straight ahead. "My car. My rules. My music," she said flatly.

"Like I said," said Peace. "Control freak."

I had to agree. Like I said, Tara has a stick up her butt half the time.

We passed the rest of the trip in silence.

By the time we reached Six Devils, the thunderstorm had worn itself out. I had never been so happy in my life to see the blue sky overhead and feel sunshine on my face again. But I didn't feel any more confident, as Nellie's directions to the bunker were obscure at best. We'd spent the afternoon driving all over God's creation, and I had to wonder if this was a tip or a trap. Nellie couldn't even tell us what year she had been there for her cleanup job. How could we trust her to remember the location of a random door buried in the ground?

Six Devils, not to be confused with the more commonly known Seven Devils town whose denizens claimed they were founded first, was an off-the-beaten-path little Appalachian resort with all the usual touristy attractions, many of which—tubing, ziplining, hiking—Tara would have said I was too old for. I could show her a thing or two! According to the hamlet's website, locals said the wind howling in the hills sounded like "devils screaming in the night"—hence the name. I hoped and prayed we wouldn't be sticking around long enough to verify that spooky description.

The hideaway was off the grid, so our GPS directions weren't much help. But eventually a satellite view and a good guess led us through a foggy wooded lot, then down a bumpy, overgrown dirt path that I hoped Tara's car wouldn't get stuck in. We arrived with just enough daylight left to reach the clearing where the bunker should have been. Just as I expected, all we found were endless weeds, dirt, and leaves.

"We're never going to find the door," I grumbled. "It's probably beneath twenty years' worth of debris. And it's going to get dark soon."

"Between the three of us I'm sure we can find it." Peace was already tromping across the glade before I unfastened my seatbelt.

When I stepped out of the car, my Easy Spirits sunk with a sloppy slurp into the mud. I was ankle-deep before I freed my foot from the suction.

"I'm stuck!"

"Here, let me help you out." Tara met me at the passenger-side door and held out her hand to guide me around the mud.

"I don't want your help. I want to go home!" I was beyond irritated after driving through a storm, ruining my shoe, and now I was probably going to miss my candlelight dinner with Rick tonight.

I hated the feeling this place gave me. Foggy serpentine tendrils wrapped around the tree trunks, and eerie shadows clung to the fringes of the clearing. It was the kind of *too quiet* that created a sense of foreboding. Like when your two-year-old stops tantruming and suddenly the house goes still, only for you to discover he's painted a poop mural all over his bedroom wall. Even the crickets were in hiding; the only sound I heard was my own shallow breath.

"I'm pretty sure this creepy place is sending me a message." My joints creaked as Tara pulled, eventually getting me safely over the muck.

"Oh? What message is that?"

"*You shall not pass*! I would rather be searching for Mordor than the bunker right now, if you want to know the truth. We don't even know who the woman in the tape is, or what year it's from. What do you expect to find here?"

"I don't know, but maybe Nellie's cleanup job was as good as she does nails." Tara showed me her already smeared fingernails. "There might be something left behind that can help us. If we can figure out the month and year, we could look up old missing persons reports to see if any sound like a possible match."

"How are we going to figure out that?" I asked.

"Well, based on some of the details in the tapes," Peace jumped in matter-of-factly, idly kicking a pile of leaves and other organic matter almost dead center in the clearing, "I think the year is 1995, probably around November or so."

Tara and I had listened to the tapes half a dozen times and still weren't sure about the year, and yet Peace listened to them once on the way up here and deduced a year *and* month?

"Well, la-di-da," I said skeptically. "How do you figure?"

"Victor was talking about *MADtv*, which I vividly remember coming out in fall of 1995 because that year for Halloween I dressed up as Alfred E. Neuman."

"Who's that?" Tara asked.

"Ooh, ooh, I know!" I exclaimed, raising my hand like a schoolgirl. When I was a teenager, you weren't cool if you didn't read *Mad.* I read it faithfully, even if some of the subversive satire was way over my head.

"Only you would dress up as a person no one has heard of, Peace," Tara teased, joining Peace at the mound of leaves.

"And only you wouldn't know basic pop culture trivia like who Alfred E. Neuman is, Tara," Peace retorted.

She pulled up a graphic of the freckle-faced magazine mascot with the jug ears, tousled shock of red hair, and goofy, gap-toothed "What, me worry?" grin on her iPhone and showed it to Tara.

"Handsome devil. You two could pass for twins," Tara deadpanned.

"Ha, ha." She had scrolled to a photo archive and pulled up a vintage scan. "Here's me as ol' Alfred. I used theatrical tooth wax to black out my front tooth and eyebrow pencil for the freckles. I got a cheap red wig, too, and wore one of Chris's old dress shirts and brown suits. Pretty rad, huh?"

Tara grinned wickedly. "I must say, you make a very convincing homely boy. And you didn't even have to flatten down your boobies. Mother Nature took care of that."

"You should talk," Peace shot back, "with those mosquito bites of yours!"

"Girls, girls!" I scolded. "I didn't get dragged all over tarnation to referee a cat fight. You two behave or there'll be no ice cream on the way home."

The two women had been like sisters since they were little girls, and just like sisters they fought all the time. Blessedly, my playful threat eased the tension.

"Vic also said he had recorded the episodes on a VHS," Tara rationalized. "So he could have recorded them and then brought them later on. We can't be sure it was 1995."

I thought for a moment, conjuring up every detail from the tapes that I could remember.

"Wait. I remember Victor talking about his car. A Nissan Skyline R33 GT-R, right?"

Tara shrugged. "You know about cars?"

"Rick dragged me to countless car shows when we were together, so I guess I picked up a few things. If memory serves, that car debuted in 1995, and if Victor was your typical spoiled teenage boy who wanted the first model when it came out, that would make the year 1995. I'm guessing like Peace said, around November. That would fit the general timeline of the television show and when the car came out."

I couldn't believe how good we were at this sleuthing business!

"Hey, it's a good start!" Tara exclaimed. "We have a

general year and month to work with, since Nellie's memory was useless."

"This dirt is really loose. I think the entrance is under here," Peace called out.

I joined the girls, who were both on their knees digging frantically in the pile of detritus with their hands. I couldn't help but be reminded of the scene in *Deliverance* where Burt Reynolds and pals buried the sodomizing hillbilly they'd killed on the riverbank, pawing at the ground like apes. Presently, a metallic *thunk* reverberated in the still, humid air.

"Did you hear that?" Peace called out. She rapped the ground, producing the same sound. "I think we found it!"

The girls dug even harder. A minute later a section of gray metal came into view.

I was bending down to help when I heard a loud crack. For a moment I thought it was my joints protesting, but it was distinctly a twig snapping in the near distance.

"Did anyone else hear that?" I asked, scanning the brush.

My gaze swung to a shape surfacing from the stillness of the thicket, and just as quickly disappearing into the shadows. Was that a man blending into the camouflage of the trees? My mind hatching violent scenarios, I peered into the lush forest where a person could hide just as easily as an animal.

"I think someone's watching us," I said, wishing I could get *Deliverance* out of my mind.

"You're just being paranoid," Tara chided me. "Come over here and help us."

Within minutes we had unearthed the entire coffin lid-sized bunker door. That description couldn't have been more spot-on. A coffin that I had no desire to investigate or get trapped inside.

Because as certain as I was that something terrible had happened here years ago, I knew we were at risk of repeating history. Someone was watching; I could feel it in my bones.

Tara and Peace yanked on the door handle, grunting as they lifted. While they worked to open the coffin lid—I mean *bunker door*—an oddly shaped mud puddle caught the dying rays of sunlight. I walked over and circled around it, then realized what it was.

"Hey, check this out!" I called out, pointing to the ground. "These look like fresh tire tracks. Which means someone's been here recently. And if someone's here, I'm not sure I want to be!"

"We're so close to finding out the truth, Ging! What if another woman is locked in the bunker?" Tara rationalized as the rusted door finally sprang open.

"Or what if it's the same woman?" With a shiver I imagined a decades-old rag-draped skeleton chained to a wall.

"Let's find out," Peace said, leading the way.

"Age before beauty." Tara trembled, then gestured for me to go ahead of her. "By the way, did I mention I'm claustrophobic?"

"Oh yeah, I'll never forget finding out that little tidbit of info *after* we got locked in a crypt when we were teens," Peace told me, taking the first terrifying step down into the darkness. "She literally passed out."

"What were you doing in a crypt?" I asked.

"You don't want to know," Tara answered.

"Then why the heck were you so eager to drag us all to this bunker?"

"I thought maybe I was over it. But looking down that ladder…" Tara shuddered. "Now that fear is all coming back to me."

"Well, I didn't come here for nothing." I plucked up my courage, such as it was, and down the ladder I went.

Outside dusk was darkening. Just below the earth, an impenetrable darkness waited. The metal rungs were ice cold against my palms. With careful steps my heels found each step until I landed on what felt like a concrete floor.

Ahead of me Peace passed her cell phone light across the room, searching the black space. Eventually she found a string dangling from the ceiling and pulled it. Miracle of miracles, the naked bulb flickered teasingly but stayed lit.

"Don't touch anything!" Tara descended behind me and pulled out her cell phone, taking pictures of the room. "We can't disturb anything, in case the police need to fingerprint the place."

When my eyes adjusted, the first thing I noticed, beyond the damp chill and steely walls, was how lived-in it appeared. Empty beer cans, not covered in dust. Grease-stained bags of fast food, the scent of french fries lingering in the air.

"It looks like someone's been living here."

"Or dying here." Tara pointed to a dark rust-red stain on the floor. Mostly likely dried blood.

A metal toilet sat behind a brick half-wall in one corner of the room opposite of where the shackles hung. "Lookee here," I said, pointing it out. "Only a sadist would plan a fallout shelter where the toilet was out of reach from the captive. Even jails have more consideration than that."

I was afraid to go too far inside, petrified the door would blow closed and lock us all in. Peace seemed to have no qualms as she searched every inch of the room, bending down to look at random objects and examining them. I caught her putting a shiny round object in her pocket, and when I glanced up at Tara, she had apparently caught it too. Before either of us could comment on her sneakiness, Peace diverted our attention.

"Hey, he's got a whole stash of blank tapes here!" she enthused, picking up a cellophane-wrapped five-pack. "Mind if I take these? I found my old tape recorder that I want to use to make a mixed tape for…for old-time's sake."

"I won't stop you," I said.

"I thought we agreed not to touch anything." Tara frowned but didn't stop her. "Just…no more touching stuff. If this is a crime scene, I don't want to give the cops any more reason to keep me on the suspect list."

The more I examined the room—the stained blood spatter on the floor, the chain on the wall—the more it became apparent that there was no *if* to this being a crime scene. It most definitely *was*.

I didn't want to imagine what horrible things had happened here, but the visions came anyway. As my brain began conjuring up all kinds of torture, a loud *bang* bounced off the walls and Tara let out a scream.

Chapter 23

My scream joined Tara's as I instinctively looked up to find the bunker door…

Open.

Thank God! I didn't need to panic…yet. But the night was still young.

"What was that clanking sound?" I squeaked.

"Sorry," Tara issued a breathless apology, "I thought I saw someone standing above me in the entrance, and I bumped into this shelf."

Okay, maybe I did need to panic.

"You think you *saw* someone? Okay, it's officially time to get the hell out of Dodge." Obviously the Valances didn't have any qualms about locking women up down here to rot.

"And how do you propose getting past whoever might be up there?" Peace pointed out.

I had no answer for that, but meanwhile a new crisis had developed.

"Shoot, the rusted edge of the shelf cut me pretty bad." Blood seeped from a gash in Tara's forearm. "Are there any Band-Aids down here?"

I found a first aid kit covered in cobwebs on a shelf and emptied the contents on a folding table. Thankfully most of the paraphernalia was sealed in clean plastic wrap; even if it was well beyond the expiration date, it would serve its purpose. As I unraveled a ball of gauze, tucked inside was a cassette—a hot pink and yellow Memorex tape like the ones we'd found in Victor's secret storage room. When it clattered to the table, I instantly recognized the 1990s music-themed handwriting across the label: *Pretty Hate Machine*

"Look what I found hidden inside." I held it up for Tara to see. "It looks like the other tapes we found. This may have some new information."

"Put it in your pocketbook and we'll listen to it on the way home."

While I flushed Tara's wound with bottled water, and treated it with watery antibiotic ointment, I kept watch on the bunker door.

"You sure you don't want me to sew it up? I'm pretty good with a needle and thread." I winked as Tara winced.

"Thanks, but no thanks."

While I finished wrapping Tara's wound, Peace headed for the ladder. "I'm going to look around outside for a minute. I'll be back."

"I sure hope so," I muttered under my breath. "What exactly are we supposed to be looking for?" I asked Tara.

I wandered aimlessly around, looking for clues, anything that might hint at who was held captive here all those years ago…and who might living be here now.

Tara was conducting her own search. "I guess just note anything that stands out to you."

"You mean like a naked guy sitting at a sewing machine making a suit out of human flesh? Will do."

We both laughed nervously.

An old mattress hugged one corner of the room, with a child's portable potty next to it. Elmo decorated the plastic rim, as if this was a playroom and not a torture chamber. A rusted chain clung to the wall with a single shackle, which was all it would take to keep a person hostage here. I wondered how—or if—anyone could survive this.

The concrete floor was dirty and stained a rusty red near the shackle, but none of it looked fresh. Then again, someone could starve to death without losing a drop of blood.

"These water bottles don't have dust on them," I observed, "and this canned food hasn't expired, so I'm guessing whoever was here is going to be coming back soon. We should probably hurry and get out of here before they do."

My phone beeped somewhere deep within my purse, and it took me a few minutes to root through the tissues and ChapSticks and hair brush and travel-size body spray to finally find it. I swiped it to life, finding a text bubble on my screen. Wearing my first smile since we arrived, I sought a moment of privacy in a corner.

Hi, beautiful. I can't wait for tonight with you. I love you. <3

"Who's that?" Tara asked.

"No one," I replied, more cheerfully than I'd intended. I did *not* want a lecture right now. I knew Tara wouldn't approve of Rick's profession of love, not until he proved himself. Which in Tara's eyes would require him to lasso the moon, George Bailey fashion.

"*No one* doesn't make your cheeks blush and turn you

giddy, Ginger. It's Rick, isn't it?"

"I plead the Fifth."

"Ginger! C'mon, you know you can't let your guard down with him. He's been in your life a quick minute and you're already googly-eyed over him. He's a piece of trash for leaving you, and he's just going to stink up your life all over again."

Aaand, cue lecture.

"Yeah, well, it's easy for you to say with your perfect, doting husband who risked going to jail to protect his family. Mine left our family for $1,000 and a dime bag of coke."

"You mean a dime bag of pot? I don't think you can get cocaine for ten bucks."

"Whatever. It was the eighties. I have no idea what kind of drugs Rick did or what they cost," I huffed. "That's not my point. Love hasn't been easy for me, because while everyone else seems to find someone so easily, it's been forty years and I'm still single, still lonely, still searching for love. The way I see it, if the man who once loved me—and yeah, also ruined me—wants to make a repeat performance, it's my decision if I want to go through it. And honestly, I have nothing left to lose. So why not? Rant over."

Tara's lips parted as if she was about to argue, then she closed her mouth, reached for me, and hugged me there in that cold, sterile space.

"You're right. I'm just protective of you because I love you too, y'know." She stepped back, hands still on my shoulders. "I'll support whatever you want, whatever you need."

I smiled at the only person who understood me. "You know, I've never thanked you for always being a constant—"

"Pain in the ass?" Tara grinned.

"I was gonna say *in my life*, but yeah, that too."

"Ready to go?" Tara asked, heading toward the ladder.

I was leading the way up the steps when I nearly collided into Peace's legs as she rushed down through the narrow opening. Her face was flushed, eyes wide with panic.

"Someone's here!" Her breaths came fast and hard.

I held back my *I told you so* and instead asked, "What do we do?" I felt my own panic rising. I wanted to clamber out of this death trap before we ended up locked in …but I also didn't know what was waiting outside of that door.

Chapter 24

Peace stood on the top rung of the ladder, searching the gloom for a person she now doubted she had seen.

"Maybe I'm wrong..." she second-guessed. "It's getting dark and hard to see."

"But is the coast clear?" I said nervously.

"Yeah, I think so. Y'all climb on up."

After we did, Tara asked, "What exactly do you think you saw?"

"I...I feel stupid even saying it," Peace mumbled.

"Who?" Tara and I asked in unison.

"You know those car tire tracks you saw?" She directed the question at me, then kept talking: "I spotted an SUV through the woods. And in the driver's seat was someone who looked identical to Victor Valance."

I wasn't sure if I should be relieved or creeped out that Peace was seeing ghosts.

"We both know that's not possible." Tara laid her hand on Peace's arm and squeezed. "We saw his dead body, Peace."

I caught a secret hidden in her body language that I didn't like. An inflection in her voice that felt off.

"What's going on between you two? You're acting weird." There was something Tara wasn't telling me, and I wasn't letting it slip by. Not this time.

But Tara's attention was fixed on Peace, and Peace's on her.

"Do you think it's trauma from the attempted rape making you see things?"

"Attempted rape?" I spluttered. "What in blue blazes are you talking about? You can't drag me all over the state searching for clues if you're gonna keep me in the dark."

Tara and Peace exchanged an unreadable look. "Can I tell her? She won't say anything to anyone," Tara asked Peace, who after a long minute nodded.

"Two nights before we found Vic's body, he approached Peace at a bar and apparently spiked her drink when she wasn't looking. He ended up coercing her into his Hummer and attacked her."

While I wasn't surprised by anything Victor Valance did, it still came as a shock. Peace, for all her flightiness, actually had a pretty tough veneer. I couldn't fathom how she held it together after an ordeal like that.

"Oh, Peace, can I hug you?" The grandmother in me wanted to reach for her and let her pour all that pain onto my shoulders.

Her eyes glistened before fat tears began to roll down her cheeks. She leaned into me unsteadily, chest heaving, body racked with sobs.

"I'm so sorry you went through that! Are you okay?"

After a short but powerful cry, Peace pressed the heels of her palms into her eyes to stem the residual tears. She met my gaze with bloodshot eyes.

"I'm okay," she said with a sniffle. "Victor didn't end up hurting me. But I can't say the same for him. A knight in shining armor showed up, and while he distracted Victor I left him with a bite mark he'll never forget…and not the kinky kind. I took a chunk out of the bastard's hand."

"Good for you! He deserved a lot worse. Did you report him to the police?"

Peace scoffed. "And tell them what? Technically nothing happened, so what was I going to say? That he *tried* to rape me but didn't succeed? One look at his mutilated hand and they'd probably arrest me instead. I felt ridiculous reporting something that didn't happen."

"But it could have! He tried! The police would have taken that seriously."

"The Bloodson Bay police that the Valance family practically owns? Get real, Ginger."

Touché.

I understood why she didn't want to report it, but by saying nothing, Victor could walk away knowing he could do it again… Except that Victor was currently lying dead in a morgue. And Peace might have been one of the last people to see him alive.

Peace continued, saying, "The last thing I wanted to do was draw attention from Victor's family. You know what they're like. I don't want to be on their shit list. They'll do anything to protect their name and image. Can you imagine what would happen if I caused Victor to go to jail…especially after putting his uncle behind bars all those years ago?"

I wanted to quip, *You'd end up in The Valance Memorial Halfway Home for Wayward Girls—with all the discomforts of hell.* But instead I asked winkingly, "Who was the knight in shining armor that distracted Victor?" Peace was almost as unlucky in love as I was.

Peace lifted one shoulder noncommittedly, then shuffled

awkwardly aside. She glanced at the floor, and I wondered what was so hard about the question.

"My brother, actually," Tara answered for her.

"Jonah?" His foreign name still felt awkward in my mouth, since his birth name, Cole, was how I knew him. I was still getting used to it, but the name was slowly growing on me. I was not, however, used to the idea of sharing him with another *mom* when I should have been the only one.

Resentment still lingered after finding out Cole—*Jonah*—had been picked up wandering on the beach during a storm almost thirty years ago, and instead of contacting the police, Tara's mother kept him and named him after the Biblical figure who had been saved from the sea. As far as I saw it, he didn't need to be saved from me. But for Jonah's sake—and Tara's—I never turned Eloise in for child abduction. It was the one thing I could do for him after missing out on so much of his life.

"I know, it's crazy to hear that my brother is a hero," Tara said proudly.

Peace grabbed Tara's and my wrists at once, yanking a little too hard. "Promise me you won't say anything to him. You know we have history together, and there has always been this stupid childish competition between him and the Valance brothers. It'll make things…weird between us if he finds out I'm telling people."

"Of course," I agreed, simulating zipping my lip.

I had to admit, though, I was proud of Jonah. After spending almost ten years in jail for attempted murder, it was good to hear that he had turned his life around. It was fitting that his first chivalric deed post-stir was coming to the rescue of the only the woman he had loved his entire life—Peace.

"Does anyone other than Jonah know what Victor did to you?" I asked.

"No, and I want to keep it that way. Ever since that night, I can't shake the feeling that Victor is still out there watching me. I know it's crazy, because he's turning into worm food as we speak, but still..."

I felt it too. That unsettling sensation, like a hand reaching out from a grave.

My phone beeped, but I didn't want to rummage through my mountain of crap again to find it in my pocketbook. "I gotta get home. I promised Rick a candlelit dinner tonight and I don't want to stand him up. We've got a very full night of activity, if you know what I mean."

"Ew, please don't make me imagine you and Rick getting it on." Tara pretended to gag.

"What, you don't want to picture us doin' the no pants dance?"

"Ugh!"

"Takin' a trip to pound town?"

"Gross!"

"Playin' hide the cannoli?"

"Stop, stop, I'm begging you!" Tara yelled, eyes clamped shut, hands over her ears. Peace and I were enjoying seeing her squirm—maybe a little too much. Translation: we were laughing our butts off.

"Tara, you always were a goody two-shoes," Peace said, when the hilarity had subsided. "I've got to get home too. Horses need to be fed or else they'll tear the barn down."

As we headed to the car, I couldn't help but consider that all of us wanted Victor dead. Tara hated him for destroying her horse rescue. Peace had been assaulted by him. And Jonah had never fallen out of love with Peace since they were teens. We all knew what Jonah had been capable of in the past, nearly killing a Valance brother over a girl and going to jail for it.

Was this his way of finishing the job?

Tape 4
Creep

1995

[Tape clicks on]

[Young male] I've been stuck here four days and there's no end in sight. I called Dad from a pay phone in town, and he screamed at me to never call him again, that he'd come when we're done here. What does that even mean? Done how? This lady is broken, if breaking her was the goal. What else could he plan to do with her? I'm afraid to find out.

[Chains rattle faintly. Woman moans in background]

[Young male] She's not looking too good. I don't know what to do. All I know is I'm tired of doing my dad's dirty work. He's allowed to bang whoever he wants behind my mom's back, while I have to babysit his mistress and watch her die when he's done with her.

[Woman, weakly] I hear what you are recording, and it was not like that, you know. I was not some *broad* he *banged.* I was in mourning, and your father found me and helped me feel something other than grief. I liked him...until I met the real him.

[Young male, hysterically] Breaking news! My dad—the judge, jury, and executioner of Bloodson Bay—is actually capable of genuine human emotion!

[Woman] And you do not have to babysit me. You can be your own man and let me go. Stop being your father's doormat and stand up for yourself...and for your mother.

[Young male] You realize that if I do that, you're dead, right?

[Woman] I am willing to take that risk. I would rather be free and take a chance at life than rot in this bunker where certain death awaits me. Because there is no way your father will let me live. Not after locking me up for this long.

[Young male] Look, you can't totally blame him for your situation. You got pregnant by a married man. What did you expect to happen?

[Woman] How dare you! What a stupid male chauvinist attitude. First of all, I had no idea he was married. And while the night we met was a bit hazy and I made my fair share of mistakes, he certainly did not wear a wedding band. I was grieving a loss, and your father used that to manipulate me. I never asked for anything of him for years...not until recently when I made one simple, tiny request. And in reply he throws me in a bunker? What kind of psychopath does that?

[Young male] You haven't met my family if you have to ask that question. We're a family of psychos! It's why my dad controls that stupid town, because all of Bloodson Bay fears him because you never know what he'll do.

[Woman] So you want to be like him? Because you are dangerously close to walking the same path, young man.

[Young male] I don't know if there's any hope for me *not* to walk the same path. It's my *fate*, Miss Alika, if you believe in that kind of thing.

[Woman] I realized you know my name but I do not know yours. I believe I have earned that, yes?

[Young male] Yeah, I guess there's no harm in you knowing. It's...Victor.

[Woman] Victor...as in *conqueror*. I suppose it suits you well.

[Tape clicks off]

Part 3

Sloane Apara

Chapter 25

A glorious dawn broke upon the periwinkle blue sky dolloped with peach-cheeked clouds. A blue heron waded in the surf on its stilt legs; another high-stepped over the ruins of a child's sandcastle, startling a ghost crab back into its burrow. Tiny sanderlings scampered along the beach, foraging for sand fleas. A black skimmer, dapper in its tuxedo-like coloration, glided majestically over the waves before snagging a fish.

My morning walks along the beach, where my yard dropped off into the bay, were the best part of my day. It was peaceful here along the shore, before the beach filled with people, as the sea foam tickled my toes and the breeze tossed my hair.

The saltwater was frigid this time of year, before the fullness of spring had a chance to draw the ocean to its warm bosom. I climbed the steps that led to my beachfront home tucked into a rare wooded lot. It had been quite the expensive coup finding this isolated lot along the bay, on a small lone hill surrounded by flat land. But the breathtaking view from my treehouse-like home was absolutely worth it.

At the top of the wooden steps a pink mist gathered around the banana trees and canna lilies and elephant ears sprouting from the sandy soil. Hidden by the haze were nature's most precious secrets. I reached the top tier of the deck that protruded from the open-floor home I had designed with the help of an incredible Deaf architect who understood my needs. While my now-dead husband never held back a complaint of how *sterile* or *cold* the home appeared, he had no idea how hard it was to be a Deaf woman in a house full of solid walls.

My vision was my awareness, my survival, my communication. If I could see him across the room, I could communicate. Walls isolated a person like me, unable to hear a phone ring or kettle whistle or a call for dinner. With open floors and glass walls, I always knew what was going on around me. Even up until we split up, Benson refused to understand. It was one of many reasons we didn't last…and then he died.

I was outside on the patio when the doorbell flashed throughout the house, a flickering special-order red bulb that I couldn't miss even if I wanted to. And right now I really wanted to.

I didn't need to answer the door to know who it was. The telltale flash-flash-flash, pause, flash-flash-flash, pause, told me exactly who it was. It was Mummy's signature "ring," if you wanted to call it that, ever since I was a kid. Although spinal meningitis left me Deaf as an infant, Mummy couldn't afford the latest Deaf technology until I hit double digits. When I turned ten Mummy finally forked out the money for a flashing doorbell. When I turned thirteen she splurged on a Text Telephone, or TTY, which allowed me to type conversations, relayed through an operator, to my friends.

These newfound freedoms didn't come without a price. All friends had to be "Mummy approved," and the flashing code was enforced to protect me from greeting strangers at the door.

Over the years I learned that "protective" in describing my mother was an understatement. Maybe it was because I was

Deaf, or maybe because I was her only child, but Mummy would do anything—and I mean *anything*—to shield me from the big, bad, evil world.

"You're here early, Mummy."

In Mummy's punctual world there was no such thing as too early, only too late. Golden morning poured in through the door, creating a halo around my mother's black silhouette. She swept past me into the house in a rushed blur of motion.

"Good morning, *omoge*," Mummy signed, using the Nigerian word for "young lady."

She stepped out of her flats and deposited them near the entry, then padded her way barefoot into the living room. After setting her purse on a table, she pulled me into a hug that felt longer, tighter than usual.

"You did not go out into public wearing that, did you?" Mummy asked as she eyed me up and down.

I glanced down at my cropped cashmere sweater and jeans with holes in the knees. Instinctively wrapping my arms around my bare waist, I covered up the sliver of belly showing. Mummy hadn't always been this conservative, or so she tells me, but I had known her to be nothing else my entire life. Our job as women, according to her, was to protect ourselves from the lecherous gazes of men. As much as I tried to explain to her that modern men were responsible for their own wickedness, not us women, she took the firm stance that if you don't give them something to look at, they'll look somewhere else.

"No, Mummy, I didn't go out in this."

"Have you eaten? I can make a bread sandwich and tea for you."

A Nigerian favorite, *bread sandwich* to her usually

consisted of mackerel in a tomato sauce, which had always startled overnight guests when I had sleepovers growing up. And by *tea* she usually meant whatever hot beverage I had on tap, though I had tried to explain the different between coffee and tea countless times.

"No, thank you. I've eaten. Sit. Relax," I urged. Even as an adult, I would always be seen and tended to as her little *omoge*.

Mummy sat on the sofa, her vibrant clothes a stark contrast against the dominant creams of my décor. Lush plants added a splash of color here and there. Behind her hung a large framed photo of Yankari Game Reserve that I had taken as a teenager during a safari with my extended family during a visit to my mother's homeland. In true Nigerian fashion, my *iya-nla*—or grandmother—had stuffed me full of jollof rice and pounded yams, and showed me the beauty of my motherland. They had even learned some ASL in order to speak with me. Part of my heart would always remain there, but my home was in Bloodson Bay.

Shifting awkwardly, Mummy glanced about the room, then grabbed a magazine from the coffee table, silently flipping through it. Mummy was only this quiet if something was wrong.

"You seem anxious, Mummy. What's going on?"

She dropped the magazine and rose to her feet. "I might as well spit it out. Something has happened and we must leave. Perhaps return to Nigeria before it is too late."

I couldn't imagine what my uber-religious mother had gotten into that would drive us out of the country.

"I don't understand. Too late for what?"

"Someone…died, Sloane, and they may think I am responsible for it."

"Wait—what? Who died?"

"I wish I could say more, but I cannot tell you, *omoge*. It would put you at risk."

There was only one person whose death seemed connected to everyone I knew...but how was he connected to my mother? "Does this have something to do with Victor Valance?"

Her wide eyes convinced me I had guessed correctly.

"Who thinks you killed him? The cops?"

Mummy shook her head. "No, his father, Ewan Valance."

"The town judge? Screw him, Mummy! He has no reason to think that! Victor's death has nothing to do with our family."

Mummy stood awfully silent for far too long.

"Right?" I pressed.

The doorbell flashed frantically, rooting me to the spot. Were the police here to arrest my mother? I crept slowly to the edge of the living room wall that led to the entry, trying to see without being seen. Damn this house of glass!

I figured they'd be barging through the door by now if it was the police, so I continued my stealthy approach toward the front door. A flash of red hair brought instant relief. It was Ginger and Tara.

No sooner had I ushered them inside than Ginger frantically signed a mess of misspelled words and random strings of thoughts I couldn't follow.

"Slow down!" I yelled, using my voice. "I can't understand you," I followed up with sign.

"We were at the bunker yesterday—you know, the one from the tapes. We found another tape hidden there in which we heard Victor say the name of the woman he had been holding captive!" Ginger finally explained in comprehendible sign.

I could feel a presence behind me and turned to see Mummy standing there, shamefaced. I returned my gaze to Ginger, who acknowledged her with a stiff wave.

"So you already know?" Ginger asked me.

"Know what?" I was so confused, I didn't know what was going on.

Mummy stepped to my side, tears streaming down as she tried to screen her face from me. When she found the courage to finally face me, the pieces fell into place.

"It was me who was in the bunker in the fall of 1995, Sloane."

Tape 5

One Sweet Day

1995

[Tape clicks on]

[Young male] Yesterday I found out I have a half-sister. I don't even know how to feel about it. A sibling running around out there that I didn't know about makes me wonder what else I don't know. Are my parents my real parents? Is my brother my actual brother? I feel like I can't trust anyone anymore.

[Woman] That is exactly my point, Victor. You cannot trust your father. Which is why you must let me go free. Once he disposes of me, he will go after my daughter, and I cannot let that happen. Please.

[Young male] Why should I trust you? I have a feeling you haven't been honest with me either. You won't even tell me my sister's name. I want to meet her. Once I meet her and talk to her, I'll let you free. Deal?

[Woman hesitates] Uh, I cannot do that.

[Young male] Why not? It's a simple request. Should be easy. Give me her name, I'll verify all this with her, and I'll let you go.

[Woman] She does not know about Ewan.

[Young male] Don't you think she should? I do. I'd want to know if I had a whole other family out there. Because no one likes being lied to their entire life!

[Woman sighs] I cannot. I am sorry.

[Young male] Then I guess I'll let my father deal with you. I'm tired of everyone lying to me. You all deserve what you get.

[Woman] Wait! If I tell you the truth—the whole truth—will you let me go?

[Young male] No lies, nothing left out?

[Woman] Yes. Every last horrid detail.

[Young male] Fine. It's a deal. Tell me everything and I'll figure out a way to get us both out of here.

[Woman inhales shaky breath] It all started the day my husband died...

[Tape clicks off]

Chapter 26

"It all started the day my husband died..." Mummy began, her impassive gaze skipping around the living room from Ginger to Tara and lastly settling on me.

We had boiled water for tea, but as I sipped, it did little to calm my raw nerves. I listened with rapt attention as Mummy continued, and I felt my anxiety ramp up with each sign.

"The man I told you was your father," Mummy clarified.

I didn't like how this was already beginning. "Please tell me Ewan Valance isn't my biological father," I signed, mouthing the words angrily.

"Please just listen without judgement, Sloane. It is a complex story, full of complex emotions. But it is what it is, and I cannot change the past."

"No one here will judge you, Alika," Ginger encouraged. "We've all made our fair share of bad decisions. Me especially. Go ahead."

"The day my husband passed truly destroyed me. I loved him more than any heart could endure. But when you experience a passion, a connection that deep, it tears you in two when it is taken from you. Especially so abruptly and senselessly." Mummy turned to Ginger and Tara. "He was murdered during an armed robbery. Shortly after that loss I met Ewan."

"Did you sleep with Ewan Valance?" I demanded.

"I did."

I didn't know how to feel about the blunt way she answered that.

"I can't believe it. You always talk about your faith and being a good person, when meanwhile you slept with the devil! I don't even know you, Mummy!"

Mummy held up her hand. "Just wait. You need to understand the whole story."

"There is nothing you can say to justify it. What about the man I thought was my father? The man you told me you would love until your last dying breath? Was that Ewan Valance?"

"Oh, daughter, you do not understand." Mummy dropped her chin, shaking her head slowly. A tear dripped onto her lap, the first bud of emotion I had seen her express.

Mummy sniffled before she continued. "A lifetime ago, before you were born, I was married to the most wonderful man, as if he was created just for me. The moment I laid eyes on him I knew he was The One, as you Americans call it. When we met, he was with Doctors Without Borders, during its early days after the Nigerian Civil War. My family had suffered greatly from that famine after that war, and he came to help us. I will never forget his proposal, when I saw the purity of his heart for the first time."

"Oooh, I love a good meet-cute story!" Ginger gushed.

Mummy cocked one sculpted eyebrow. "Meet-cute?"

"You know, like in the movies when a couple meets for the first time under some charming or zany circumstance, and you just know they're destined to fall in love."

"Ah, I see. Yes, it was very cute. He took me to a beach along the Lekki Lagoon and hid an engagement ring in a shell on the sand…but he had forgotten which shell it was. So we spent the entire day searching for a specific shell, and I had no idea why. He never once got angry or upset—we simply laughed and enjoyed every moment together. Eventually he dropped down on one knee and proposed without the ring, and after I said yes, he happened to step on the shell, injuring his bare foot. But there was the ring! And he hobbled home, promising he would endure anything to ensure my happiness."

Sitting next to her, Ginger couldn't contain her feelings as she wept, grabbing tissue after tissue from her sleeve, babbling over the sweetness of such adoration.

"We quickly fell in love, and he asked me to leave Lagos and come to America to build a life with him. I could not say no, because I would have given up everything for him. In fact, I did. And I would do it again in a heartbeat."

"You've told me this story before many times," I reminded her. "Is it all true?"

"Yes, of course it is true. Let me finish, *omoge*. Because his parents left him a house in Bloodson Bay, we moved here while he finished his time with Doctors Without Borders. Eventually we got pregnant—with you, Sloane, my darling daughter. But within a month of finding out, he was killed when a man tried to rob him at gunpoint and the gun went off. It was a horrible trauma to me, and I felt like my world had ended. I was left here in America, with no family, newly pregnant, and unemployed. I was heartbroken and falling apart. This is when I lost my mind."

"What do you mean, Mummy?"

"It was only one night, but I had been grieving terribly. I was not in a good—uh, what do you call it? Head space?—so I went out for a drink. I knew better. I was pregnant and of course should not have done it, but I had lost my will to live. I did not want to raise a baby without the man I loved. I met Ewan Valance at that fateful bar. He seemed so comforting and nice and helped me forget my pain, if only for a few hours. And I made a terrible decision that night when I allowed him to seduce me."

"Oh, Mummy," I groaned, using my voice.

"I know, it is awful. I instantly regretted my indiscretion and prayed for forgiveness. I thought I could put it behind me, but I would soon learn my troubles were only just beginning, and I would rue the day I ever set eyes on him."

"What happened?" Ginger sat on the edge of the sofa, one knee tucked up under her, the other bumping my mother's legs, she was so close.

"I did not seek Ewan out or speak to him after that one night, nor him to me. Until one day, when I was near my due date, we saw each other passing by on the street. He instantly recognized me, and when he looked at my huge belly, I could see the fear and anger on his face. All that charm and kindness were gone. He was furious with me."

"Did you tell him the baby wasn't his?" Tara asked.

"I did not get a chance to say anything. He stormed up to me, grabbed my arm so tight it left a bruise, and whispered in my ear that if I told anyone about the baby, he would kill me. If I asked for money, he would kill me. If I tried to blackmail him, he would kill me. And then he left. For fifteen years I never saw him again and raised Sloane on my own."

I felt a *but* coming on…

"But one day, out of the blue, I got a letter from his wife."

"How did his wife find out?" I could barely force my fingers to move, I was so floored.

"I do not know how she discovered what happened, because I never told a soul. But she wrote me a letter telling me I should call out her husband and demand child support for my daughter so that I could give you a good future with abundant opportunities. She must have known or heard that I was a poor, single mother, but I did not want a thing from that family. It was almost like she wanted me to disgrace her husband. Maybe she wanted an out and needed my public confession in order to do that. I will never know for sure, but I imagine being married to Ewan was a mortal punishment she wanted to end."

"What did you do?"

"I felt badly for her, and I did what any desperate woman would do. I wrote Ewan a letter requesting child support in exchange for my silence."

My obvious shock must have shamed my mother, because she instantly went on the defense.

"You have to understand, Sloane, we were in a terrible financial place at that point. I was a single mother, with no decent job prospects here, and no money to afford to return home to Nigeria to be with our family. I wanted to make sure you could go to college and do better than I could give you, so I decided to ask for just enough to cover your first year of college tuition."

"I'm guessing that didn't go over well," Ginger cut in.

"Correct. Shortly after that I came home after work to find our house torn apart. I realized in that moment that it was a message—a threat. So I scraped together what money I could and sent you to visit our family in Nigeria while I stayed behind to fix things."

"Mummy, why didn't you come with me?"

"I did not have the money, daughter. I barely had enough to buy a single ticket for you. And life in Nigeria at that point was not much better as the government was in upheaval." Mummy shook her head sadly. "I had hoped I could explain everything to Ewan. But I never got that chance. Right after you left, Sloane, I woke up one night to a masked man holding a cloth over my mouth, knocking me out. When I came to, I was chained to a wall in the bunker with Victor Valance in charge of keeping me alive. I was degraded, treated like an animal, and if it was not for God's protection, I would be a skeleton still chained in that bunker."

Imagining what Mummy had gone through—the loss of my father, raising me alone, held captive…it was just too horrible. I shrank down to a ball at her feet and sobbed in her lap.

"I am so sorry, Mummy, that you went through that!" I cried into her legs as she ran her fingers through my hair.

When I looked up, my hands shaking as I tried to sign, her expression was so cold. So hard. So terrifyingly calm.

"What happened down there, Mummy?"

She glanced away, toward the window where the noonday sun beat down.

"I watched Victor Valance change from a boy to a monster."

Tape 6

Mo' Money, Mo' Problems

1995

[Tape clicks on]

[Young male, whispering] I'm recording this as proof of what actually happens tonight. My dad is on his way, and I have no idea what he's planning to do, so this is my testimony of the facts.

[Woman, frantic] Victor, there is not much time! Please free me before he gets here! Please do not let him kill me!

[Young male] There's nothing I can do to save you, lady. It's in my dad's hands now.

[Woman] Listen, you must not tell your father that the baby was not his. Please. The only reason he has not killed me yet is because of her—because he thinks he is her father. Please promise me you will not tell him the truth.

[Young male] You want me to lie to my dad? He'll know I'm hiding something. And when he finds out...

[Woman] He will *kill* me if he discovers she is not his. My blood will be on your hands!

[Squeal of a door opening in background]

[Older male's voice, distant] Son, you down here?

[Young male] Yeah, Dad, I'm down here with that lady.

[Footsteps growing near]

[Older male] Good, good. Did she tell you anything?

[Woman] I told him nothing, Ewan.

[Older male] Was I speaking to you, whore? You keep your mouth shut until I give you permission to speak!

[Young male] No, she didn't tell me anything.

[Older male] So she didn't tell you how she's making up lies about me cheating on your mother, then threatening to blackmail me for money?

[Young male] No, Dad, she hasn't said anything about that.

[Older male] I find that hard to believe. But if what you're saying is true, I guess we can finish this. Now, tonight you're going to show me what kind of man you are, son.

[Young male] What do you mean? I don't want to be part of this.

[Older male] It's too late for that. You're already a big part of this. And it's time to finish it.

[Young male] Are you...are you telling me to...*kill* her?

[Older male laughs]

[Older male] No, son, we're not going to kill her, but she's got to learn a lesson about keeping her mouth shut. Do you think your mom deserved to hear all these lies about a one-night stand that led to an unwanted pregnancy and have her heart broken? Especially since it didn't happen?

[Young male] No. But Dad—

[Older male] Exactly. But somehow your mom did find out, and now her heart is broken. All because of this blabbermouth who had the gall to ask for child support money after fifteen years. You follow the Bible's teachings, don't you, Alika? Then you should know that the love of money is the root of all evil.

[Woman] But I did not tell your wife, and I do not want your money! If you let me go, I will disappear forever. You will never see me again.

[Older male] Oh, I already plan to make you disappear. It's time we teach her a lesson about greed, don't you think, son?

[Young male, fearful] Dad, I don't know...

[Woman] Ewan, wait! I was not the one who told your wife. She is the one who contacted me. I even have her letter as proof!

[Older male] Who cares about a stupid letter or how she found out, Alika? Because it doesn't matter now. What's done is done. You still can't be trusted. If I were to pay you, you'd only come back for more to keep quiet. So you've forced me to have to...*deal* with you.

[Woman] What if I told you there is more to the story? Something you should know. Perhaps it will change your mind.

[Older male] I don't need to hear anything you have to say, Alika.

[Woman] Someone else knows about us, someone who is trying to hurt your family. Do you not want to know the truth?

[Older male] Truth is what we decide it to be. And I've decided that you need to be punished for breaking my wife's heart and nearly destroying my family's good name. And if someone else wants to attack me, I'll destroy them too. Simple as that.

[Woman scoffs] You do not find it hypocritical that a man whose sole duty it is to find the truth and pursue justice—a judge—does not want to know the truth?

[Older male] Maybe more time in the bunker to think about all that truth will help you sort it out. You're lucky I'm not going to kill you, because I'm a merciful guy.

[Woman breaks down sobbing with relief] You are not going to kill me?

[Older male] Not yet, at least. But when you get out of here, you're to stay in Bloodson Bay where

I can keep an eye on you. You try to run, I'll find you and kill you and your daughter. Got it?

[Woman sniffles] I understand.

[Older male] I still have the issue of your money demands to deal with... How do I know you won't run to the police or the media about this?

[Woman] Because I will end up dead is why I won't.

[Older male] Ah, you're learning!

[Young male] Dad, this is getting crazy! She can't ruin your name because she has no proof of you two being together. It's her word against yours. No one would believe her anyway.

[Older male] Alright, I'll give you your freedom, Alika. But at a price. Son, take this hammer, and if you can break the shackle free, she can go home. Let's see whatcha got, boy.

[Young male] But I'll break her wrist if I hit it...

[Older male] Then she can rot here for all I care.

[Woman] Wait! Just do what your father says.

[Older male] I don't need to remind you, Alika, that if word of this ever comes out, or you try to run away, Sloane will die. You will die. I will go all the way to Lagos, Nigeria, to kill all of your family if I have to.

[Woman stutters] H-h-how did you know Sloane is in Lagos?

[Older male] I know everything, Alika. My power is absolute and my reach is long. So if you tell anyone—even Sloane—it will be the last thing you say.

[Older male] Alright, it's time to see what you can do, boy. Get to swinging!

[Young male] I'm sorry, lady. You know I don't want to have to do this, but it's the only way to get you out of here.

[Older male] Don't apologize to her! Let's get on with it.

[Young male grunts as the sound of metal on metal reverberates and woman cries out in pain]

[Older male laughs] Harder, son! Those chains won't break themselves!

[Woman screams] God have mercy on me!

[Tape clicks off]

Chapter 27

I pictured my mother's face contorted in a silent scream as the hammer snapped her wrist. I was an emotional sponge, soaking up the sadness and squeezing it back out.

"What did he do to you?" I asked but didn't want to know. I wanted to shoulder her pain as much as I wanted to hide from the truth.

Mummy told us about the cruelty Victor Valance had carried out against her. Denying her food and water, while greedily partaking of same as she looked on. Forcing her, under his leering eye, to relieve herself in a child's potty, while he used the bunker's sanitation system, which afforded him the privacy she was denied. And the final indignity: being either too stupid or too wicked, maybe both, to find a more humane means of removing her shackles, instead subjecting her to the gut-wrenching pain of the hammer's inexact blows.

"Why could he not find some means of removing my bonds to free me?" Mummy asked tearfully. "Why did he not go to the police? To this day, my mind wrestles with these questions. Instead he seemed to relish my pain, or at least to ignore it, which is just as bad. And all because his accursed father bade him to. I understand well the love of a son for his father, the burning need to please him, at any cost. But my captor was a coward. He did not have to do the things he did to me..."

I felt brittle in her embrace as I sat before her, a hollowness in her eyes I had never seen before. For her it had happened years ago, but for me her wounds were fresh and still bleeding.

She patted my head like when I was a little girl. "It is okay, Sloane. I am okay," she soothed. "It was long ago. I have healed."

"How could you ever possibly heal from that?"

She smiled down at me the way that only mothers can. "The human spirit is fiercer and stronger than any pain our flesh can endure."

I sat with those words for a long time. So long that I noticed Ginger shifting uncomfortably and Tara itching to check her phone.

A blink of the doorbell light jarred me upright. Every demanding burst was now a threat.

"I'll get it," Ginger offered, but I waved her to sit back down.

Whatever was waiting on the other side of that door, I had to face it myself. I imagined Ewan Valance—or one of his fancy-suited thugs—waiting on the other side, ready to drag Mummy off to finish what they had started so many years ago.

I strode toward the front door, shoulders high and back straight. Ginger and Tara got up and walked behind me like an entourage, while Mummy hung back in the living room sipping her tea.

The light flashed again, and a vaguely familiar face appeared on the other side of the glass.

"Detective Hughes," Tara signed the name I couldn't place.

I had a dreadful feeling I knew why she was here. I opened the door, feeling the support of Ginger and Tara behind me.

The detective's mouth started moving, but I couldn't read her lips.

"I'm Deaf and use sign language," I signed and spoke at the same time.

The detective looked to the women around me, and I deduced she was searching for an interpreter. Ginger stepped up and started signing while the detective spoke.

"Is your mother here right now?" the detective asked.

She already knew the answer to that question. My mother's car was parked in the driveway next to hers.

"Why?" I asked.

"I need to speak with her."

"About what?"

"Miss Sloane Apara, is it?" the detective asked, but didn't wait for me to confirm my maiden name. "I need to come in right now." Her hand rested on her gun holster, and I stepped back.

What had Mummy gotten herself into?

As the detective pushed past me into the house, I scurried behind her. She headed straight for the living room, hand still on the gun holster. Only now did I notice the other officer waiting on the porch, who followed her inside. The same man we had seen in Victor's basement. As he passed I read his metal name badge: *H. Alonzo*

They made a beeline for Mummy, standing now, firmly but not roughly spinning her around, but I couldn't hear anything that they were saying. I looked to Ginger for clarity.

"They're telling her she's under arrest for the murder of Victor Valance," Ginger explained. "And they're reading her her Miranda rights."

I tried to push past the detective to Mummy's side, but her arms were pinned behind her back, leaving her unable to sign. All I could read from her lips was, "It will be okay. Everything will be okay."

Everything was chaos. Constant movement I couldn't follow. Noise I couldn't hear. I shook my head, screaming with my voice because my hands wouldn't obey, "Stop!" I felt the word vibrate in my chest, the only assurance that I had been heard. "My mummy is innocent!" I needed her to explain what the hell was happening and wished the detective would just stop for a moment to listen to me.

I grabbed the detective's arm, trying to force her to look at me. "Can I speak with my mummy in private?"

The detective seemed to understand me and shook her head, looking to Ginger for assistance. "After we finish our interrogation and take her statement you can speak with her. But not until we're done."

"I am safer in jail, Sloane," Mummy mouthed to me. "Ewan cannot get to me if I am in there."

But I knew better. He could get to anyone anywhere.

The detective funneled Mummy past me, pausing only for a moment as Mummy spoke something in Ginger's ear. Then the detective and the other officer escorted Mummy down the front steps, while I trailed helplessly, silently behind.

I looked to Ginger, the one Mummy had entrusted her secret to.

"What did she say to you?" I asked.

"She said you must protect yourself from snakes in the grass."

"Protect myself?" I reiterated to Ginger. "From what? From

who?"

Until I could speak with Mummy, I had no idea who I was running from and why.

Chapter 28

I was familiar with attracting enemies. I'd gained my fair share of trolls on social media, the price one paid for internet fame. For every follower there was a detractor. Some people got their jollies from seeing success stories crash and burn. But this was different. This was personal. Targeted. And not toward me but my mummy.

"We need to find out what the cops have on your mom," Ginger announced after the detective's car backed out of my driveway, stealing Mummy away.

"She didn't do it," I signed. "She didn't kill Victor Valance."

"Well, the cops seem to think she did, and they wouldn't have arrested her unless they had some kind of compelling evidence. So we need to find out what it is so we can prove her innocence."

"Are you sure she's innocent?" Tara looked scared to ask her dumb question, and she should be. Anyone who knew my mummy understood she was incapable of hating a man, no matter how evil he was. Praying over him? Certainly. Killing him? Certainly not.

Then again, I hadn't thought my mother capable of sleeping with the devil either, and I was wrong about that.

Tara continued blabbing on, tempting me to slap her…or at

least grab her hands to stop signing at me like she knew me or my mummy. "Vic refused to free her when he could have. It might have taken her fifteen years to finally get vengeance, but wouldn't you want to kill someone who held you captive?"

Ginger's lips curled with skepticism. "But why now—after so long? Or why not kill Ewan instead—the one who orchestrated it all?"

"Maybe something happened recently with Vic that set Alika off?"

"My mother is innocent!" I yelled. I refused to watch them talk about my mummy like she was a killer. "And I'll prove it. Let's go."

"Where are we going?"

"Where else but to her house? There's got to be something there that can help us."

Mummy lived only five minutes away from me, the perfect distance for her impromptu pop-ins to make sure I ate dinner, or had a stocked pantry, or—well, it usually involved making sure I was well fed.

Ginger drove us to Mummy's quaint teal and white beach cottage, as I was too shaken up to drive. My hand trembled as I turned Mummy's doorknob, surprised to find it unlocked. I wondered at what point the police would arrive, assuming they would any minute if they hadn't already been and gone. If there was something here that could save her, I needed to find it first. Luckily Bloodson Bay had a small, understaffed sheriff's department, which hopefully bought us enough time.

The minimalist house didn't show any signs of being torn apart, so either the cops were neat in their search, or we beat them here. We all three split up, each taking different rooms searching through drawers and cabinets and dressers, not sure what we were looking for. Nothing we found proved her innocence, but neither did anything prove her guilt…that I knew of. What exactly did the cops have on her?

I thought of the facts we had put together so far. That Victor's head had been blown off by a shotgun. My mummy had never fired a gun in her life, and never wanted to, after my father had been killed by one.

Then there was the horse euthanasia drug found in Victor's vehicle, which Mummy would know nothing about.

Mummy's account of the harrowing ordeal she'd endured in the bunker, as Victor refused to seek help from the police, kept running through my mind. If that was all they knew about, it certainly seemed more like circumstantial evidence than ironclad proof to me.

I wandered into my mother's office, where the old teletypewriter, or TTY device, I had used as a teenager still sat in all its ugly beige glory. It was essentially a typewriter with a telephone handset on top, and a narrow LCD screen that electronically displayed the conversation in scrolling green letters. I remembered typing my very first phone call on it—to Peace Christie, in fact—and marveling at how my keyed message went to an operator who spoke the message to Peace on the other end of the phone line. While hearing people often found the complicated conversation frustrating, to a Deaf girl it was simple freedom.

Any time the TTY lit up I would get a thrill of excitement that this little sliver of normalcy—of being a teenage girl chatting on the phone with a friend—was finally mine. Being the only Deaf girl in a hearing public school brought a terrible loneliness, until Peace came along, sleeves rolled up and ready to fight me over a boy neither of us had a chance with. It was the first time another girl felt threatened by me, rather than pitying me.

Neither of us got the guy, but we got each other, which was a far better deal. She learned about sign language, and I learned about friendship. Late-night phone calls, catty gossip, no-sleep sleepovers, terrible nineties fashion, cheesy nineties movies—closed-captioned, of course…I had it all, along with someone to share it with. While Peace would never fully understand my life, she embraced my uniqueness and I embraced hers.

My eyes were drawn to the messy desk, which Mummy usually kept fastidiously neat. As Mummy would say, *Cleanliness is next to godliness…but with you, dear daughter, it is next to impossible.* The top drawer was wide open, everything inside in disarray, as if Mummy had been rooting through it in a hurry.

But she was never in a hurry. And never too rushed to close a drawer.

I continued searching, reaching for the handle of the lower drawer where Mummy stored keepsakes from my father's Doctors Without Borders days, along with pictures and correspondence. I remembered my anticipation as she unlocked the drawer with a beautiful antique brass key, and pulling out the bundle of their love letters, bound with a pink ribbon. She would read them to me as I sat on her lap, luring me into their whirlwind romance as my father traveled extensively, both eager for the day they could finally wake up every morning together.

To my astonishment, the drawer opened with a slight tug.

For as long as I could remember it had always been locked, but perhaps after I moved out Mummy no longer felt the need for privacy. I imagined she visited this drawer more often after I left, finding comfort, on lonely nights without end, in my father's handwriting.

I lifted out the bundle of letters and rifled through them, noticing the letter on top wasn't the one I had remembered. Did my memory deceive me? It should have been the very first letter she had written him after he left Lagos. This letter looked to be a much later one. I couldn't be wrong about this. She had read them to me so many times. So where was it? Mummy was nothing if not organized. A creature of habit.

Had the cops taken it? And if so, why? I was unable to equate the woman in these letters to the one sitting in jail for murder. Was my reminiscence flawed? Had I distorted reality? Mummy's horrific confession had jumbled everything good I remembered about our mother-daughter bond.

I tucked the letters into my purse for safekeeping, in case the police returned. These were personal and precious, and I couldn't risk any more being lost. For Mummy's sake. It was all she had left of the love of her life.

I had just closed the office door when Ginger came running up to me, signing frantically: "Blood, blood!"

I followed her to the bathroom, where Tara, pale as a stick of chalk, was doubled over, gripping the sides of the sink. Her pants were dark with blood, especially around the crotch. At her feet was a small red puddle.

Tara's lips parted in a distressed O before she collapsed. Ginger was momentarily frozen with shock. I instinctively fell to my knees and cradled her limp body against my chest.

"She's unresponsive!" I shouted, wheezing out words I couldn't hear.

"I'm going to call an ambulance," Ginger signed, leaving me alone with this bleeding woman who I barely knew.

Tara's arm hung over my lap, her cell phone in her hand. Her fingers twitched; the phone came to life, and a text message bubble popped onto the screen:

I know what you did to her, and you're not going to get away with it.

I tapped the phone with my fingertip, the blood making the screen slippery. There was no name associated with the contact, only the word "Unknown" next to the text.

Who was the *her* the text referred to? Had Tara done something to my mummy? It all felt too coincidental. Mummy in jail for murder. Her missing letters. Tara's secret text. And now Tara was dying…

Part 4

Tara

Chapter 29

I lolled along in a thin sleep, eventually waking up in an unfamiliar place full of unfamiliar light and unfamiliar sounds. Even my body felt unfamiliar with thin tubes stuck to my skin.

The plastic feel of my gown and stiff bleached sheets gave it away. I was in a hospital bed. I vaguely remembered why. Being in Sloane's mom's house, feeling sick and running to the bathroom, then cramping and blood. Something had alarmed me, but I couldn't retrieve the missing memory from the fog. After that everything went blank.

"Look who's finally awake." A woman in blue scrubs came to me, her soft, kind face smiling down as she checked the beeping machine above my head. "You'll be glad to know the baby is fine, Mrs. Christie."

Turning my groggy head to the side, I expected to find some other patient that this nurse was talking to, but it was only me in this hospital room. Only me and apparently my…baby?

"Let me put your mind at ease, hon—cramping and bleeding is common in early pregnancy. Nothing to worry about, but you need to start taking better care of yourself." Now that I was slowly regaining consciousness, I followed the nurse's focus from my eyes down to my wrists. I tried to cover the marks, but I only seemed to attract more interest. "Are you self-harming? It's nothing to be ashamed of. I see it all the time.

But it's something you really do need to address."

I had no recollection of hurting myself. "No, that's not what it is. At least not intentionally. It happens while I sleep."

"Hmm." She locked her eyes on mine. Deep concern there. Maybe some doubt too. "You stressed much?"

Stressed didn't even begin to cover it. "A little."

I turned over my bruised wrists, where open gashes had replaced the thin pink lines. I was literally tearing myself apart.

"You need more rest, honey. And if the stress is too much, we might be able to find something pregnancy-safe to take the edge off. I'll send the doctor in to speak with you."

Trying to wrap my brain around what she was telling me, it all felt jumbled. I remembered the body-heaving nausea after finding Vic's body. Then the overpowering smell of chemicals at Nails by Nellie. The self-inflicted stress scratching. And now this bombshell!

I had totally missed the signs, chalking it up to the stress of becoming Vic's murder suspect. Having been pregnant with Nora, you'd think I would have recognized the signs!

I was pregnant. After years of trying for baby number two, it had finally happened…when we weren't trying. When we were trying anything *but* having another baby. We were about to put Nora through college. Sell the house and move. How the heck was I going to break this news to Chris? Mentally he had already checked out.

My mother once told me that a baby was always good news, but I wasn't sure Chris would see it that way. Well, there was no turning back now—the bun was in the oven, and that was that. The thing was, though, I had no idea how I felt about the whole thing myself.

Chris and I had given up on the idea of a second baby years ago when we had tried to get pregnant after Nora was born, and kept trying while she toddled around, and continued trying even as she went through middle school. Eventually our horses became our babies since another human one wasn't in the cards.

Apparently God had decided to shuffle the deck.

"Make sure you start taking prenatal vitamins," the nurse added on her way to the door. "And take it easy, okay? It's not just about the baby, but about mama too!"

"I will." Though I didn't know how I would possibly accomplish that when my friend's mother had been arrested for murder and it rested on Tara's Angels to help prove her innocence…if she was, in fact, innocent.

The nurse had just opened the door when a thought occurred to me.

"Wait!" I called out. "You didn't tell my husband about the baby, did you?"

"No, ma'am. Privacy laws don't let us unless you consent first."

Speak of the devil…a light rap on the door was followed by Chris rushing past the departing nurse, straight to my bedside.

"Honey, are you okay?" After setting a bag down at the foot of my bed, Chris barely finished his sentence between kissing my forehead and scanning my body for injuries. "I came as soon as Ginger called. What happened?"

He nudged himself between me and the edge of the bed, holding my hands, face flushed with worry. I didn't know where to begin. I knew he didn't want another baby. He had made it abundantly clear when he finally emptied all of Nora's baby things from the attic and hauled them off to Goodwill. Year upon year of hoping for a son had left him weary and jaded.

And with his job in limbo, our medical coverage was too. Which I now realized would make this brief hospital visit a huge financial burden rather than a minor inconvenience.

There was no way I could tell him I was pregnant. Not when everything was already spinning in chaos. Then I remembered an ad I'd been seeing on TV a lot lately and the perfect explanation came to mind.

"I'm okay," I assured him as he squeezed my hand tighter. "I've got uterine fibroids. Don't have a stroke, they're not cancerous and they're completely treatable. The nurse said they're often caused by stress."

"This is exactly why I'm glad we're leaving. This town is nothing but pain and stress. I'm more convinced than ever that leaving will do us both a world of good."

And then there was that. He wanted to sell our Bloodson Bay home, motor our way to a new life. My pregnancy would crush the cross-country dream he had finally grabbed hold of that gave him any kind of hope.

"Let's get you home, honey. I brought you clothes. Tonight I'll start planning how to get us the heck out of here."

While Chris headed to the nurse's station to figure out the paperwork, I slipped out of my hospital gown with a cold rush of air smacking my butt. By the time I was dressed in the fresh clothes Chris had brought me, Ginger popped her head in.

"How's my girl?" she asked.

I gave her a thumbs-up. "I'm feeling better."

"Bless your heart, you're one tough chick!"

A moment later Sloane slunk through the doorway, as if she didn't belong here. But she was why I was alive instead of bleeding out on her mom's bathroom floor. I eagerly waved her in.

"Thank you for helping me," I signed.

"Of course! Never do that again, though. You gave us a scare."

"Sorry," I signed sheepishly. "All good now, though."

Of course, Ginger and Sloane pressed me for details on my condition. I wasn't ready to share the "good news" with anyone, so I gave them the same bogus uterine fibroid routine I'd given Chris. They bought it without question. When did I become such a quick-witted and convincing liar?

Somewhere in the room I heard my cell phone beep with a text. I searched for my purse, which after a moment I located on the pale blue hospital-grade synthetic chair exactly like the one Chris had slept in after I gave birth to Nora. I picked up my purse and found my phone.

The missing memory bolted back. Two texts appeared on the screen. On top was the one I had gotten from an unknown number while at Sloane's mom's house:

I know what you did to her, and you're not going to get away with it.

Below that another text. Dread tied my stomach in knots. After reading the message, it looked like I wasn't going home to rest after all. I wasn't sure what exactly it was about, but I didn't want to drag Chris into it until I found out.

I turned to Ginger. "Mind if I ride home with you? I need to make a quick detour that I don't want Chris to know about."

"What don't you want me to know?" Chris said as he glided

through the door.

I sputtered the first place that came to mind that Chris absolutely detested going to with me—usually because I spent too long there and too much money:

"Target. I need to go to Target to pick up some things that the doctor recommended."

Chris slipped his arm under mine, guiding me down the hallway to the lobby. "Are you sure you don't want me to go so you can rest? I'll endure a trip to Target for you."

"No, babe, I really don't mind going. The list is pretty long."

Before Ginger could ask what I was talking about, I shot her a conspiratorial look. "Ginger doesn't mind, right?"

"You know I'm always up for Target!" she agreed, shaking her head subtly behind Chris's back.

"And then you'll come straight home?" Chris persisted.

"For sure."

"Text me when you're on your way home and I'll get a bath started for you. Then how about a back massage tonight to help relax you?"

I knew I was the luckiest woman in the world when it came to love. "You know I can't resist that offer," I said, which was the only truth I'd told in the past thirty minutes.

After Chris left and Ginger, Sloane, and I were sitting in Ginger's car, Ginger turned to me with a reproving glower. "So where are we *really* going, and why did you lie to your husband?"

Chapter 30

The Bloodson Bay Police Department had all the charm of a roach motel. Harsh fluorescent lighting bleached the large squad room packed with cubicles separated by threadbare newborn-baby-poop-green carpeted aisles.

Oh no. I already had baby on the brain. There was no way I could keep this secret to myself.

I wound past a handful of empty desks, waving a quick hello to Officer Speers, before I reached the corner desk with the little gold name plate that read *Detective Martina Carillo-Hughes*. I had told Ginger and Sloane to wait for me in the car, because what I needed to do wouldn't take long…I hoped. So I stood. Standing was my signal to Marti I didn't plan to stay long.

I held out my phone screen, showing her the text she had sent me while I was at the hospital:

We need to talk. Come down to the station as soon as you can.

Marti looked up at me. "Sit. You're making me nervous just standing there."

So I sat. I guess I was staying.

"You beckoned?" I jumped right in.

"Yes, I *beckoned*. We've had a new development in the

Victor Valance murder case that I felt you needed to know about."

"Let me guess. You figured out Alika Apara couldn't possibly be Vic's killer?"

Her eyebrow rose in a little arc. "What makes you say that?"

"You have to ask? Alika has never been to my house. I've never even met the woman until today. So it makes no sense for her to bury a body on *my* property. And you said you found my Somulose kit in Vic's Hummer. Well, Alika has no idea what horse euthanasia is, let alone how to use it. So like I said, it wasn't her. I'm assuming the only reason her name got dragged into it was through an anonymous tip. Am I right?"

Marti chuckled.

That's what I thought.

"Well, you're partially right. We know Alika wasn't on your property."

"Tell me something I don't know."

"Did you know that the body buried on your land wasn't Victor Valance? Last night Leonard Valance found the real Victor dead in his home."

Where was my shocked expression when I needed it? Because Marti picked up on my lack of surprise instantly and pounced.

"You already knew your body wasn't Victor, didn't you?"

It wasn't a question, because now we both knew what I had been hiding.

"I might have known. I wasn't 100 percent sure, but I guessed as much."

"How?" Marti asked. "What gave it away?"

"Someone I know bit a huge chunk out of his hand two days

before we found his body—well, whoever's body it is. With all the dirt I couldn't tell that the hand was messed up until you showed me the autopsy photos. I assumed the hand wouldn't have healed that quickly, which made me think it wasn't Vic."

"Who is this *someone*? And why didn't you tell me before now?"

Because telling you would have incriminated Peace, I couldn't say. But I told Detective Hughes as much as I safely could. Like I said, I still didn't trust anyone in the BBPD as far as I could swing a bull by the tail, as Ginger would say.

"I can't tell you who. They swore me to secrecy."

"This isn't The Babysitter's Club, Tara. There are no secrets between friends when dealing with a murder investigation. You can't keep details about a potential suspect from me. That's obstruction of justice."

I stiffened in my chair that felt like I was sitting on a rock. I wondered if it was intentional keeping "interviewees" as uncomfortable as possible.

"I know my rights, Marti, and I don't have to provide that information. I've got my lawyer on speed-dial, if you want to start having to go through her to speak to me. I'm working with you in every way, but I don't have to tell you a friend's personal business."

Detective Hughes pursed her lips. I knew that look. She was manipulating her way around my blockade. "Even if it could help Alika Apara's case?"

"I thought you ruled her out."

"We still have a witness who saw Alika leaving Victor's house yesterday, around his time of death."

"What witness?"

"You know I can't tell you that, Tara."

"So some random anonymous witness says they saw Alika leaving the crime scene, and that's all the evidence you have against her? What about the body on my property, which was clearly designed to look like Vic? The killer even put Vic's ring on his finger! Alika couldn't have done that!"

"We're still looking into the connection. But we found additional evidence at Victor's house that supports Alika's motive. It's enough to make an arrest, Tara."

I glanced across her desk, cluttered with papers and folders and half-eaten food and evidence bags. One clear bag had a crumpled tissue in it with the words *Recovered from V. Valance residence* neatly printed on the label.

Friggin' A! Judge Valance must have found Ginger's used tissue in the secret storage room and planted it for the police to find. I had to get ahead of it. I couldn't let Ginger get dragged into this too.

Sitting next to the snot rag was another plastic baggie containing a cassette tape—the very same brand we found in Victor's basement. And in the bunker. The word *Exposé* was scribbled on the label in the same handwriting as all the other tapes.

So there were more. Probably also planted by Judge Valance. It had to be one of the tapes from Alika's captivity, which provided the motive Detective Hughes referred to.

I had really hoped we had found them all. How many confession tapes did one kid need to make? Though considering how modern teens were obsessed with selfies and vlogs and TikTok, teenage Vic circa 1995 would have fit right in with Generation Alpha. Except for the torturing an innocent woman part.

"We also discovered something interesting about the cause of death for the first victim," Marti said, referring to the body found on my property. "Based on the petechial hemorrhage found at the base of his neck, he was killed by suffocation, which I suspect is why the killer blew his head off. To hide that little fact."

"Why are you telling me this?" I asked.

"Because you're off the hook, as far as I'm concerned." Marti slapped the desk lightly, signaling we were done here.

I didn't know how stupid it was to ask, but I had to know. "May I ask *why* that takes me off the hook?"

"Because I don't think you're capable of suffocating a grown man…and I have a hunch this body is linked to Victor's death. And while I don't like how you attract trouble, Tara Christie, I don't think you're a serial killer."

"Well that's a relief."

"Don't get too excited, Tara. Because while I don't think you killed Victor, he died from noncardiogenic pulmonary edema."

I gazed blankly at her. I had no idea what that meant or why I shouldn't get excited about it.

"It means he stopped breathing…and the condition is usually associated with a barbiturate overdose. Which we'll determine once the toxicology report comes back. I'm not letting Judge Valance intercede this time around."

Crap on a stick. I knew what barbiturate overdose meant—the Somulose kit. It had come back to bite me after all.

My innocence was at least proven…sort of. We could check that box off the to-do list. Now for the bajillion more I needed to take care of…

I remembered I had wanted to ask about the disturbing Duke sweatshirt that had been left on my porch.

"Do you know which officer was camped out in front of my house two nights after we found Vic's body?"

Marti shifted forward. "How do you know it was an officer?"

"Are you kidding? Chris spotted the unmarked car right off. Whoever the cop was, he was pretty dumb and careless. Should have been more discreet."

Marti did a slow burn that had me squirming in my seat. "Actually, Mrs. Christie, *I* was in that unmarked car. I saw no reason to be discreet. I've learned that when it comes to dealing with your, shall we say, unorthodox family, discretion is seldom a useful tactic."

Open mouth, insert foot. "I'm sorry, Mar—Detective Hughes, I didn't mean any disrespect."

She waved her hand. "Forget it. Why do you want to know?"

"Well, I was just wondering—did you happen to see anyone come up to my house and drop something off? Chris found a Duke sweatshirt with what looked like bloodstains on it sitting on our porch." Marti's expression brightened with interest. "No, it wasn't blood—a food stain of some sort. Otherwise I would have brought it in. I just hoped maybe you had seen who dropped it off. It felt like a threat to Nora, because it was identical to her Duke sweatshirt, but it could have been a prank by an old classmate."

Marti shook her head. "No, I didn't see anyone. It might have been dropped off after I left. Did Nora recently break up with a boyfriend, perhaps?"

"Actually…yes! That must be it! I hadn't thought of him doing something like that. Keanu is usually a really nice kid, but I guess you don't know how someone will react when they get their heart broken."

What a relief! The most logical explanation was that Keanu had childishly lashed out at Nora when she'd rejected him. At least I could rest easy that no one was targeting my daughter.

Feeling quite a bit lighter, I stood up to leave, when I realized I hadn't asked the biggest question of all:

"So if Victor wasn't buried in my yard, who was?" I met Detective Hughes's stare. She looked as confused as I felt.

"And here I was hoping you could answer that…"

Tape 7
Jagged Little Pill

1995

[Tape clicks on]

[Young male] There's a lot of blood. And her bone is sticking through her skin real bad. I think I see muscle. I'm worried she's going to bleed to death.

My dad left without us, telling me to head home once I finished bandaging her arm, but it's dark out, and I'm not exactly sure how to get home from here. In case she doesn't make it, this tape is evidence that my father, Ewan Valance, forced me to do this against my will and I had no way to save her.

[Woman] Victor, stop talking to that damn thing and help me! I will talk you through bandaging my arm and getting us home.

[Young male] It looks really bad.

[Woman] Yes, and it hurts really bad too. But at least the shackle is off. Listen carefully. First I need you to wrap this gauze around my wrist to stop the bleeding. You know how to get to town, yes?

[Young male] Yeah, it's not that far.

[Woman] Good. Once we stop the bleeding we will drive to town where we can ask someone for directions to the highway. If you get to the highway, can you find your way home from there?

[Young male] I think so.

[Woman] Okay, good. Grab that water bottle and help me clean the wound out. I am shaking too bad to do it myself.

[Water splashing on floor]

[Woman sucks in strained breath] Now use that bandage and wrap it really tight, then tie it as tightly as you can.

[Young male grunting]

[Young male] Like that?

[Woman] Yes, good. Do you have any pain medicine?

[Young male rifling through pill bottles]

[Woman] What is that in the bottle you're holding?

[Young male] No, you can't take these. These are roofies.

[Woman] Roofies? What is that?

[Young male] They'll knock you out, or at least make you more...compliant. Those are what I gave you when you kept screaming for help that first night. I dissolved one in your water.

[Woman] As if holding me against my will was not enough, you had to drug me?

[Young male] You wouldn't shut up and kept crying. I needed sleep!

[Woman] I cannot believe your family. Have you no morals?

[Young male] Any morals we had were beat out of us as kids, lady. So I have to know...are you gonna go to the police about this?

[Woman] Your father knew where my daughter is, Victor, which *no one but me* knew. I will not risk our lives trying to take down an unbeatable giant. I am afraid I am no David. Nor do I want to live on the run. Besides, as long as Ewan thinks my daughter is his, he will not harm us.

[Young male] But what if he finds out the truth?

[Woman] He must not. You are the only other person who knows the truth, and you must never tell him. I will do whatever it takes to bury this secret in order to protect my daughter.

[Tape clicks off]

Chapter 31

The bath and back massage were exactly what I needed, but they weren't enough to soak or rub the insomnia out of me. Too many thoughts clunked around in my brain, so here I was, just shy of five o'clock in the morning, hearing Chris saw logs in our bedroom while downstairs I played the last tape from the collection again and again, thinking the same thing over and over:

Maybe Alika Apara killed Victor Valance after all. She had threatened as much:

> *You are the only other person who knows the truth, and you must never tell him. I will do whatever it takes to bury this secret in order to protect my daughter.*

Was killing Vic "*whatever it took*" to keep him silent about Sloane's true paternity? Maybe Vic blackmailed Alika for money. Sloane was rich as hell, so he might have seen this opportunity as the perfect golden ticket. Round and round I went with suppositions...but there was only one truth. And it was out of my reach.

If Alika's pointed threat was on this tape, I wondered if

something even worse was on the *Exposé* tape that sat on Detective Hughes's desk. Abduction. Torture. Vengeance. Murder…Could anything on that tape be worse than what I had already heard?

Mixed with all these thoughts was the growing reminder in my belly that a baby was coming. At the most inopportune time. While Chris online shopped for used RVs that we could tour the country in.

It was no wonder I couldn't sleep.

These thoughts unnerved me, and when I felt unnerved, only one thing calmed me: my horses.

Although dawn was still another couple hours away, Peace would already be up letting the horses out to pasture. There was something at her house I needed to find anyway, something that might help me figure everything out. I'd make some excuse to go into the house while she was occupied and nab it from the attic. After grabbing two to-go cups of coffee, I headed out.

The sign for the Rockin' C Ranch swung back and forth under a strong breeze as I drove past it up the driveway. The ranch was ocean-spray air and dew-soaked grass, horses grazing lazily over sandy loam fields, a salt-chewed house in need of paint.

The barn lights were off, and the house was dark except for the lamp Peace always kept burning for security reasons in the foyer. Peace's personal car, a secondhand Toyota Prius—the hybrid was just one example of her ongoing "save the planet" crusade—was gone, which was odd this early in the day. Looked like homebody Peace might have finally gotten a social life. If so, all I could say was hallelujah and congratulations.

The vintage farm truck, a 1965 Ford F100, was in the

rickety garage. It had its share of dents and dings, but Peace kept it in tip-top running condition, and the original Caribbean Turquoise paint job still looked showroom fresh. It was the same truck Chris and I had tooled around in even before he got his driver's license. He liked to show off by bumping along washboard dirt roads and cow paths all over the farm at breakneck speed. Our heads would bounce off the roof of the cab and we'd laugh like idiots. Chris thought he was hell on wheels. I thought so too. Guess I was a lot easier to impress back then.

It was still dark outside when I let myself inside with my spare key, which I generally only used in emergencies. I decided the best plan was to slip in and out before Peace returned home. As I closed the front door, Puffin proved how terrible a guard dog she was as there was no sign of her. I figured she was asleep in Peace's bedroom and out of earshot.

I was pretty sure Peace was out, but I needed to be absolutely certain. In the foyer I called: "Hello? Peace? Hey, sleepyhead! I brought coffee!" No answer. That was a good sign. Emboldened, I crept catlike up the stairs in the dark. Luckily I knew every creaky board in the place, having spent a good portion of my girlhood in this house, hanging out with my best friend Peace and flirting with my other best friend Chris, until we fell in love.

When I reached the landing, I saw that Peace's bedroom door was ajar. I peeked inside; her bed hadn't been slept in. *Oooo! Maybe somebody got lucky tonight!*

I wasted no time climbing the second flight of stairs to the attic. I yanked on the string, and the lone lightbulb cast a dull glow over cobwebs and dust and clutter. I rummaged through a few boxes until I found what I came for. It would speak the words I didn't know how to say.

I shoved it in my purse and headed down to the living room, past the cracked hallway window. It had never been repaired after my brother, Jonah, hit it with a rock in a misguided declaration of love he'd copied from a cheesy 1990s flick, mistaking the hallway for Peace's bedroom. A lot of broken hearts went unhealed back then, and a lot of broken things went unfixed after Peace's parents died.

My little escapade had made me thirsty, so I slipped into the kitchen and flicked on the overhead light. There was nothing in the refrigerator but bottled beet juice (yuck!) and some funky health drinks, so I opted for a bottle of sparkling water.

As I sipped, I glanced around Peace's kitchen. For such an environmentally-conscious chick, Peace was a real slob. The floor looked like it hadn't been mopped in months, there were crumbs all over the counters, and the sink groaned under a week's worth of dirty dishes. I couldn't imagine how she could stand to live in such a biohazard, but being what Ginger might call a spinster, I guess maybe she had just stopped giving a damn what people thought. The breakfast table was a mess—granola bar boxes, a vegan cookbook, a stack of *Mother Jones* magazines …and something very, very odd.

The most unexpected thing to find here, in health-nut Peace's house.

A smokeless tobacco tin. The brand that Vic chewed. I knew this because I'd watched him chewing and spitting disgustingly for the last dozen or so years as we fought over horses at the kill pens. But Peace didn't touch the stuff—well, duh!—so why was a tin of it here?

A tiny piece of a memory peeked out at me. I knew I had seen this tin before. Recently. But where? *Right—in the bunker.* I had caught Peace pocketing a shiny round something or other—and Ginger noticed it too. This had to be what she had grabbed; it would easily fit in her pocket. There was only one possible explanation for why Peace would have grabbed it, though it felt like a stretch. Did the tin have something to do with what Vic had done to her? Perhaps her DNA was on it? Or it could have been evidence of some sort…

Random facts swirled around in my head. Peace's Victor sighting, which meant she knew he was alive. My Somulose kit in Vic's Hummer, with the missing syringe. The warm fast food in the bunker…and this tobacco tin. Vic had to have been alive, hiding out in the bunker, and I think Peace knew.

The question was, where was the syringe that killed him? I didn't want to entertain the possibility that Peace was behind Vic's death, but she would be the only other person who would know what it was and how to use it.

The heaping garbage can caught my eye; did I have time to spill the contents all over the floor, search them, and put them back before Peace got home? Probably not.

Fortunately, I didn't have to.

A full garbage bag sat next to the can, waiting to be taken out. Another chore Peace hadn't gotten around to. Fruit flies buzzed around the bag and as I got closer, I wrinkled my nose at the stink. "Hello, what's this?" I said aloud. *I spy with my little eye…*a syringe, plainly visible at the bottom of the clear bag.

I hastily untied the bag, shoved my arm down through the conglomeration of household nastiness, and plucked out the syringe. I was angry at Peace for hiding this. Angry with myself for finding it. Printed across the prescription label was my name and address, then below that the word *Somulose*.

After retying the bag I quickly washed my hands and turned off the kitchen light, then placed the syringe and tobacco tin in my purse. The best course of action was to confront Peace about this later in the day, after I figured out what the heck I was going to say to her.

I had just headed into the living room when the front door flew open and a white blur came stampeding straight for me.

Chapter 32

"Down, Puffin! It's only Tara." Peace stood in a halo of light, her finger still on the light switch.

The dog—all eighty-five pounds of her—was standing on my chest and stomach. I could barely breathe. Finally Puffin recognized me and gave me a great big tongue kiss across my face before scampering over to her master.

"Now I know what it feels like to be tackled by the Hound of the Baskervilles," I deadpanned, clambering to my feet.

"Sorry about that. She was out with me," Peace said. "When I was pulling in I saw a light in the kitchen and sent her into the house first—I'm not about to surprise a burglar without my bodyguard." She bent down to ruffle the dog's fluffy neck affectionately. "Go on outside, Puff. I'll feed you in a little while. Scoot!" The dog trotted through the open front door.

"Didn't you see my car outside?" I said innocently.

"Yeah, I saw it. I figured you were in the barn. You weren't." Peace folded her arms across her bony chest. "I didn't expect to find you poking around my house while I was out. Mind telling me what the hell you're doing here?"

She sounded incredibly pissed to find me here, even though it was pretty routine for me to show up unannounced most mornings. But I admit, it wasn't usual for me to practically—okay, literally—break into her house. With Grinch-like genius,

I thought up a lie and I thought up quick.

"Uh, we run a farm together, remember?" I said. "I saw you weren't home when I got here, so I thought I'd get the coffee started so we could have our pow-wow about business stuff over breakfast—like we do every day."

I thought that would satisfy her. It didn't. "Oh, really? I don't smell any coffee brewing."

Oops.

"Uh…I couldn't find the coffee beans," I lied (again), then quickly switched gears. "Oh, but I did bring you a to-go cup that's in my car. So, you're just now getting home, huh?"

"Yeah, I was out."

Her terse reply wasn't unexpected. Peace had always been discreet about her love life, especially back when my brother Jonah had been part of it. But this wasn't just a matter of her privacy being invaded. This was something else altogether.

"Well, I can't stand here yakking all day," she said, and turned toward the kitchen.

"Wait!" It was time to give up the charade. I reached into my purse and took out the syringe and tin and held them out in my leveled palm.

She exhaled a long, raggedy sigh, resigned to whatever was about to come. She knew that I knew. All over her I saw guilt.

"Peace," I blurted out, "what did you do?"

Instead of spilling her guts, she threw my accusation right back at me.

"No, the better question is what did *you* do, Tara?" She slipped into the dining room, then returned with a manilla envelope. She shoved it at me. "This showed up in my mailbox two days ago. Right after we got home from the bunker."

I pocketed the syringe and the tin and grabbed the envelope, flipping it over. On the front was written: *I thought you might want to know what your family is doing behind your back.*

I opened the envelope and slid out the papers. It was a real estate document. A cold shiver ran down my spine as I read the title on the first page:

BUYER AGENCY AGREEMENT

At the bottom was Chris's signature with a date scribbled beside it. It was signed the day after we found the sweatshirt on the porch. Peace's betrayal and my puzzlement eventually folded together into a long silence.

"This whole ranch sale is an overreaction, Peace..." I started.

"An overreaction to what?"

"Chris had found a sweatshirt with what looked like bloodstains on it—a sweatshirt just like Nora's. It felt very threatening, and ever since then Chris has been talking about moving. But it's a lot more complicated than just that."

I couldn't explain what I didn't know. Why did Chris hire this person without talking to me and Peace first? How had this even gotten out—especially without my knowledge?

"What's so complicated about it?" Peace's neck splotched pink with anger. "You planned to sell the ranch out from under me."

Where to begin? It went as far back as Victor Valance thwarting my every effort to rescue and rehabilitate neglected and abused horses for resale to loving homes. If we couldn't save horses, we couldn't sell them. It was simple math, and a hard truth.

"The ranch is going under, Peace. We're losing more money every month. So Chris and I were talking...and...and Chris just mentioned he was going to talk to an agent about selling. I didn't think he'd actually get a contract started. Honestly, I'm as surprised by this as you are."

I set the paperwork on the coffee table next to Peace's vintage tape recorder that I recognized from our youth. In the deck was one of the blank tapes she had swiped from Victor's bunker.

"No one knows about this yet?" Peace verified.

I shook my head. "No one knows. Not Ginger, not Nora. Not even me. I don't know how someone else found out."

"So then you don't know who left this for me."

"I'm guessing it's the same person who has spent a lifetime trying to destroy our business, buy our land, and run us out of town. The only person who seems to know everything about everyone's business."

We both spoke the name together: "Judge Valance."

I had been so sidetracked by the real estate contract that I had almost forgotten about the syringe in my pocket, which I now held out to Peace.

"I need you to explain this, Peace. And hopefully in a way that proves you didn't kill Vic."

"I'm sorry, Tara, but no matter how I say it, it looks bad."

"Can you at least try?" I urged.

Peace had just walked over to the front door to close it when I heard bootsteps tromping up the walkway, then out of the gloom a figure coalesced in the doorway.

My jaw dropped to my knees.

Chapter 33

Leonard Valance put his arm around Peace's waist and gave her a peck on the lips. Then he seemed to notice me for the first time. "Oh, hi, Tara. Didn't expect to find you here."

I had no words. As Valances went, Leo was just about the cream of the crop—which wasn't saying much. I hadn't forgotten he had helped Tara's Angels when we'd broken into his brother's secret lair. And back in the day, girls flocked to him for his Luke Perry-ish dreaminess.

He was still boyishly handsome, but he was a *Valance*, for goodness' sake! They were my family's sworn enemy. Seeing him standing there, canoodling with my friend, my confidante, my business partner, my sister-in-law, and knowing his vile brother had tried to rape her—well, it was like finding out your mother's prom date had been Adolf Hitler.

Peace guided Leo into the house and closed the door behind her. We stood in a tight little circle in the living room. It felt like the scene in *The Good, the Bad, and the Ugly* when the three saddle tramps found themselves in a stand-off.

Leo fished a cell phone out of his pocket and handed it to Peace. "I found this in the back seat of my car. You must have dropped it when we were at the drive-in. Knew you'd be wanting it."

My brain was turning cartwheels. "The back seat of your

car?" I repeated robotically, not sure I'd heard him correctly. And *very* sure I didn't want to know what they were doing in it. But I had a pretty good idea anyway.

"Yeah," Leo said. "More room to spread out back there, ya know." He grinned lasciviously at Peace.

"Good thing we didn't take my Prius," she added. "No room at all."

They broke into giggles, pawing all over each other like teenagers. Finally Peace noticed my expression of mingled discomfort, disbelief, and disgust.

"Okay, so the cat's out of the bag," she said. "Yes, we're dating, as if it's any of your business. We met in town, took in a late movie at the new drive-in they restored, and then stopped by Debbie's Diner for a snack. It's not the end of the world, Tara."

"It's not? I think maybe it is. How can you stand to be with him after what his brother tried to do to you?"

"Leo knows everything, Tara." Peace grabbed Leo's hand and held it.

"Everything as in…?"

"He knows about what Victor did to me."

"You mean spiking your drink and attacking you?" I wanted to say it for clarity, in case Peace had forgotten what kind of people the Valances were.

"Yes. Leo knows."

"Why would you tell him? If his father finds out, what if he tries to turn this around as a motive for *you* murdering Vic, Peace."

"I would never tell my father, Tara," Leo interjected. "I helped you sneak into my brother's house, didn't I?"

It was one thing for me to request a one-time favor from Leo, but a whole other thing for Peace to make him a fixture in our lives.

"And I appreciated your help, Leo, but the two of you together...you know it could never work. Our families are practically enemies."

Leo took a step toward me; Peace tugged him back. "It's awfully hypocritical of you to call my family the enemy, Tara. Did you tell Peace how you're trying to sell the ranch out from under her?"

Mouth agape, Peace backed away from him. "How did you know about that?"

"What do you mean?" Leo floundered.

"I mean Tara didn't even know about the real estate contract, so how did you know?"

Leo sighed. "Okay, guess I'm busted. My dad has had feelers out in case you ever listed your farm, and the moment he found out about it getting signed with an agent, he told me. I don't understand—are you mad at me?"

"Were you the one who put this in my mailbox?" Peace reached for the manilla envelope off the coffee table and held it out to him. He didn't accept it, only acknowledged it with a glance.

"I thought you should know," he said, his voice as thick as cream. "But I didn't want to put myself in the middle of it, so I figured this was the best way to tell you. They shouldn't get away with stealing your dream, Peace."

The way the words wound together felt familiar. I'd heard that exact phrasing recently. Or had I read it? A text from an unknown sender. The grip it had on me, shocking my body until it surrendered and fell on the bathroom floor in a puddle of blood. It came back in a vivid green bubble:

I know what you did to her, and you're not going to get away with it.

"Was that you who texted me that threat?" I yelled.

"It wasn't a threat, Tara. It was a simple fact!" Leo yelled back. "I'm not letting you or Chris, or whoever you want to blame it on, take away what rightfully belongs to Peace!"

"If it wasn't a threat, then why did you text it from an unknown number? Because you didn't want me to tell Peace?"

"I have more than one cell phone, Tara. One for personal use, and one for business. I wasn't trying to hide anything," Leo spat back.

"Enough!" Peace threw her hands up between us. "Tara didn't know about the real estate contract, Leo. And Tara, you're going to have to get used to me and Leo being together. If you can't figure out a way to trust one another, then we're going to have a problem."

I popped a hand on my hip, daring her. "If you want me to trust Leo, prove to me why I should."

"Okay, you want proof?" Peace said, cocking her head. "First of all, you went to Leo when you needed help getting rid of Vic's recording of your threat against him, right? And Leo helped you out, didn't he?"

"That's still to be determined," I huffed. "No one ever found that recording or destroyed it, as far as I know. So who knows if it'll turn up to bury me."

"Well, then you're going to have to trust *me*, Tara. Because we really like each other and I'm not going to base my love life on your approval."

"What about Jonah?" I asked. "My brother is crazy about you and this will destroy him, especially after he saved you from Vic that night."

"About that," Peace faltered. "It wasn't Jonah who came to my rescue that night. It was Leo who saved me."

"What? Are you for real? How?"

"I was out for drinks that night with Leo, not Jonah. Then Vic showed up and started picking a fight with Leo about dating me. At some point during the night Vic must have spiked my drink when Leo had taken a call outside while I was still at the bar with Vic." Peace stopped here, and I knew why. I had heard most of this already—an edited version, at least—and she had cried then as she cried now.

Between shaky breaths and wiping tears, Peace continued. "Suddenly I was feeling woozy, like I was blacking out, and I woke up in the back of Vic's Hummer with him on top of me. I started screaming and kicking, biting the shit out of his hand. That must have pissed him off even more, because Vic…saw red. That's the only way I can describe the way he looked, his face all contorted and eyes leering at me like he was about to kill me."

Peace broke down into full-blown sobs, and I wanted to reach for my sister-in-law and hold her and comfort her and shield her from these terrible men.

"Just when I thought I was about to die, Leo showed up, trying to pull him off me." She had wrapped herself up in Leo's arms now, and for a moment I was happy for her. That moment was short-lived, though.

"And that's when I jabbed him with the Somulose syringe," Leo concluded.

"I'm sorry—what?"

Had Leo just confessed to killing his brother? The confession that would have freed Alika. Damn, why hadn't I thought to record this whole conversation on my phone!

"You killed your brother?"

"No!" Leo yelled. "It was just a tiny dose—barely enough to knock him out."

Whoosh—there went his confession.

"I couldn't overpower him. He was drunk and high out of his mind, and when Peace bit him, he snapped. So I grabbed the first thing I saw on the front seat of the car, which was the syringe, and jabbed him with it. Then I drove him back to his house and made sure he woke up okay. I swear he was alive and cussing me out when I left him there."

Leo sounded earnest, and I believed him.

"The thing that I couldn't understand, though," Leo continued, "was how *your* Somulose kit ended up in my brother's car."

Leo waited, and I knew he had me. A line had been drawn between truth and lie, and if I wanted the truth I needed to step up to the edge. None of us were leaving this room until I told them. The truth and nothing but the truth, so help me, God.

"I gave the kit to Vic. We had made a…deal. I was supposed to help him euthanize one of your racehorses so he could file an insurance claim on it. It sounded like he was going to be on the run and he needed money. In exchange for helping him, he'd leave the ranch alone. We never ended up doing it, though. After he attacked Peace, our whole plan kind of…fell through the cracks."

I had been lying to everyone, hiding this from the police. Peace had been lying to me about that night. We all had been lying. About everything. I couldn't trust anything out of her mouth, just like she couldn't trust anything out of mine.

"Wow, insurance fraud," Leo said. "That's…pretty low. Even by my standards."

"Are you going to turn me in to the police?"

No one answered as daylight peered in through the yellowed venetian blinds behind Leo.

"I won't say anything as long as you don't turn me in for what I'm about to tell you…"

Chapter 34

"Let me say something first," Peace said to Leo, tugging him to the sofa to sit. The promise of sunrise, a faint pink crawling across the walls, almost fooled me into believing this was a normal morning. "Before we tell her everything, I think she needs to know how serious we are about each other."

Serious enough to keep each other's secrets? First Ginger and Rick, now Peace and Leo. At this rate I wouldn't be surprised if my mom suddenly said to me, "Tara, I want you to meet my new beau: Lucifer."

I hesitated to follow them and get comfortable, but I wasn't sure how much longer my legs would hold me up. Between low blood sugar, sheer exhaustion, and a pea-sized baby, I couldn't risk another tumble. I sank into the sofa as Peace looked at *me* while holding *him*.

I politely held back my revulsion.

"Leo and I have wanted to tell you and Chris about us for a while now, but there was never a good time."

"Ha! There is never a good time to tell Chris you're dating a man whose family made our lives a living hell. And whose brother is so hated that his list of murder suspects keeps growing by the hour."

"It's not like we planned it," Leo came to Peace's defense, and I shot him a scowl. "It just happened."

"Regardless of your newfound *love*"—I nearly spit the word out—"you said that you jabbed Vic with the Somulose but he was still alive when you left him. So…I don't understand the timeline. Was Victor alive this entire time?"

"Okay, that story isn't quite as simple," Peace said, sighing. Nothing about this story was simple. "Well, I don't know about y'all," she added, "but I could use a cup of coffee. I'm assuming the usual overabundance of cream and sugar for you, Tara?"

Closing my eyes, I imagined the roasted, nutty, caffeinated goodness rolling over my palate. I wasn't sure I had ever needed it as much as now. Then I remembered I was pregnant. I didn't know how many of the prenatal rules from when I had Nora still applied, but I definitely recalled not being allowed caffeinated coffee. No coffee for nine months was crueler than morning sickness.

"Got decaf?" I asked.

"Since when have I ever had decaf? And since when do you drink decaf?"

"Um, I'm trying to cut back on caffeine. I'll pass. I'm not feeling like it today."

Peace stumbled back dramatically, horror-struck. "No coffee? You must be in really bad shape to turn down your morning caffeine hit."

"Well, I *did* just find out you're dating…this guy. I kinda lost my appetite." I aimed a thumb at Leo, the smile I forced like a razor cutting into my face.

"Okay, I'll make some for Leo and me then. You just sit here with 'this guy' while he explains everything. Back in a jiff."

Peace left Leo and me alone, and I decided right then and

there I wouldn't let him off easy. I wanted answers, and I would drill until I hit gold. I was one tap of my phone away from calling the police.

"So, Leo, let's hear it. The truth this time." From across the table I pushed the syringe and tin toward him. "Are you manipulating Peace to help you cover up Vic's murder?"

"First of all, that's not my tin. I haven't chewed tobacco in years. And I already told you I didn't kill my brother. What you're implying doesn't make sense."

"Then make it make sense for me. According to the police, you're the one who found Vic dead in his home. And they told me he died from a barbiturate overdose." I picked up the Somulose syringe, only now realizing my fingerprints were all over it. "If Vic was alive when you left him, then why bother hiding this in the garbage? And is this all connected to the body I found on my property?"

Leo sighed. "I guess I might as well come clean. It all started a few weeks ago when Victor had gotten himself in real bad debt with some people who gave him a choice: pay up or die. Of course Vic goes running to my dad for help, but this was bigger than my dad's ability to protect him. These weren't Podunk thugs. These were big-city criminals. That's when my dad came up with an idea.

"He sent Vic into hiding up at the bunker while we figured things out. He was supposed to stay put while my dad took care of the details. A passport, faking his death, setting up a place to live, things like that. We never expected Vic to return to Bloodson Bay and make things worse..."

"Worse how?"

"The night he came back was the night he attacked Peace.

Which like I said, I had given him a quick jab of Somulose to knock him out before I took him home. That night I had tossed the syringe in his bathroom garbage can at his place when I dropped him off. It wasn't a murder weapon at that point, so no big deal, right? But he was alive when I left. He even cussed me out the door after he woke up. I swear I had barely used any of the syringe—certainly not a lethal dose. Plus that was days before I found him…" Leo choked on the sentence, barely able to finish it, "dead in his home."

I tried to keep in mind that Leo and Vic were brothers who loved each other, even if Vic was a sleazeball. Vic the brother who taught Leo how to body surf as kids. Vic the man who held a woman captive in a bunker. Two versions, both equally real. Just different faces of the same person.

"So Vic was just running around this whole time while the police thought he was dead?"

"That means the plan worked. We needed to ensure these guys didn't go after our family, so we faked Vic's death."

I had a bad feeling I knew where this was going.

"And in order to fake his death you needed another body…"

Chapter 35

"The body buried on my farm…it was Marvin Valance, wasn't it?"

The deadbeat brother of Judge Ewan Valance, Marvin only blew into town when he needed money or a place to hide out from his creditors. With numerous drug convictions and eventually a murder charge hanging over Marvin's head, Judge Valance seemed only too happy to hide his embarrassment of a brother behind bars.

"How did you figure it out?"

I told him how I'd heard the judge had released his brother under the Compassionate Release Program. "It didn't make sense to me…until now. Your father let Marvin go so he could kill him in order to save his son's life. That's it, isn't it?"

Leo sighed. "Yeah. It was all orchestrated by my dad. Dad had been wanting Uncle Marv dead for a while now, and he turned out to be the perfect victim. With a little payoff to a doctor to diagnose him with terminal cancer, my dad used his connections with the prison warden to arrange Uncle Marv's release. No one would miss him. He deserved to die anyway. And it gave us a body that was about the right size. All we had to do was put a bullet in his head so that his face wasn't identifiable, then plant Vic's ring on his finger."

My rage was volcanic and ready to erupt.

"Then you buried him on my land! If you cared at all about Peace, which you claim to do, you would have picked any other place to unload him—the friggin' ocean would have been a better spot!—instead of my property. Once again your family throws mine to wolves in order to save yourselves!"

"I had nothing to do with where he was buried, I swear! My dad put Vic in charge of burying the body—but we needed it to be found so that Vic's death made headlines. I had no idea Vic would choose your land. It was probably his way of sticking it to your family, and for that I'm really sorry."

"He more than *stuck it to us.* We were potential suspects! I was interrogated about his murder!"

"Which is probably exactly what Vic and my dad wanted. I would have stopped him had I known. I never wanted you or Ginger to get caught up in this."

Peace returned to the living room with two mugs of coffee and handed one to Leo. She took the seat beside me on the sofa and placed her mug on the table.

"That's actually why I took this from the bunker." Peace picked up the tobacco tin and handed it to me. "Open it, Tara."

I twisted the lid off and looked inside, finding a folded paper towel. Tucked into the folds was a plain gold wedding band.

"What's this?" I asked.

"It's Rick Mallowan's wedding band," Peace stated simply, as if it weren't the most bizarre thing she could say.

"Whoa, waitaminnit—did you just say Rick Mallowan? As in *Ginger's* Rick?" She nodded. "I should have known he was involved."

At this point Leo took up the narrative.

"After my dad hired Harry Alonzo to kill my Uncle Marv,

Rick and Victor were in charge of burying the body."

"Alonzo—as in the police officer?" I reiterated.

"Yeah, that's the one. Anyway, because of all the blood after the, well, you know—" Leo mimed a gun with his fingers, pulling the fake trigger and making a guttural *boom* sound "—Rick had given Victor his wedding ring to hold on to so it didn't get blood and scratches all over it. Plus he was shoveling dirt, so I'm assuming he didn't want to get blisters from it. Anyway, Victor put it in the tin for safekeeping and took it up to the bunker with him and forgot it there."

"Leo had told me about the ring and how Rick was asking where the tin was," Peace cut in. "So when I saw the tobacco tin had blood on it, I had a feeling it was the one with Rick's ring inside. I didn't want Ginger to see it and recognize it, especially after she said they were getting back together. I figured she didn't need to find that and get hurt all over again after Rick told her he mended his criminal ways."

Poor Ginger. Rick had breezed back into her life with promises of white picket fences and happily-ever-afters, but the truth was he was the same old selfish jerk. I didn't want Ginger to know that stab of betrayal again.

"That's actually what caused the fight between Rick and Victor," Leo explained. "When Rick realized he never got his ring back, he confronted my brother about it. I guess Vic wanted to keep it as insurance, maybe to frame Rick in case anything came back to him. Anyway, he wouldn't give the ring back, and Rick ended up stabbed over it."

It sounded like Vic had planned to pin his fake murder on Rick…but it still didn't explain who actually killed Vic.

"Do you think Rick might have tried to retaliate and kill

Vic?" I asked.

Peace glanced at Leo and inhaled a shaky breath.

"No one knows who killed my brother, but my parents are determined to find out," Leo said. "I know they had tried to interfere with the initial investigation when it was Marvin's body, but now they want answers for Victor. And my dad wants heads. All I know for sure is that whatever the cops told you about the Somulose causing it, it wasn't me."

It sounded like Leo was trying to convince himself along with me.

"But you said you threw it in Vic's bathroom garbage. So how did it end up *here*?"

"When I stopped by Vic's two days ago and found him dead, I knew the cops would search the place. My prints were all over it, so I grabbed the syringe from the bathroom and brought it here. I was planning on burning the garbage to get rid of it, but I got a little distracted by your sister-in-law..."

Peace bristled. "Gee, thanks, Leo. Planting incriminating evidence in *my* house. What the hell were you thinking?"

"Chill out, willya? This was the last place I thought the cops would look."

"Yeah, yeah. Next time don't bring murder evidence to my place, okay?"

"Next time?" I dared ask.

"You know what I mean," Peace said, glancing back at Leo.

It did my heart good to see them embroiled in a lovers' quarrel.

Meanwhile, it seemed no one was any closer to finding Vic's actual killer, while the fate of Sloane's mother hung in the balance. Alika didn't deserve to go to jail for something she didn't do. My own husband had been in that same spot only recently, so I knew how hopeless it felt.

A hazy plan formed in my mind as I stood, realizing the morning was slipping away and none of the farm chores had even been started yet.

"Leo," I said, "if you're sincere about being with Peace, then you need to help me do something."

He tilted his head and frowned. "What exactly?"

"I'll meet you back here in an hour and I'll explain everything. Oh, and you need to come too, Peace."

I sat in the driver's seat of my car, rolling the window down to let the morning air wash over me as I mentally reviewed the revelations I'd just heard. Leo had insisted he had only injected Vic with a small amount of the drug. I slipped the syringe out of my purse and held it up to the sunlight. It was completely empty. So either Leo was lying, or someone else had used it to finish the job. Obviously I wasn't going to get a confession from him, but if I dug up enough facts on my own, the truth might reveal itself.

Whoever was behind this couldn't cover up what they didn't want found any longer. I wasn't letting Alika Apara take blame that didn't belong to her.

Leo stood on the porch.

"Hey, Tara!" he called to me from the top step. I looked up at him. "Just a reminder that now we both have something on each other. So if I go down, you're coming with me."

Chapter 36

Most people thought the gate surrounding the Valance estate was intended to keep thieves out. To my mind, its sole purpose was to tuck this family of criminals away from prying eyes. As Peace, Leo, and I barged through their wrought-iron fence topped with rows of deadly spikes, I was about to pry every last detail open.

The sun-drenched mansion, awash in morning's rich orange glow, and its surrounding property took up nearly two blocks of prime beachfront real estate. I turned to Leo as we stepped up on the veranda. Finding what we needed at Judge Valance's house would have been nearly impossible if it was just me. But with Leo on our side, it was as easy as walking through the massive double front doors and into the lair of Mrs. Bette Valance, wife of my sworn enemy.

Then the wife of my sworn enemy hugged my sister-in-law.

"Peace, darling!" Bette sang out. "What a welcome visit! And who is this?"

I felt Bette's gaze pivot to me, but I couldn't force my eyes past the black silk blouse hanging on her twig-skinny shoulders.

"Mom, this is Peace's sister, Tara Christie."

"Tara Christie..." My name hung on her plump coral lips, which stood in such sharp contrast to her skeletal face that it was like looking at a cadaver who'd just gotten a Botox injection.

"Oh, yes. You're the gal who found that body on your property, aren't you?"

If that was all I was going to be remembered for after years of saving horses and serving my community, shoot me now.

"Yes, that's me. Nice to meet you, Mrs. Valance."

I cupped her chicken bone hand lightly. A 4-carat diamond set into a 24k gold wedding band winked at me in the sun. I knew well the *I'm better than you* contempt that people like Bette hid behind their kindly smiles, but I politely smiled back.

"Mrs. Valance was my mother-in-law. Call me Bette." She pulled me into a hug with a zombie's preternatural strength, thankfully releasing me before my lungs popped. "I'm familiar with everything your family went through, especially when they thought the body was…Vicky's. I'm so sorry you had to get dragged into it. I truly am."

I was beginning to think I misjudged this woman. I recalled the interview she had done on the news, pleading into a bouquet of microphones for the public's help in finding her boy's killer, tears streaming down her face. For the first time I noticed the dark half-moons under her red-rimmed eyes; she'd been crying again, recently—maybe she'd never stopped crying since Victor had been found dead. Her grief was real. I felt like crap for doubting her seemingly genuine warmth.

"No need to apologize. And I'm sorry about Victor. I can't imagine how hard it is to lose a son."

"Thank you, darling. That means a lot." Then Bette turned to Peace, circling her arm around her shoulder like a mother might. "You should come around more often. It's good to see you. Though I wish it was under better circumstances, of course."

More often. Apparently everyone but me knew that Leo and Peace were dating.

"Come in, come in," Bette insisted, nudging us inside the atrium. A manor like this didn't have such commonplace spaces as an entryway.

As Bette led us to the living room, I calculated that about four of my houses could fit into the first floor of hers. One wall was designed with ocean-facing windows so crystal clear a bird would mistake them for open sky. I stood at the window wall, taking in the view of her backyard.

Tropical trees and shrubs not native to this area sprang from carefully tended rock beds leading to a courtyard along the front of the house. Sparkles of marble edging and patches of inch-tall grass added variation to the backdrop. Bending around these floral islands were wooden pathways leading to gazebos, pagodas, outdoor bars, in-ground pool, hot tub…you name it, they had it all. Along with their own private beach access. The endless blue seascape conspired to leave me breathless.

A baby grand piano in the corner drew my attention. Atop its lid were framed photos from Vic and Leo's boyhood. Tan-skinned cherubs tossing a Frisbee on the beach, with a frisky beagle pup in pursuit. Arm wrestling on the kitchen table, eyes fierce, tiny biceps bulging. Hurtling down a mile-long backyard Slip and Slide, screaming in ecstasy, arms and legs flying. Adorable in their Cub Scout uniforms, arms draped over each other's shoulders, showing off their merit badges. Sitting on Santa's lap in matching snowman sweaters, Vic tugging mischievously on the jolly old elf's beard. I was reminded of how closely the brothers favored each other. Their voices were also remarkably similar, sharing the same cultured drawl as their social climbing parents.

It was a shrine to the cute, wholesome, happy boys they'd once been, before they'd grown up and realized that upholding the Valance birthright meant goodbye to innocence. Forevermore.

"Don't you wish they could stay little forever?" Bette asked, catching me looking at the pictures. "I suppose that's the tyranny of time. We just do the best we can as parents and hope they turn out nothing like us."

I glanced back at her, watching her eyes water. While our lives were nothing alike, mother to mother we weren't so different.

Bette visibly shook off the nostalgia. "What kind of hostess am I? I should offer you tea. Or do you prefer coffee? Maybe a glass of wine?"

Wine? And it wasn't even noon yet.

"Do you have any of that homemade blueberry wine you make?" Peace was already getting comfortable on the sofa next to Leo.

"Of course. I've been living off of it since my Vicky died. Tara, would you like a glass?"

"You ferment your own wine?" I asked, impressed. I had imagined her turning her nose up at anything that sold for less than $1,000 a bottle.

"Vicky and I vinified it together, until…" She stopped, as if she had only just remembered he was gone. "Anyway, it's delicious. This was the last drink I shared with Vicky before he…"

Oh boy. This was going to be a tough conversation to get through.

Bette's focus drifted away, somewhere outside the wall of windows where the water stretched so far it captured the whole sky with it. She returned to the present as swiftly as she left.

"Do you want to try it?" she asked me.

I almost accepted, because weren't blueberries healthy? And a glass for breakfast sounded perfect for taking the edge off…except that I had a baby the size of those blueberries now. "No, thank you. Water's fine."

After Bette left with Leo to get the drinks, I turned a confused stare on Peace. "How long have you been seeing Leo that you know what kind of wine these people make?" I whispered.

Peace rolled her eyes, as if my question was intrusive.

When Bette and Leo returned carrying fancy crystal glasses filled with water and wine, I chose a large leather chair, with Bette in a matching one beside mine, while Peace and Leo sat across from us on the sofa, their hands clasped together.

"So," Bette began, one manicured hand clutching her wine glass, the other neatly resting on the lap of her wrinkle-free pantsuit, "Leo tells me you wanted to talk about something involving Vicky."

Bette sipped while I explained.

"Yes, ma'am, that's why I came. I understand there were…nefarious…circumstances surrounding his death," I began, treading carefully. This was a grieving mother, after all. "I'm just trying to piece together what might have happened, because a friend of mine was arrested over this, but I don't think she did it."

Bette set the glass down beside her, then folded her hands primly. "You're referring to Alika Apara, aren't you?"

"So you know."

"Of course I know. I make it my business to know about everything that goes on in my husband's tow—*in this town*. And Alika deserves to be behind bars for what she did." Her stare was intense; those prim hands curled into fists of rage upon her thighs.

"I don't understand, Bette. You actually think she killed your son?"

Bette gestured airily like someone shooing a fly. "Oh, darling, I know exactly what that woman did."

Chapter 37

I floated in Bette's rage, wondering what she would say next.

"Alika Apara may not have held the weapon that killed my Vicky, but that doesn't make her any less responsible for his death. Did you know she blackmailed him?"

"For what—money?"

"Of course for money. What else would you blackmail someone over?"

I thought of Sloane. With her huge house and thriving event planning company, she would have felt right at home in this massive, luxurious place. Alika didn't need money when she had a daughter perfectly happy and willing to give her anything she could ever want.

"I find that hard to believe. Alika doesn't need money."

Bette huffed. "Oh, darling, everyone always wants more money!" She tipped her wine glass back in a long swallow, leaving a pink lipstick heart on the glass. "Besides, I have proof. A week and a half ago I found a letter she sent my husband—right there in my mailbox along with my electric bill. She didn't even bother to send it privately to my husband's office in town so that I wouldn't find out. I suspect she was hoping I'd read it so she could hurt our family any way she could."

"What were the blackmail demands?"

"A million dollars or else she'd tell the media about his

affair and illegitimate daughter from a lifetime ago. Can you believe the unmitigated gall? She wouldn't just be hurting Ewan, but her own daughter along with him. What kind of mother does that? I'll tell you what kind—one that deserves to rot in jail!"

"I'm guessing your husband read it."

"Of course. I wouldn't hide that from him. He needed to know she was threatening him."

"Did you give that blackmail letter to the police?" I asked.

"Not at first. I didn't want to smear Ewan's name. I'm not going to sit here and pretend I don't know about the vicious gossip in this town about our family, some of it aimed at me personally. Some people think I'm nothing but a gold digger." She paused, perhaps waiting for me to correct her. I didn't. "But when Vicky was found dead...well, I had to. The letter was evidence."

"Did they confirm Alika wrote it?"

"They couldn't find any fingerprints, which was no surprise. But the handwriting matched hers exactly."

I found it strange that the threat was to expose Judge Valance's affair rather than the abduction and captivity. What would Alika want with a million dollars, anyway? It didn't sound like the decent and humble woman I had met, who desperately wanted the past to disappear like the morning fog. Why stir things up now, after all these years?

"You said that Alika was the reason Victor died. I don't see how blackmailing your husband was connected to his murder."

"Oh, that. The police told me someone called in with an anonymous tip that Alika was seen leaving Victor's house the day he died. Whether she killed him or not while she was there is anyone's guess."

Bette gulped the rest of her wine, lifted high the empty glass for Leo, like a servant, to fetch her a refill. Her hand wobbled so badly Leo had to snatch the glass before she dropped it. Her cadaveric face flushed as she stifled a hiccup. *Someone* had no qualms about getting tipsy in front of company.

"But then came the tape."

I scooted forward in the leather chair. "What tape?"

"The tape where Alika essentially threatened that if she didn't kill Victor, someone else would. So, whether or not she was the one to poison Vicky, she is still the reason my son is dead."

My mind blew up with questions. I needed that tape to piece together the remaining gaps in the puzzle.

"About this tape—where did you find it? And do you still have it?"

Bette fixed her eyes on the piano where Victor was still young and innocent and happy.

"The police found the tape. I chose not to listen to it. I don't need anything else ruining my memory of my son. They were not the last words a mother wants to remember from her dead child. Anyway, the police told me a condensed version."

"Would I be able to listen to it?"

Red blotches surfaced on her neck like an angry rash. The sharp knuckles of her clenched hands threatened to pierce the onionskin flesh. She was clearly uncomfortable, as if she was in a mental debate.

"I'm sorry, but the police have the only copy."

Except she didn't sound sorry.

"What about the blackmail letter? Do you have a copy of

that I can read? I'm not trying to impose, but I'm having trouble aligning all of this with the woman I know."

"One moment while I get it." After tottering to her feet, she managed to veer around the chair, almost bumping her hip against the corner of a table, then disappeared into the cavernous belly of the house. A long, awkward silence between me, Peace, and Leo later, she returned carrying two pieces of paper. On top was a photocopy of the letter, the crisp and neat handwriting reminding me of my kindergarten teacher's.

"This arrived April 13, and nine days later Vicky was found dead. And you tell me there's no connection."

I read it while Bette emptied another wine glass, then slipped my phone out to snap a quick picture of it:

Dear Mr. V,

It's been a long time since we've spoken, and I disappeared like you asked. But since then, I've thought a lot about our history, our secret. I kept this close to my heart for all these years, not just for my benefit but yours and your son's as well. Now I've finally realized it's time I get what I'm owed. I birthed your daughter, I raised her well, and I asked for nothing in return. Now it's time to reward me for my loyalty.

1 million dollars. That will buy my silence and ensure this secret stays buried forever.

Along with this promise I will destroy evidence I have of what you and your son did to me in the bunker. A tape with your voice, your threats against me.

If you pay me I will never speak of this again, and you'll get to keep what's most important to you: your power and reputation. Your son can live his life freely. But if you don't, I'll leak the truth to the police, starting with the tape I guarantee you don't want anyone to hear.

I hope you'll see how reasonable this request it.

Give the wife my regards,

Alika

I shuffled the photocopy underneath the next page, finding another letter, this one an original. Sepia yellow and crinkled with time.

"What's this?" I asked, holding it up to Bette.

"That, darlin', is the other letter she sent years ago, back in October 1995. Also from Alika Apara, mother to my husband's bastard child, asking for child support. Exact same handwriting, if you look at it."

After another quick snapshot, I read it. Sure enough, written in the same neat kindergarten-teacher script:

I understand this letter comes unexpected and perhaps unwanted years after you discovered my pregnancy from our tryst. But after your wife reached out to me, she encouraged me—as one mother to another—to seek your help.

As my daughter grows older and soon will be preparing

for college, I held hope that you might want to support her academic pursuits in order to give her the most opportunities possible. I do not wish to tell anyone else about our affair, nor her paternity, but I do hope you will consider my humble request with an open heart.

Alika

"Satisfied yet?" Bette stood in front of me, listing slightly to the left. There was ice in her tone. "The woman is a greedy, homewrecking, lying whore who told my husband *I* reached out to *her*. Clearly she was delusional! And then she drags my son into her mess…and now my boy is gone…"

I handed her both pages. "I know you don't believe me, Bette, but these prove nothing. Alika didn't do what you think she did. Don't you want to know who actually killed your son?"

"There's no point in finding out, Tara. My son had a lot of enemies. Including you, so I hear. I don't particularly want the cops digging into Vicky's…business activities and publicizing them. We all know he was no angel. But at least let him rest in peace without his criminal history being the last thing the public reads about him."

"Even if it puts an innocent woman behind bars?"

"A woman who deserves it!"

By this point I could barely control my anger. I caught Leo's subtle head shake, Peace's beseeching glance, both urging me to keep my cool, not make a scene. They should have known better.

"You choose to turn a blind eye to your husband's crimes,

don't you?"

Bette lifted her chin imperiously. Her eyes snapped with indignation that anyone would have the audacity to impugn her husband. At the same time, I had the sneaking suspicion that a carefully hidden hatred for the man at least partially motivated her.

"Don't sit there in judgement when you know nothing about my life. You want me to open my eyes? They're wide open, Tara! I don't have a choice, do I? I know who I'm married to. It's not like I can walk away. And do I really want to see the devil behind the mask? No, I don't. So don't sit there giving me your self-righteous pep talk until you've lived my life for a day."

"I'm sorry," I stuttered. "I didn't mean—"

The sound of breaking glass reverberated along the endless white marble stretching from the atrium to the living room.

"Everything's fine, Mrs. V!" a servile voice called out—from where in this sprawling Xanadu, it was impossible to tell.

"Sheer incompetence!" Bette seethed. "I hope to God she hasn't broken another piece of my Wedgwood china, or there'll be hell to pay."

At that moment Judge Valance swaggered into the room, brandy snifter in hand, wearing his signature double-breasted Armani suit. As we didn't move in the same social circles, it wasn't often I viewed him in the flesh; the close call in Victor's secret storage room had afforded me only a glimpse. Now here he was, the proverbial lion in winter, in his own den, silver-maned, jowly, carrying a bit of a paunch. But he retained the piercing blue eyes and hawkish nose, and his bearing was still erect and commanding. Old lions, though claws and fangs dulled by age, are still highly dangerous, especially when there is wickedness in their hearts.

Bette hastily hid the letters behind her back. Ewan glanced at me, and for a fleeting second I worried he'd recognized me, before his gaze shifted to his wife. I was a nobody in his sight, beneath his notice—just one of the hoi polloi. I counted that as a blessing.

"One of your ham-handed maids has broken a dish," he reported disinterestedly, swirling his brandy like a character in a drawing-room mystery.

"Ewan, how nice of you to make a cameo appearance in your own home," Bette slurred. "Not the Wedgwood, I hope."

"No. One of the everyday dishes. The ones from Walmart, I believe." The judge gave a low chuckle, seeing Bette's mortified expression. "Sorry, my dear, I guess I let that slip." He favored the room with a strained half-smile and left.

"I need to have a word with that clumsy woman," Bette murmured wearily. The fight had gone out of her. She turned to me. "Look, I appreciate what you're trying to do for your friend, Mrs. Christie." Suddenly we were back to formal address. "But Alika Apara is not as innocent as you assume she is. And whatever she claims my husband did to her, there are always two sides to every story."

"What do you mean?" I felt like I was just as empty-handed as when I arrived.

Bette walked ahead of me to the two-story tall front doors, my cue to leave. When she opened the door and turned me, there was an unexpected defeat in her gaze. She was back to being a faded Southern belle clinging to empty social niceties.

"I've told you more than enough. I think it's time for you to leave. And please…let my son keep his dignity."

Tape 8
Exposé

1995

[Tape clicks on]

[Young male] This is my last confession. At least I can finally say that after everything that's come out, everything that happened, me and Alika came to an agreement that I think we both can live with. She's gonna keep my secrets, and I'm gonna keep hers.

[Woman] That is because you gave me no choice, did you, Victor?

[Young male] Oh, don't act like such a victim, Alika. You made your bed, now lie in it. You're the one who brought this on yourself.

[Woman] Brought this on myself?

[Young male] Yeah, by trying to extort my dad for money. You know blackmail is illegal, don't you?

[Woman] I felt sorry for you when I first met you, because I thought you were just as much a victim of circumstance as I was. But I can see you actually *enjoy* this. You deserve whatever hell you get, Victor. And I hope it is extra painful for you.

[Young male] Ha! You think I'm scared of hell after what I've seen?

[Woman] You should be.

[Young male] And what, do you want to be the one to send me there?

[Woman] If I were a stronger woman, maybe I would. But I have a feeling you will have many enemies one day, Victor, who will gladly take on that job.

[Tape clicks off]

Chapter 38

"This doesn't sound like Mummy at all." Sloane had just finished reading the photocopy of Bette's blackmail letter I had taken a picture of on my phone. She stared at the screen for several minutes, shaking her head as she read, signing the word *no* again and again while scrolling down each paragraph.

The floor-to-ceiling windows framing Sloane's living room looked out upon a moonless black night. The interior space was cheerful and bright, with white walls and stark overhead lighting, a necessity for conversation when you relied on your hands to do the talking.

Ginger was seated on the love seat, her back to the window; Sloane and I sat across from her in matching rattan armchairs. As Sloane signed, I watched her gestures mirrored against the dark glass behind Ginger. While the porch screen door let the sound and scent of the ocean waft inside, the shore was hidden from view.

"You don't think this is your mom?" Ginger asked.

Sloane's lip lifted as she considered the question, then she shook her head. "While it does look like her handwriting, she doesn't write like that—so informal. She learned the American style of English as a second language and never got the hang of contractions. She speaks and writes with very proper grammar. This is *not* her."

Sloane handed my phone back to me.

"Plus, why would Mummy blackmail the Valances for money? Maybe back in 1995 when she needed money to support me, but definitely not now. She has never cared about money, only about her faith and living right. This…no…it's all wrong."

There had to be a way to prove this to Detective Hughes.

"Do you have anything personal of your mom's that shows how she writes? Something we can give the police to prove it's not her?" I asked. Using Alika's 1995 child support request as proof was out of the question.

Sloane tapped her fingertip on her chin. "Oh wait! Yes, I have something." She held up a finger and rooted through her purse, producing a bundle of letters and placing them next to my phone. "These love letters from Mummy to my father are old, but the way she expresses herself hasn't changed since she wrote them. Even her handwriting is the same…"

She explained how, in a nostalgic mood, she had revisited the letters recently. Suddenly her busy fingers paused mid-air.

"And one of her letters was missing!" she signed excitedly. "Someone must have stolen it from her house in order to copy her writing!"

This sounded promising. With all these details put together, we had a chance of proving Alika's innocence. A small chance, but at least a chance.

All three of us examined the handwriting, dismay slowly filling me up as I compared the script.

"I'm worried this isn't going to be enough. While it might not sound like her, the handwriting is spot-on—in my amateur opinion, of course. Even the way she writes her V's."

Sloane's smile drooped. "You don't think the police will

believe her, do you?"

I shook my head. Stacked against us was a bogus witness testimony, a forged blackmail letter, the incriminating *Exposé* tape sitting on Detective Hughes' desk, and a police force paid off by the man who wanted her behind bars. It felt hopeless.

"Mummy was right." Sloane shoved herself up from the chair, pacing to the window. When she turned back to face us, her arm movements were sharp, jarring, full of anger. "She once told me our name was our curse. *Apara*—in Nigeria it means 'one who comes and goes.' She believed that was why my father came into our lives, then left so tragically, because of her last name. For a long time I thought that was nonsense. But then Benson came into my life and also met with tragedy. And now watching my mummy leave my life so unfairly…maybe she's right. Maybe we're cursed. Maybe no matter how many facts we line up, no matter how good a defense we provide, Mummy is fated to leave me."

"Girl, you can't give up!" Ginger joined her at the window, hugging Sloane as she hung in her arms. "Even if your mom goes to trial, what jury would convict her based on this garbage? It's circumstantial, isn't it?"

"I can't leave that up to chance. My mummy is a Black foreigner in a small, tightknit town. What do you think a jury of her peers is going to see when she gets on the stand?"

There had to be something more concrete to prove Alika's innocence. It was just a matter of finding it.

"We all know there's no way your mom killed anyone," I stated plainly. "Which means there *has* to be proof that someone else did it. If we narrow the list down, maybe we can find that proof."

"Whoever wrote this must have known about the bunker as well as Ewan's affair," Ginger said. "That list can't be long. It was only your mom, Victor, and Ewan."

"And don't forget Leonard," I added.

While our suspect list wasn't promising, at least it was a starting place. Someone had to know something that could help us find our killer.

My phone beeped with a text. Ever since the body showed up in my yard, every beep, chime, or ring made my heart stop, but when I saw Nora's name next to several silly emojis, it resumed its beat. I must have been glowing, because Ginger picked up on it right away.

"What's got you grinnin' like a possum eatin' a sweet potato?"

I chuckled. "It's Nora. Apparently she just discovered television commercials and is grumbling about how annoying they are. She grew up on Netflix, so she didn't know they existed until she started living with my mom."

"Kids today…it's no wonder they have no patience!" Ginger replied. "By the way, I meant to ask. Did you ever figure out where that creepy sweatshirt that was left on your porch came from?"

"I'm pretty sure it was Keanu's. I'm guessing he must have been upset after Nora broke up with him and was returning it…with a few new intentionally placed stains."

Ginger looked doubtful. "Are you sure?"

"What other explanation could there be?"

"It's just that Nora told me Keanu has been up there staying with her and your mom for the past week."

"They're back together?" I couldn't hide the jealousy that

Nora had told Ginger and not me.

"Actually, they never broke up. She only told you that so Chris would stop hounding her about how much she didn't need to be dating. But please don't tell her I told you! She swore me to secrecy."

"So if the sweatshirt wasn't Keanu's…" Then maybe it wasn't so innocent. Maybe it *was* a threat.

"Don't let your mind go there," Ginger said. "I'm sure it's nothing. It's a sweatshirt, not a bloody knife. What are they going to do—smother you with it? Force you to watch Duke basketball?"

Ginger had a point. Maybe I was reading too much into it. The more pressing matter was figuring out who wrote this blackmail letter, since my gut—which felt like it was already showing my pregnancy—told me whoever wrote the letter was behind everything.

"Maybe I can talk Peace into getting some info out of Leo," I suggested, fresh out of ideas. "Or maybe one of the staff overheard something."

Then a tiny little lightbulb flickered in my brain—a nightlight glow. I swiped back to the picture of the blackmail letter. My gaze rolled over the threat, analyzing each sentence, how they fit together. All the facts rose up in front of me with startling clarity.

"I think I know who's behind it," I announced. "Who was close with the family, was privy to private information like what happened in the bunker, had access to Vic's tapes, and hard up for money?"

Ginger and Sloane exchanged a confused look.

"Don't you see? The answer was right in front of us all

along. It was—"

A sharp crash splintered the air. I screamed, throwing my arms over my head to shield my face from the lacerating spray. Sloane ducked out of the way, and with a muted cry, Ginger crumbled to the floor.

Chapter 39

Eventually Sloane's one-story-tall window stopped raining down on us, leaving a jagged black hole in its place. There were no words painted on the rock we found at Ginger's feet. No paper message attached to it. It was just an ordinary rock that fit comfortably in the palm of my hand; small enough for most anyone to throw, heavy enough to bust the window.

Seated where we were, Sloane and I had been lucky. Ginger, sitting directly in front of the window, had not. The rock had left her with a bloody goose egg on the back of her head but, as she quipped, it had failed to knock good sense into her. It could have been a lot worse, had distance and impact not slowed the projectile's velocity. Or if it had been not a rock, but a bullet.

As it was, Ginger had taken the brunt of the glass shower, and had what seemed like a thousand cuts to show for it. She refused professional medical care and submitted to Sloane's and my amateur doctoring like a trooper. Sloane and I suffered only minor cuts.

"That's the last straw! We need to stop," I decided as I drove Ginger home while Sloane stayed back to clean up her living room.

"What about '*Goonies never say die*'?" Ginger insisted. "We don't give up, Tara. *You* don't give up."

"Maybe it's time I started. My involvement is only making

things worse. I know I tend to meddle. And have control issues."

"Don't forget you're a huge pain in the ass," Ginger added lovingly.

"That too," I agreed with a wry grin. "I had always just considered those character flaws, but now they're putting people I love at risk."

"You're saying you love me? Can't live without me?" Ginger cooed playfully.

"You already know I do. Which is why this rock through the window thing is the only warning I need. Let's walk away and let the police do their job."

"Oh, you mean the police who are helping Judge Valance cover up a crime? Those police?"

I shrugged. What else could I do? This wasn't a hill I wanted to die on—or Ginger either, for that matter. "Not my problem anymore."

"Whoever did it can kiss my go-to-hell! It really burns my biscuit that you want to give up now when we're so close, Tara."

"You call this close? We're running in circles, Ging."

"No, honey. You don't get a rock thrown through your window unless you're on to something. They're trying to scare us off their scent, but they didn't realize they're dealing with Tara's Angels..."

Ginger gave me an encouraging hug as I dropped her off, but I didn't have the heart to tell her I planned to disband the group.

I left Ginger, bandaged up like an Egyptian mummy, under Rick's care. I was moved by his genuine concern, but I hadn't forgotten his role in the clandestine burial of Marvin Valance—and who knew what other recent shenanigans that Ginger was still in the dark about. I warned Rick to wait on her hand and foot…or else *my* foot would be up his ass.

Behind me the sun rose, casting orange sparkles over a calm bay, as I pulled into the empty parking lot at Nails by Nellie. Good, the place would be empty this early in the morning. I breezed in and made a beeline for Nellie, hunched over a pedicure tub with a scrubbing brush.

"Back so soon for another manicure? Pedicure? Or both? I've got a buy-one-get-one deal."

"Actually, I'm here to talk to you."

"Talk to me about what? You changed your mind about your toenail color?"

"No, Nellie. How did you know that I was the prime suspect in Victor Valance's murder?"

Nellie scowled, deepening her wrinkles enough to insert a quarter in them. "What? I don't remember saying that."

"Well I do. Right there in your supply closet you gave me that tape and told me it would help clear my name. How did you know the cops suspected me? I looked, and my name wasn't publicized anywhere online."

Nellie rose creakily to her feet. "I just assumed they did, since the body was on your property."

"Don't lie to me, Nellie. There's too much at stake, and too many people have been hurt already. I have a feeling you knew because you still work for the Valances, don't you? You overheard them planning everything."

"You have no proof of that." She took a threatening step toward me, her fingers clenching the scrub brush.

"I think I do. When I visited Bette, there was a crash in the dining room. Something broke. I heard a voice cry out,

'Everything's fine, Mrs. V.' It sounded vaguely familiar. Now I'm sure. That was you, wasn't it?"

"I'm not saying it was, I'm not saying it wasn't. You ain't got no proof!"

I had to remind myself that I had youth and strength on my side, and all she had was a loud mouth. "Maybe. But I do have proof of something else."

"Like what?"

"Something you sent to Judge Ewan Valance, Nellie. I think you know what I'm talking about."

"What about him?"

I pulled out my phone, showing her the screenshot of the photocopied blackmail letter. She flinched so imperceptibly I almost missed it.

"What's this have to do with me?"

"You wrote this a couple weeks ago, didn't you? And that letter is the reason an innocent woman is behind bars for murder."

"Murder? I don't know what you're talking about, but I didn't kill anyone!" Nellie raised her hands, swollen and chapped.

"You blackmailed the judge for a million dollars, didn't you? And don't deny it—I *know* this is you! I heard you call him *Mr. V* when we were talking the other day—and Ginger heard it too. Just like this letter addresses him as *Mr. V*."

"So what? That means nothing…"

"Oh, I'm just getting started! And you're the only person who knows about the fallout shelter, and who could have swiped one of Victor's tapes while you were cleaning it, and I know you're eager to retire and get out of here…and I'm sure a million dollars would do that for you."

"Look, I admit I wrote that letter, but I had nothing to do with no murder. Or Alika getting put in jail either."

"But this letter put her on Ewan's radar!" I wanted to wring her bony neck. "Because of you, he lied and framed her for his son's murder, all because of your blackmail demand. I don't understand—why Alika? Why not some fake name?"

Nellie tossed her brush in a bucket of soapy water and cracked her knuckles.

"It wasn't originally my plan to use Alika's name in the blackmail letter. But I needed a real enough threat to get Mr. V to pay up. He's too smart to fall for a fake name. And he silences mistresses by the dozens. Then I remembered the bunker tape I had found—with his voice being proof of what he'd done. Abduction's a serious crime—jailable. It was the only thing I had on Mr. V that could scare him. So I snuck into Alika's house and found a letter in her desk that I could use to match her penmanship. Real sweet love letter, too. I felt bad for taking it afterward."

"You knew how dangerous Ewan Valance was and you put an innocent woman's life at risk!"

Nellie turned away, shoulders slumped. "I'm sorry. I know it was selfish. I just wanted to get paid and get on my way. I'm tired of bustin' my hump working for them for almost five decades with nothing but this crappy salon to show for it. You know I still have to work for that damn family, don't you? I'm dead tired, Tara! But I can't leave—I know all their secrets, and they know I know. So I'll be stuck working for them until my last dying breath. Do you know how miserable an existence that is?"

"I can imagine how hard your life has been. But you still have to come clean to the cops. Alika Apara needs to be set free. Right now she's sharing a cell with a purse-snatcher who smells like he hasn't had a bath in a year. Does that sound fair to you?"

"No, it don't. But neither does you sending me to jail for blackmailing a criminal who treated me like garbage!"

"You've got it all wrong, Nellie. I'm going to send you to jail for *murdering* a criminal who treated you like garbage."

Nellie uttered a string of profanities I need not repeat. "Murder? I may be a blackmailer, but I'm no killer, Tara. I wanted what was owed to me, that's all. Not blood on my hands. I have no idea what happened to Victor, but I guarantee he got what he deserved. I just wasn't the one to dish it out to him, I promise you that. I was only trying to look out for y'all. Protect the little people. That's all I've ever tried to do."

It suddenly occurred to me that Nellie saw herself as some sort of self-styled vigilante—a geriatric Robin Hood. She knew Alika's name, knew her past, knew she was the one from the bunker. Which meant that she might have also been the one who back in October of 1995 suggested Alika ask for child support in the first place.

"What do you mean, you were looking out for the little people?"

"Mr. V has taken advantage of women his entire life. He gathers mistresses like trophies, then screws 'em and dumps 'em. He cheats on his wife and brags to his buddies about it. So yeah, I may have nudged things along to get Alika some financial help back when her daughter was growing up."

"What exactly did you tell her to do?"

"I just pretended to be Mrs. V while encouraging her to ask

for child support. And I may have subtly exposed to Mrs. V who her husband really was. But I didn't expect Mr. V to throw Alika in a dungeon! That's why I tried to warn you to leave Bloodson Bay. I don't want to see something happen to you or your daughter."

Fear paralyzed me. What did Nellie know about Nora?

"Are they planning to go after Nora?" My voice came out as a squeak. "Someone left a sweatshirt on my porch..."

"Oh, honey, that was me. And yes, I was trying to scare you off. At Debbie's Diner I overheard you talking about Nora going to Duke, so I got the idea to plant that on your porch to scare y'all the hell out of Dodge. It ain't safe having a Valance for an enemy."

For as worn out as Nebby Nellie claimed to be, she sure had enough energy to run all over town causing trouble.

"Did you also throw the rock through Sloane's window last night? Because that was too much, Nellie."

Nellie cackled. "Honey, last night I had a date with Jack Daniels. Hell, we ended up in bed together."

I should have felt elated that I was one step closer to solving this mystery and freeing Alika. But someone was still after my family, after Sloane's family, and they had already killed once. They could easily kill again.

"So you'll go to the cops with everything you did and help get Alika out of there?"

"Yeah, I'll set it right. Prison would be better than working for the Valances anyway. But just so you know, me coming clean about everything ain't going to free her. You know that as much as I do. Not with Mr. V pulling the strings."

"I just wish you would have said something instead of

pulling all these cloak-and-dagger stunts, Nellie. You really made a mess of things."

"Well, I'm sorry, and I'm saying it now: Leave this cursed town! Run as far away as you can. Before it's too late."

Chapter 40

The Bloodson Bay Police Department was on the way home, and I had been meaning to talk to Officer Speers privately the first chance I got.

I realized that I couldn't take back anything I told him today, and maybe I couldn't trust him like I hoped. But I was desperate, and this was my Hail Mary pass.

I found his cubicle nestled in a far, lonely corner, almost as if it was designed to be in permanent timeout. This worked to my advantage because I had wanted to avoid being spotted by Detective Hughes.

Officer Speers stood up to greet me with a sincere smile as I approached his desk. I glanced at the photos pinned to his fabric cubicle: Speers in a camouflage jacket kneeling beside a ten-point buck he'd bagged; two bluetick coonhounds asleep in front of a campfire, while Speers and a pal drank beer; a pretty woman with windblown chestnut hair on the deck of a skiff, her arms around a little boy and a girl. Joe Speers: outdoorsman, family man—and, I hoped, my friend.

"Thanks for making time to speak with me." I sat, my leg nervously bouncing.

Officer Speers crossed his beefy arms on the desktop and leaned forward interestedly. "It sounded pretty urgent. Is everything okay?"

"I came to you because I don't know who else I can trust. Someone's after me. First the body planted on my property, then last night a rock was thrown through my friend's window while we were sitting next to it."

"You think Judge Valance is behind everything, don't you?"

I nodded. He knew, which probably meant everyone knew.

"I've done my research," Officer Speers continued. "I know he's been after your farm for ages, and your rivalry with Victor over the kill pen horses isn't exactly a secret around town. So what do you have for me?"

"It's about Vic's murder, and the body you haven't ID'd yet." I had carefully chosen the facts I wanted to share. But if there was any chance of carving out trust between us, I would need to come clean and throw myself on Officer Speers' mercy.

So I confessed to my plotted insurance fraud with Victor. And Victor attacking Peace, and how I knew from the moment I saw the autopsy photos of the John Doe that it wasn't Victor, due to absence of bite marks on the hand. I told him the dead body was in fact Marvin Valance, lowlife extraordinaire, and that Judge Valance was behind it. I even explained how Nellie wrote the blackmail letter after years of service to that family, unable to leave because she was bound to the Valance vault of secrets.

But I left out the bunker. Until I knew Officer Speers was completely trustworthy, I omitted everything having to do with Alika, because she was the one I was trying to exonerate. Her name couldn't be in any way tied to the Valance family.

"Wow." Officer Speers hadn't said anything as he listened without expression. "That's quite a…story."

"A *story*? It's not a story. It's all true."

"I believe you, Tara. Except for one detail." He patted my hand comfortingly, though I wasn't sure why. "I don't think you conspired with Victor Valance on that insurance fraud. I'm pretty sure he stole the Somulose kit and planned the insurance scam himself."

It took a moment for what he was saying to register. Maybe it was pregnancy brain, maybe it was disbelief, but it sounded like he was letting me off the hook. It was my word against a dead guy's. No prison time for me. Officer Speers was going to help me expose the truth, and he would protect me while doing it.

Officer Speers tapped his desk, glancing back at the rows of cubicles filled with ears and eyes.

"I wish I could do something with this information, but without any hardcore proof of the judge's crimes…"

This was it. This was the moment.

Reaching into my purse, I pulled out a sack that clattered as I sat it in front of him.

"Here's your proof."

He opened it and peered inside. "What it is?"

"Cassette tapes. Victor recorded these back in 1995 when his father forced him to abduct Alika Apara and hold her prisoner to silence her about an affair he had with her years before."

I had handed over the only thing that could put Judge Valance behind bars. All of the tapes except for one that I had saved—*Pretty Hate Machine*. It depicted the worst of what Victor had done to Alika during a particularly horrific day near the end. Starving her, taunting her, vowing to kill her just so he could go home. In it he sounded more like a madman and less like a human. I had something else planned for this tape.

In whispers I told Officer Speers the complicated details of what he would piece together from these tapes. How Alika had gotten pregnant right before the one-night stand, but Judge Valance assumed the baby was his. How she let him believe it, because he threatened her life and the only thing keeping him from killing her was that he thought the child was his. I even explained how Nellie—pretending to be Bette Valance—wrote to Alika advising her to ask for child support in a misguided effort to help out the widowed single mom. And how that sole monetary request marked Alika as Judge Valance's target, which resulted in her being kidnapped.

All Alika had done since then was avoid that man, keep that dark secret, and protect her daughter.

"Now this"—Officer Speers lifted the bag of tapes and held it aloft—"*this* is the evidence we need to take that whole corrupt family down."

"What about Bette Valance?" I wondered aloud. I felt bad for the woman, being sucked into that black, evil hole, unable to escape.

"I'll see what I can do. She might not have known anything. And if she did, if she was forced to go along with it out of duress, we can protect her."

I grabbed Officer Speers' hand, squeezing it with more gratitude than words could express. "Thank you. Thank you for protecting me…and helping Alika. Thanks for being one of the good guys."

"Tara." He stopped me as I turned to leave. "I think you should have this."

He opened his desk drawer, pulling out a case file, a small Walkman, and a tape. It looked like one of Victor's tapes, with my name written across the top: *Oh Tara*

"What's that?" I asked just as I answered my own question.

Victor couldn't resist his trademark play on words as he referenced "Oh Tara" by The Knack. Ginger and Sloane had speculated Vic might have recorded our argument—which included my agreement to Vic's insurance fraud—at the kill pen on one of his tapes. Turned out they were right; this had to be it. Since Officer Speers had been in possession of it, he also must have known what I did all along. And he never turned me in. *Bless his heart*, as Ginger would say.

"One of the guys saw an older woman leave this on my desk. But I think it belongs to you." He handed it to me, in essence giving me my freedom since it was the only piece of evidence of what I had plotted to do. I knew exactly who had turned it in, but I wasn't worried about her telling anyone. Nebby Nellie had enough secrets of her own to worry about. "And just so you know, you can trust Detective Hughes. She's one of the good guys too."

I left feeling equally weightless and heavy. I had one more thing to do, and it just might be the greatest challenge of all.

Tape 9
Oh Tara

Present Day

[Tape clicks on]

[Horses nicker and snort in the background]

[Victor] Thanks for meeting me here. I wasn't sure you were gonna show.

[Click of approaching boots on concrete]

[Tara] What's this about? Have you thought over my offer?

[Victor] You mean your offer to let me buy the horses from the kill pen low, and you'd buy them off of me for a small profit? Yeah, your offer sucks. I've got a better one.

[Tara groans] Okay, I'm listening.

[Victor] I'm leaving the game. Leaving Bloodson Bay...for good. But I need money, and you need me gone if your farm stands a chance of surviving. So I came up with a way where we could help each other out. It's a win-win for us both.

[Tara] Why do I have the feeling that whatever it is, it's illegal?

[Victor] Do you want to save your ranch or not?

[Tara] Fine, what do you want me to do?

[Victor] I need you to help me kill a horse.

[Tara scoffs] Are you crazy? You know I *save* horses for a living, don't you? I'm not going to kill one for you.

[Victor] Just shut up and listen for a minute! I have a racehorse that's insured for over a million dollars. If I could somehow euthanize her—

painlessly, okay?—without the insurance investigator finding out, I'll be out of your hair forever. I'll take the money and run. All I need from you is a euthanizing kit that's not traceable, so it don't come back to me.

[Tara] No way. I'm sure you know a crooked vet you can pay off to give you one.

[Victor] That's the one thing I don't have.

[Tara] Sorry, but I don't want anything to do with this. You're on your own.

[Victor] Then say goodbye to your life's work, Tara. All those sick and abused horses you want to save? Consider them dead. All because you think the life of a racehorse you ain't even met is worth the hundreds more you could have saved. This is your last chance to help me...or you'll be seeing a lot more of me as I watch you burn everything down.

[Long silence between them]

[Tara] Those are my choices—commit insurance fraud, which is a felony offense, by the way, or lose my ranch?

[Victor] Yep, take your pick.

[Tara sighs] I hate you, but I'll help you, Vic, because I never want see your face again. But if I do, you better believe I'll blow it right off your head.

[Tape clicks off]

Chapter 41

The warm April evening was pitched perfectly between the teeth-chattering winter and boiling summer. Nice weather for a glass of wine—nix that; a glass of juice—on the back porch as I told Chris I was ready to pack up our lives and leave Bloodson Bay. And terrible weather to break it to Ginger what Rick had done. That he had been a party to Marvin's burial on my property. That the man she loved was still a criminal, not reformed like he had told her. I decided to give her his wedding band and she could choose for herself what she would do about him. But I wouldn't be around to watch it all crumble. I would be gone by then, living another life. That confession would hurt the most.

I still didn't know who killed Vic, but now that I knew for sure it wasn't his body on my property, I almost didn't care. *Almost.* Because a part of me wanted to know who had the guts to face off with a Valance...and win. Though that terrible thought meant maybe I wasn't much better than them.

There was one last thing, and one last tape, that needed to be dealt with before I walked away. Something only another mother would understand.

The driveway was lined with pink cherry blossoms that complemented the sunset. As I pulled up to the house, I was surprised to see Peace's car parked there. I wasn't sure I would ever get used to her and Leonard Valance being together, but again, I wouldn't be around to worry about it. For once I wouldn't make other people's problems my problems.

By the time I stepped up on the veranda, Bette Valance was already opening the front door, bony fingers wrapped around the stem of a full wine glass, before I could even ring the bell.

"Oh, it's you. I saw a car coming up the drive. I'm surprised to see you." Bette looked disappointed, as if she had been expecting someone else.

"I just wanted to apologize. Mind if I come in?" I asked, then thought better of it. "Unless your husband is home. If that's the case, I'll speak my piece right here."

"No, no, Ewan's not home. Come on in."

Bette led me back through the grand atrium. My gaze skimmed the first floor for a sign of Peace, until I heard her familiar laughter coming from somewhere outside. As long as she was happy I would be happy for her.

Then I looked at Bette. A woman with a fabulous mansion, hired help waiting on her hand and foot, endless money, unchecked power, the finest clothes, and yet her life was hollow and meaningless—a masquerade of sophistication and gentility that fooled no one, probably not even herself. I wouldn't change places with her for anything.

She led me into the living room, but I wouldn't be here long enough to sit down. I stood at the piano shrine next to her, both of us gazing at the photos rather than each other.

Bette's greatest moments were trapped behind picture frames, where her boys were young and carefree, a simpler time with simpler needs. Now all she had to keep her company was the lonely tip-tap of her own footsteps on these cold marble floors.

I felt a swirl of emotions for this mother who had managed to raise a monster. And yet she still clearly loved him until the end.

"How did you do it?" I asked. My voice sounded tiny in this palatial room.

Her blank expression morphed into one of shock and fear. "What do you mean?"

"How did you manage to love a son who so clearly turned out so…bad? I'm not trying to scratch at your wound, but you obviously knew what your son was up to, all the lives he destroyed, and yet you still saw the little boy he used to be." I gestured to the sweet child in the pictures.

"Oh, I don't know. I guess that's a mother's love, isn't it? Unconditional. Sometimes we have to look the other way…" As she said it, her gaze shifted, hiding from me.

"Even if they hurt people?"

She shrugged. "We protect them as long as we can, but that's when tough love comes in, I guess."

I wondered if Bette had ever given Vic tough love in his entire life. Or maybe that's all he knew.

"That's actually why I'm here. I know how much you loved him and wanted to protect him, so I'm giving you this."

I handed Bette the last tape, the one we had found in the bunker that I couldn't turn over to Officer Speers: *Pretty Hate Machine.* The name basically said it all.

The other tapes had portrayed Victor as a shared victim of his father's malice, but this one portrayed his darkest side as he tortured Alika. I'd let that version of him get buried with him.

"You probably won't want to listen to this. It's

pretty…graphic. But I felt you wouldn't want anyone else to see this side of your son, so I'm giving it to you, to do with as you will."

She flipped the tape over, gaze settling on his handwriting. "From one mother to another, thank you, Tara. That means a lot to me."

She set the tape on the piano bench and picked up a photo of Victor as a baby. Tears brimmed in her eyes, what I took to be a Steel Magnolia resolve kept her from sobbing in my presence.

"I know what it's like to want to do anything to protect your child. I went through it with Nora. But in the end, life has a way of holding us accountable for our choices."

Bette looked thoughtful for a long moment. "Yes, life has a way of doing that, doesn't it?"

I left with that thought following me out the front door, an uneasy feeling washing over me. Something felt so strange about this conversation, but I couldn't quite put my finger on what. Bette trailed me out to the veranda, still holding her wine. A shield that kept people away.

As I descended the granite steps, the plant lover in me paused to admire the lush gardens surrounding the mansion. Pink dogwoods were in glorious bloom, as were azaleas in shades of red, salmon, and white. Beds of tulips in a rainbow of colors competed for attention with plots of cheery gardenias and violets. A marble water nymph poured water from a tall jug into a two-tiered fountain in which black-capped chickadees frolicked and preened. Anthropomorphic critters—a frog playing a fiddle, a golf-playing squirrel, a bespectacled snail hitching a ride on a turtle's back—made me smile, in spite of my somber mood.

Then I noticed the landscaping rocks. River rocks, if I wasn't mistaken—I'd seen them plenty of times at the garden center. Smooth, oval, a variety of natural colors. At the base of the steps I stooped to pick one up. It was the same color, a brownish-gray, as the one that had been thrown through Sloane's window. I bounced it in my palm. It had the same heft too; plenty heavy enough to bust a window…

"Bette!" I called out.

She halted in the doorway, her back to me. When she turned around and saw the rock in my hand, pink splotches crawled up her neck. Her hand shrunk into a balled fist.

That was the moment the final puzzle piece went *click.*

Chapter 42

"You threw a rock like this through Sloane's window last night, didn't you?"

Bette recoiled as if I'd slapped her. "No, of course not. What a ridiculous thing to say!"

"You could have killed Ginger. The rock hit her in the back of her head, and she was cut up very badly. Was that the goal? To scare us away from digging a little deeper? You must have been pretty drunk to pull a stupid stunt like that!"

Bette squared her shoulders. Perhaps it was the wine talking, but her tone took on a cruel haughtiness. "You're out of line, young lady! Our gardener installed those stones. They are not rare. You'll find them not only on fine estates like mine, but no doubt also on drab, common homesteads—like yours."

I ignored the jab. "Then I take it you wouldn't object to me having the rock that could have killed my friend examined for fingerprints—yours, that is."

Her hand trembled, spilling wine at her feet, and her plump lips quivered for a moment in mute fury. At length she yelled, "Leave my property right now or I'm calling the police!"

Stomping to the bottom of the steps, I glared up at her. "Go ahead. I'm sure Detective Hughes would be happy to help sort this out."

Bette, jaw clenched, held my gaze and her resolve. She

refused to drop the mask. I'd have to find a way to break through it.

"Why? Why are you trying to stop us from uncovering the truth, Bette? Do you really think your husband is worth protecting?"

"My God, will you ever stop, Tara Christie?" she screamed.

"Not until you tell me why you're letting Alika go to jail for a murder she didn't commit. Are you covering for someone? I know you're trying to protect Victor, but he's gone. Alika still has a daughter who needs her. Don't ruin their lives because you're angry."

That did it. Bette slumped to the veranda floor rather ungracefully, spilling more of the wine, but she had the presence of mind to smooth out her pantsuit. Sitting cross-legged, she downed the remainder of her drink in one gulp.

"I'm not angry, Tara. I'm…lost."

"Because Victor died? You had to know his lifestyle would eventually lead to that. He had a lot of enemies, but Alika wasn't one of them. Tell your husband to retract his bogus testimony against her. You had to know what Ewan was up to, trying to hide Victor from those people who were after him. Your husband is not a good man, Bette, and you know it because you've been trapped here under his thumb your entire marriage."

"I know…"

I glanced at my car, torn between leaving and staying. Peace's car parked next to mine reminded me that one day she could end up facing the same dismal fate as Bette.

I walked up the steps to the veranda and sat down next to her. When I took her hand in mine she squeezed it, and continued to hold it, running her sandpapery thumb along the edge of my palm.

"If you care at all about Peace, which it seems you do, you'll put Ewan behind bars where be belongs so you don't drag my sister-in-law into this mess."

"Peace is so easy to love." Bette cracked a small grin. "And I never meant to hurt your friend Ginger. I just…I've not been thinking straight, and you're stirring up a hornet's nest, Tara. You have no idea what kind of danger you're putting yourselves in."

"I think I do, Bette. But just like you want to protect your loved ones, I want to protect mine. And for both of us that includes Peace."

"She's got such a pure heart." Bette's gaze dropped to her lap. "She certainly didn't deserve what Vicky did to her."

Bette knew about the attack? I thought Peace had said no one knew but me and Leo.

"As a mother," I hoped to reach our common ground, "you set the bar for how your kids will turn out. They're watching you for an example. Even now Leo is looking for you to guide him. Do the right thing and fix this if you want to give Leo and Peace a chance at a happy future. You're his last hope, Bette."

She looked at me, eyes watering. A plaintive sound, like the whimper of a child, came from deep inside her. It was a drawn out moment before she was able to speak.

"It was me. I did it."

She whimpered some more. I let the remark hang in the air, waiting respectfully for her to elaborate after she'd collected herself.

"I killed Vicky. My own son."

Only after several shaky breaths did she continue.

"We had told him to go to the fallout shelter and stay put until we could safely arrange for his new life. But no. Vicky could never follow orders; he was too proud. And when he came back and saw that Leo had connected with Peace and was finally happy building a new life for himself, Vicky just couldn't handle it. He had to try to take her for himself. Poor Peace…I just couldn't shake off what Vicky had done. So much like his father…animals, both of them, just animals."

Only now did a tear fall, one perfectly round droplet that joined the splashes of wine she knelt in.

"So I decided to let him go gently, on a mother's terms. I didn't even know I was going to do it until I went over to his house to talk to him first, bringing a peace offering. Blueberry wine, our favorite. When I realized he would never change, I went to the bathroom to wash my face—I had been crying and my mascara was running down my cheeks. That's when I saw the Somulose syringe in the garbage, mostly full. We have horses, so I knew what it was for. And the idea came to me. Lace the wine and let my son go peacefully and painlessly, as you would a beloved pet. It was the least I could do for him as his mother."

I was too shocked for words. As I stood and helped Bette to her feet, I needed to know that she would do the right thing.

"Will you tell the police…so I don't have to?"

Bette looked away in refusal. "I can't, Tara. Everything Vicky did would come out. My husband would be forced to step down from his position. And what about me? What would everyone think if they found out I killed my own son?"

"They'll think you did what you had to do to stop him from

hurting more people. You can't let someone else go down for your crime."

"I'm sorry, but this confession never happened."

As Bette turned to walk inside, I heard another voice call out, "Bette!"

She stopped. I turned.

"I recorded every word." Standing inside the arched entrance that led to the rear courtyard, Peace, with Leo beside her, held up her vintage tape recorder. It was funny how the tapes came full circle.

"Mom," Leo said, "you know what the right thing to do is. This is your chance to break our family cycle. Please…do it for yourself. Be the good person you've always wanted to be."

He walked toward her, arms outstretched, like he was ready to catch her when she fell. It was going to be a long fall from grace, but I had a feeling she'd land on her feet.

Chapter 43

It didn't take long for Bette's confession to set Alika free. We were celebrating at Alika's home with authentic Nigerian dishes that Ginger raved about, particularly the *akara*, a bean cake deep-fried in palm oil. It tasted like french fries to me, but I didn't exactly have the most sophisticated palate.

I hadn't seen Ginger this happy in a long time as she and Sloane laughed over inside jokes that made me feel left out. Apparently Rick had come clean to her about everything and was in the process of restitution...*especially in the bedroom*, Ginger added simply to watch me squirm.

As for Rick's plans to come clean to the police, once that ball got rolling, there was no telling what it would crush, so he wasn't in any hurry to talk. There wasn't enough forgiveness in the world for me to ever be willing to take someone like him back, but Ginger was a better person than I was.

Everything was finally right with our little world. But I was about to smash it to bits as I prepared to tell them the news that Chris and I were selling the house and moving. I just hadn't found the right moment to destroy the good feelings.

"Tomorrow Rick's taking me to dinner at the place he took me to on our first date," Ginger gushed.

"That's so sweet!" Sloane signed.

"We were young and broke, so it's not anything five-star,

but it's special to us," Ginger explained with a blush.

Nothing in Bloodson Bay was five-star, so the bar was set cheap and low.

Flames danced merrily in the cute brick fireplace set against the exterior living room wall. It was too warm outside for a cozy fire, even with the sea breeze, but we weren't here to bask around the hearth. Ours was a more ceremonious purpose.

"You ready?" Ginger asked me. Nodding solemnly, I came and stood next to her in front of the fireplace. Sloane and Alika joined us.

I held the *Oh Tara* tape Officer Speers had given me over the flickering flames, relishing for a moment the pleasant heat until it became intolerable; then, with a little gasp, I tossed it in. The fire fed on my offering. As I watched the plastic case blister, then slowly melt, I felt Ginger's arm encircle my waist. I responded in kind. In a few moments all evidence of my self-incrimination was a molten puddle, bubbling in the cleansing flames.

"It's over!" I exclaimed, exhaling a breath I felt like I'd been holding for over a week.

There were hugs all around, of course, with all of us relieved to put it all to rest. Afterwards Ginger seemed sheepish; I knew she had something to get off her chest. Suddenly she steeled herself and blurted out, "I have a confession to make, Tara. Sloane and I have been keeping something from you."

I had a feeling about it, but I had never found the courage to confront them. Who was I to be jealous of the connection they shared over losing Benson?

"I already know."

"Know what?" Ginger asked.

"That you're both still resentful of my family because of what happened to him, and you know I never liked him. I get it."

Ginger laughed and Sloane looked amused.

"No, that's not it at all! I don't blame you for Bennie's death. We're just in a book club that we didn't invite you to join. A murder mystery club. I know you're not keen on the genre, so I didn't mention it. But I felt bad excluding you."

It was my turn to laugh. "A book club—that's the big secret?"

"We all know how protective you get over me, Tara. Plus I didn't want to hurt your feelings."

"But to make up for it," Sloane interjected, "I have a surprise for you." She made a T with both fingers, then raised her arms in the sign for *strong.* "Your sign name—Tara. Because you're one of the strongest women I've ever met."

Now they were making me cry, making it so much harder to say goodbye. How could I leave the only people who understood me and still loved me?

"'A cord of three strands is not easily broken,'" Alika said, patting me on the back. "From Ecclesiastes 4:12. You three were destined to be friends."

"How about a selfie to commemorate this day?" Sloane held up her phone's camera while we four piled into the frame. "Mummy's free, Ginger's got her beau, Tara's got an official sign name, and Feel the Noize was booked by a Hollywood client you won't believe! So I'm treating us three gals to a trip to LA!"

Ginger squealed like a little girl and bounced like a little puppy. A trip to Hollywood? Was this my actual life now?

Sloane navigated to Instagram to post the picture when Alika yanked the phone from her, eyes widening with terror.

"Go back to that picture of that woman and man." Alika's fingers were trembling as she flicked and tapped at the phone frantically.

"Mummy, stop jabbing at it! You're going to break my screen. Are you talking about Peace and Leo?" Sloane found the picture that had caused Alika such alarm and showed it to her. "Is this what you're looking for?"

"Yes! That is the man who abducted me. Victor Valance. How is he alive and standing with your friend? I thought he was dead."

"No, that's Leonard, his brother."

Alika shook her head vehemently. "I am telling you that man looks *exactly* like the one who held me captive. I will never forget his face. Unless they are twins…"

"No, they're not twins," I said. "Look closer. Leo has a cleft chin; Vic didn't. There are other subtle differences too, though I can see how you might mistake them. Even their voices sound a lot alike. Are you sure it's this guy here?"

Alika studied the photo. "Yes, I remember his face vividly. My captor may have told me his name was Victor, but he was most definitely this man, Leonard."

My heartbeat quickened as I thought of Peace in a romantic relationship with this imposter. Leonard, the man who pretended to adore Peace and befriend me, had been hiding a dark reality. That he was as much a monster as his brother, maybe worse because at least Victor had worn his villainy plainly.

"Do you think Leo planted the tapes in his brother's secret

man cave?" Ginger asked.

"Probably," I guessed. "He hates his father and wants him behind bars. I wouldn't be surprised if he led us directly to them so that we'd turn them in to the police in order to get his dad out of the picture. Especially now that he's dating Peace."

"I'd venture to guess he might have also wanted you to find the tapes so you could prove someone else had motive to kill his brother—to help clear *you* from the suspect list," Ginger speculated. "After all, you're going to be kin soon." She chuckled, but I found nothing humorous about Leonard Valance potentially becoming my brother-in-law.

Peace would never believe me when I told her what Leo had done, and I knew Leo would deny it to the death. I couldn't leave Bloodson Bay until I exposed his lies and fixed everything the Valances had broken.

Or should I fix *myself* first? I thought of all the lies I had told. To Chris. To Ginger. To Peace. To everybody, it seemed. There's an old saying: the journey of a thousand miles begins with a single step. Might as well take it and get it over with.

"Listen, everybody, I've got something to say. You know I was in the hospital…"

"Uterine fibroids, right?" said Ginger. "You said it was no big deal."

"Uh, well, it wouldn't be, I guess, if that was what had been wrong with me." I took a deep breath. "Gang, I'm pregnant!"

I signed the news for Sloane as Ginger let out a loud woot. "Preggers? Dang, girl, that's fabulous! Come here and let Aunt Ginger give ya a big hug!"

Well, that was easy. Now, how did I tell Chris?

Chapter 44

"We need to talk." I spoke the four most dreaded words in a relationship and watched my husband flinch.

Chris and I sat on the back porch watching our mini-pony Havoc graze lazily in a field bursting with violet henbit and golden evening primrose. Ginger and Sloane hung out on the other side of the porch sipping Zima malt beverages that I had found at a specialty beer distributor. I couldn't let the bunker tapes spoil the 1990s for us, so I bought the popular—and college-kid affordable—alcohol that every American drinking-aged kid from the nineties knew and loved...because our taste buds didn't yet know better.

Sloane was entertaining Ginger with a story about her and Benson's early marriage days, which gave me the privacy to finally tell Chris what I had been dying to get off my chest. At my feet was my purse, and inside the cognac leather the item I had found in Peace's attic that I was relying on to get through to him. It was a gamble how tonight would go, an inevitable game of Risk.

My thighs pressed up to Chris's jeans as we slowly rose and fell in the porch swing. I nursed a sweet tea while holding Chris's hand, while yellow-rumped warblers serenaded us. It was an intimate moment that Chris and I closed almost every evening with since back when we were teenagers dating. Hand pressed into hand, thigh pressed up to thigh, my head on his shoulder. We hadn't lost these precious daily habits together over the years, and I clung to his palm a little tighter as I realized everything was about to change.

In the distance I could make out the buttery rectangle of caution tape fencing off where Marvin Valance's body had been found. The crime scene tape flapped in the wind, one end ripping loose from the post the police had attached it to. I hadn't found the courage to tear down the flimsy police barrier. My stomach still lurched just thinking about those gray fingers reaching up from the earth, and that caved-in skull filled with dirt and bugs.

On the bistro table at the other end of the porch was the latest issue of the *Bloodson Bay Bulletin.* Splashed across the front page was soon-to-be-dethroned Judge Ewan Valance's face, but not the media glory he was used to getting. A somber expression donned his features as the article detailed the investigation into his alleged murder of Marvin Valance and kidnapping and abduction of Alika Apara. I didn't like how the defense had already gotten him released due to lack of evidence. It would take more than one battle to bring him down; it'd be a war.

Next to Ewan's page one photo was Bette Valance's, along with the formal charges and arrest based on her confession for the murder of her son Victor Valance. True *partners* in crime—pun intended! The shockwaves were almost palpable throughout the town as Bloodson Bay's golden family was in fact covered in pyrite.

As far as Detective Hughes knew, Alika's abduction case was solved, but for me, Ginger, and Sloane, it hung wide open.

With Leonard as Alika's *real* captor, not Victor, the crime had fallen on the wrong guy, a dead man who couldn't set the record straight. And we were the only ones who knew the truth.

"Why do I feel like you're about to drop a bomb on me?" Chris asked.

"It's not as bad as you're thinking. Not a nuclear bomb or anything. More like C4, or maybe a stink bomb." I shot him a grin, but he only grimaced back at me.

"Either way, it doesn't sound like I'm going to be thrilled with this news, so detonate away." Chris reached for his beer.

I almost got up to grab him another, hoping the alcohol might temper his reaction. But I needed him sober for this conversation.

"There's medium bad news and really bad news. Pick which one you want first."

"Do I have to pick either one?" Chris rolled his eyes at the choices. "Let's get the really bad news over with first."

Being married for over twenty years, I had figured as much.

"Your sister is dating Leonard Valance," I began.

Chris's mouth popped open. "What? You've got to be kidding me. How the hell did that happen?"

"I don't know, but it gets worse. You know those bunker tapes from 1995 we found?"

"Yeah," Chris created a gap between us as he shifted to face me, "the ones where Victor and Judge Valance held Sloane's mom captive."

"It turns out it was Leonard all along, and he deceived Alika into thinking he was Victor. And now he's letting his dead brother take the fall for it. Judge Valance knows and is protecting Leo. So Peace is officially dating a kidnapping torturer."

Chris took a moment to let it all in. Propping his glasses on top of his head, he ran his hands down his face. "I…I don't even know what to say to this." He flipped his glasses back on the bridge of his nose, staring earnestly at me. "Did you tell Peace yet? Or Detective Hughes?"

"I only just found out when Alika ID'd Leonard as the guy from the bunker. We're trying to figure out what to do. Alika's terrified of what Judge Valance is going to do to her if she exposes Leo. It's his only remaining son, and his family legacy. If Leo goes down for this, there's no telling what price we'll pay."

It was a terror all too familiar, a vengeful battle lasting generations between my husband's family and the Valance's.

My thoughts drifted to a heron flying overhead, its majestic wingspan casting a passing shade over the yard. Maybe I didn't need to worry about Leonard. Chris was determined to leave Bloodson Bay anyway.

"Do you think Alika will deny what happened?" Chris asked.

"I have a feeling that in order to protect herself, she won't cooperate with the police. I can't say I blame her."

No matter how much I wanted the Valance family taken down, they held a grudge like a tick on a dog. The Valance Family Hit List was a very real threat, and there was no way to escape it once you got on the list.

"You at least need to tell my sister what Leonard did," Chris insisted.

"I know. I need to figure out how. I don't want to push Peace away. Their relationship is more serious than I realized..."

"It can't be *that* serious."

At this point Ginger perked up and blurted out, "They're already talking marriage. I was thinking maybe we could stage an intervention or something."

Chris's throat rumbled with a bleak laugh. "There is no changing my sister's mind once it's set. And it doesn't help that she's got a savior complex. The worse they're broken, the more determined she is to fix them. We'll need to get creative and let Leonard show her his true colors before it's too late."

Draining the rest of his beer down his throat, Chris dropped the empty can at his feet. "I'm not sure I can handle any more bad news today, Tara."

Oh yeah. I still had the medium bad news to get through.

"You're gonna want to hear this, trust me. Especially before you go selling the farm."

Shooting me a sideways look, I saw the mixture of confusion and curiosity in his expression. I released his hand as I reached into my purse and pulled out the item I had taken from Peace's attic. When I finally held it up, I placed it on my stomach.

"What...what am I looking at?" Chris asked.

"You already forget what a onesie is?" I teased.

"I know what baby clothes are, Tara, but why do you have Nora's onesie that we brought her home from the hospital in?"

My husband was the smartest dunce I'd ever known.

"We're pregnant, Chris." My voice shook as I said the words I had longed to say for over a decade...and suddenly it didn't feel as too-little-too-late as I thought it would. It felt...like perfect timing.

"Are you serious?" He looked shellshocked. I felt worried. He didn't seem happy.

"As serious as a heart attack…or an unexpected pregnancy."

"Girl, you're making it impossible for me to mind my own business, but did you finally spill the beans?" Ginger squealed from the other side of the porch. "Not that I was eavesdropping or anything…"

I smiled so big I was sure my lips would split. Behind Chris's glasses I watched his eyes glisten, lightening from their usual dark hickory to a shade of bright oak. Chris rarely showed emotion, let alone cried.

"Please tell me those are happy tears, because I was really hoping you'd think this was a good thing—"

I hadn't finished getting the words out before Chris jumped up from the swing, scooping me up in his arms and sweeping me off my feet. Literally.

"This isn't a good thing, Tara. It's the greatest thing!" He squeezed me so tight I thought I'd pop, planting kisses all over my cheeks and forehead and neck.

"Easy, tiger." I giggled. "Baby in the oven, remember?"

"Wait a sec. You told Ginger before telling me?" Chris asked with mock offense as he gently set me down on the swing. "I'm the one who should get top billing since I *am* the one who helped make him…or her."

Already I could see his eyes spark with visions of blue onesies and toy trucks and playing catch.

"As they say, hos before bros," Ginger chimed in.

Chris tenderly interlocked his fingers with mine, stroking my hand with his thumb. "I don't understand. How did you think this was bad news?"

"*Medium* bad," I reiterated. "You wanted to move, and now that I'm pregnant, I don't think it's the right time. I want to raise our baby here, surrounded by our friends and family." I gestured to the corner where Ginger was beaming. "I thought with our struggling finances and the farm and wanting to start fresh that maybe you wouldn't be thrilled—"

Chris placed his fingertip to my lips. "Hey, we're not going anywhere. We'll figure out the money and farm, but this baby is the best freshest start I could ever ask for. We've got a new life growing inside you! Our family is our story, Tara. The problems, the finances—all of that is just margin notes."

The back door was open, the screened storm door letting cool air waft across the porch into the kitchen. As I settled into Chris's arms and we rocked steadily back and forth on the swing, I heard the doorbell ring through the house. Chris must have felt me shift to get up, because his hand tightened around my waist.

"No, don't. This moment is ours. Whatever that is can wait," he said.

I resisted the urge to check when the doorbell rang a second time in as many seconds. When it ding-donged a third time, I glanced up at Chris.

"Fine, go ahead."

"To be continued," I promised him with a kiss, then I headed inside.

The front door hung open, which I absolutely knew with certainty I had locked when I got home. Ever since Marvin's body had been unearthed in my yard, I steadfastly secured every door and window, something I had never had to worry about before, living in the country.

I stepped up to the threshold, expecting—hoping—to find someone standing on the front porch, but no one was there. No car in the driveway, either.

"Who was it?" Chris asked from behind me.

"I don't know. I didn't see anyone, but the door was open. Did you forget to close it?"

"I suppose I could have. I don't remember, to be honest."

I swung the door to close it, when Chris grabbed the edge, stopping it. He pointed to the porch floor. "Look. There's a package."

A thick white envelope had *Tara* written across it in black Sharpie. I picked it up, scanned the empty street, and brought it inside.

"No more mysterious packages!" Sloane bemoaned.

"I don't want to open it." I handed it to Chris, who tore the packet open with a swift rip.

He peered inside, handing it to me. "I think you need to see this."

Reaching in, I pulled out the same brand of tape as the ones we had uncovered in Vic's basement and at the bunker. On this one was written: *Hit Me Baby One More Time.*

I found it odd that Victor—rather, *Leonard*—would have referenced a Britney Spears song, but it fit with his theme of torture, I suppose.

"I can't, Chris. Can you listen for me?" I retrieved the Walkman I had bought right after we had found the tapes so I could listen for clues without driving Chris up a wall. Handing it over, Chris loaded the cassette inside and popped the headphones on.

He pressed play.

My heart raced.

He squinted curiously.

I strained to listen.

Then suddenly Chris's hips began to move. Dare I say *gyrate*. His head bopped. His shoulders popped. And I had no clue what the heck was happening.

I yanked the headphones off him, sliding them over my ears. Through the uncomfortable sponge-covered plastic I heard the familiar Spice Girls song "Wannabe," and I spurted out a laugh as I took off the headphones, the sound growing tinny as I set the Walkman down.

Inside the package I found a card. In retrospect, I should have started with this:

To my favorite (and only) sister (duh!):

Sup! This mix tape commemorates some of my favorite memories with you when we were teens. I'm sure you'll agree these are the bomb diggity. ☺ You may want to hit me one more time after I get these stuck in your head, but it'll be totally worth it. Any time you need to get jiggy with it, you'll have this hella mix tape that's not OPP, homey. As if!

Peace out, my phat sister from another mister (you gotta give me snaps for fitting so many nineties phrases in one letter...psyche!)

Love, Peace

Written below Peace's silly note was a playlist of songs that flooded me with a wave of nostalgia, our youthful soundtrack chronicling myriad adventures from concerts to road trips to coffee shop nights to dance club escapades.

Pressing my palm to my stomach, I vowed to ensure similar beautiful and reckless and carefree memories for this baby, a life without Ewan Valance casting his shadow of terror on us. I glanced at Ginger and Sloane—we would take him down, finally making Bloodson Bay safe again.

All three sets of eyes shifted to me—Ginger's full of hope, Sloane's full of assurance, and Chris's full of support. Instead of the suffocating grip of fear, I felt a strength preparing me for the fight of my life.

Epilogue
Ginger

Tables for two, aglow with flickering candles and decorated with tiny vases of flowers, dotted the dining room on the other side of the tinted window of Luna's Steak and Seafood Restaurant. A distant memory pulled me in as I caught my reflection against the brown glass. At this very restaurant, fifty years ago, I fell in love for the first time.

I had been young and passionate and maybe even a little stupid when I agreed to let bad-boy Rick Mallowan take me out on a date. But passion and stupidity were a birthright of the young, weren't they?

Rick was the boy who never graduated high school and was instantly met with my parents' disapproval from the moment they saw his Bee Gees-inspired red leather jacket—which was probably stolen, my dad insisted—and his tacky gold medallion necklace—which was too flashy for a boy his age, my mom grumbled. Despite the parental warnings, the love felt as real as a blade to the heart—and that's exactly what Rick ended up doing to me. Gutting me. But I was a believer in second chances, and tonight was a night of do-overs.

Dressed to the nines, Rick left my house earlier this afternoon, reminding me to meet him at seven o'clock sharp while he ran some errands.

"You remember where we had our first date, right?" he asked on his way out the door.

It was an elaborate—and oh-so-romantic—scheme to rekindle the flame we had sparked so long ago, as he booked the same table for two where we had sat gazing at each other on our first date.

A heady rush of adrenalin quickened my heart as I cast one last approving look at myself in the glass and opened the door.

I had spent two hours touching up my gray roots and staining the bathroom tub red. And another hour perfecting my makeup, wearing my signature cherry lipstick and pale blue eyeshadow.

"Do you have a reservation?" the hostess asked as I approached her podium.

"The reservation is under Rick Mallowan."

"Yes, ma'am. Follow me, please."

The soft sound of "Escape" by Rupert Holmes—better known as "The Pina Colada Song"—trailed as the hostess led me to a table with a bouquet of flowers in the center, and a wrapped gift box at my place setting. I sat and examined the box, imagining what could be inside. It was a little large for an engagement ring, but around the right size and shape for a necklace. Well butter my butt and call me a biscuit, I was getting jewelry!

I considered waiting for Rick before opening it, then eagerly pulled the ribbon, loosening the bow. The bow dropped to the table as I opened the lid. But no fancy necklace was inside.

Instead I was looking at an old newspaper article. I picked up the clipping of what looked like an ad from the 1970s classifieds:

AVON REPRESENTATIVE WANTED

Looking for classy, self-motivated, well-kept woman to handle increasing supply and demand. Must be willing to learn and have available schedule. Sales skills needed. Contact Mick for general details.

Had Don Draper written this sexist garbage? I didn't understand what this was supposed to be, until I noticed the randomly underlined letters that seemed to spell out a message:

r i c k i s m i s s i n g

"Rickismissing?" I muttered under my breath. Rick is missing!

The contact name associated with the ad couldn't be a coincidence when you figured in Rick's infatuation with Mick Jagger. I scanned around the room, looking for Rick, hoping this was just a stupid boyish prank. The restaurant was packed with patrons, but none of them were my husband.

Getting up and taking the box with me, I headed to the hostess stand where the girl greeted me with a chipper smile. I held out the box.

"Did you see who left this at my table?"

She shook her head. "No, ma'am, sorry. It's been a busy night."

Of course it wouldn't be that easy. I walked back to my table, wondering what it meant, who had left it, and why. When I flipped over the box, taped to the bottom was a tiny sliver of paper with a typed note:

> If you want a future with Rick, you will have to search through the past.

**

As Rick's past catches up to him, will Ginger get caught in the crosshairs? Will Ewan Valance finally be brought to justice? And how will Peace take the news that her new sweetheart wasn't always so sweet?

Find out in **WHAT SHE DOESN'T KNOW**,
the next book in the
IF ONLY SHE KNEW MYSTERY SERIES!

Head over to **www.pamelacrane.com** to order your copy now!

About the Author

PAMELA CRANE is a *USA Today* bestselling author and wrangler of four kids who rescues horses and has a writing addiction. She lives on the edge and writes on the edge...where her sanity resides. Her thrillers unravel flawed women with a villainous side, which makes them interesting…and perfect for doing crazy things worth writing about. When she's not cleaning horse stalls or cleaning up after her kids, she's plotting her next murder.

Join her newsletter to get a free book and updates about her new releases and deals at **www.pamelacrane.com**.

Enjoy what you read?

Then You'll Love *A Slow Ruin*

An Instant Bestselling Book Club Pick

April 1910. Women's rights activist Alvera Fields mysteriously vanishes from her home one night, leaving her newborn baby and husband behind, the case never solved.

April 2021. On the anniversary of her great-great-grandmother's disappearance, Alvera's namesake Vera Portman vanishes in an eerily similar manner.

Six months later, the police recover a girl's body. While the family waits in the horror of finding out if it's Vera, Felicity Portman clings to hope that her missing teenage daughter is still alive. Despite all odds, Felicity senses a link between the decades-apart cases—a mother feels such things in her bones. But all suspicion points to the last person who saw Vera alive: Felicity's sister-in-law, Marin.

Marin, with her troubled past.
Marin, the poor woman who married into the rich family.
Marin, the only one who knows Felicity's darkest secret.

As Felicity makes a shocking discovery in Vera's journal, she questions who her daughter really is. The deeper she digs, the more she's ensnared in the same mysteries that claimed their ancestor in a terribly slow ruin.

A Karin Slaughter Killer Reads Pick:
Little Deadly Secrets

The deadliest secrets lie closest to home...

From *USA Today* bestselling author Pamela Crane comes an addictively readable domestic suspense novel about friendship, motherhood ... and murder.

Three best friends. Two unforgiveable sins. One dead body.

Mackenzie, Robin, and Lily have been inseparable forever, sharing life's ups and downs and growing even closer as the years have gone by. They know everything about each other. Or so they believe.

Nothing could come between these three best friends . . .
Except for a betrayal.

Nothing could turn them against each other . . .
Except for a terrible past mistake.

Nothing could tear them apart . . .
Except for murder.

One of POPSUGAR's Must-Read Thrillers: *The Sister-in-Law*

She stole my husband. So I'd steal her life.

The Wife
Lane won Candace's heart over chocolate martinis and karaoke. But weeks into their whirlwind marriage, Candace realized Lane came with burdensome baggage in the form of his possessive live-in sister and her eerily watchful six-year-old son. Lane had a secret that seemed to hold him hostage, and Candace would do anything to uncover it.

The Sister-in-Law
Harper was the kind of woman who cooked homemade meals and dusted under the furniture. It was the least she could do for her brother after her husband's mysterious death, and Lane took her and her kids in. Then Candace showed up like a tornado passing through, threatening and destructive. But Harper had other plans for her new "sister," plans Lane could never find out about.

The Husband
All Lane had ever wanted was a white-picket-fence life. The wife. The two-point-five kids. The happy little family. Everything seemed to be falling into place with Candace ... until Harper's jealous streak got in the way, again. But choosing between his sister and wife would be costly ... and knowing Harper, the price would be blood.

Printed in Great Britain
by Amazon